MR. BIG SHOT

S. E. LUND

ACADIAN PUBLISHING LIMITED

CHAPTER 1

Alexa

The email dropped into my mailbox about nine thirty on Tuesday night.

The little ding caught my attention, drawing me away from the dry journal article in front of me titled, "Confidence Building Measures and the Cold War" by Professor someone from somesuch think tank. It was required reading for my comprehensive exam for the International Relations MA at Columbia.

I ignored it at first. I hadn't used that email address for almost two years. It had to be spam.

Candace, my BFF from my high school years back in Oregon, my constant partner in crime and the one person who could talk me into almost anything, sat beside me at her own desk, one knee tucked under her chin. Her dark hair was tied up into a messy bun, and she wore black horn-rimmed glasses that exposed her as the geek that she was. To top it off, she wore a Watchmen t-shirt, tattered grey sweatpants and old slippers that had seen better days.

I wasn't much better in my own Bucky Barnes t-shirt and pajama shorts, finished by fuzzy purple socks. In high school, people called us the Nerd Twins, and we were, except that I had fair hair and was short while she was dark and tall. Other than that difference, we were two geeky peas in a pod.

We had been inside all week, drinking coffee by the gallons, eating takeout food instead of cooking, because cooking required shopping, preparing and cleaning. In comparison, the remains of a takeout meal went right into the refrigerator for later consumption or into the trash.

I should have ignored the email. It had been so long since I used that address, I was surprised that the email service hadn't cancelled it. But my OCD got the best of me and I just had to open the email to get rid of the bold button. Besides, I needed a break, so I clicked on the mailbox and checked out the subject line in the preview.

Re: Emergency

"That's strange," I said and checked the date, wondering if it wasn't one of those ghost emails that show up months or even years after they were sent due to some mix-up with the server.

Candace glanced over at me. "What is it?" she asked, crunching on a Cheeto.

"It's an email sent to my old 9-1-1 address."

"Whoa," she said, her brown eyes wide. "What's it been – almost two years since you worked there?"

2

"Yep." I opened the email even though I'd promised myself I wasn't going to check my email for a full two hours. First off, pretty much all the email I received was spam. Second, everyone I knew used texts, and finally, everyone who mattered knew I was busy studying for my comp for my MA, and was not to be bothered – not even on a Tuesday night. The comprehensive exam was the following week, and I was still studying.

So, when the email notification sounded, I thought it must either be a real emergency or spam.

I was wrong. Well, not technically. But it was neither.

To: Lexi911@yahoo.com
    Reply-To: mrbigshot69@icloud.com
    Re: Emergency

Hey, is this Sexy Lexi? I got your email from John. I have a 9-1-1, and need your services. Big family dinner on Saturday at the ballroom, Cipriani Wall Street, and will be surrounded by family and business associates. John said you were really high class and brainy. In other words, not your usual escort. If you're available, wear something amazing but conservative. John showed me the menu. I'll take a standard date with no add-ons. The usual conditions apply. Cheers, MBS

"Oh, my *God*..." I was in awe that anyone could write an email like that and use an email address like that.

"What?" Candace scooted over next to my desk in her rolling desk chair. She craned her neck and squeezed even closer.

"It's from – get this – Mr. Big Shot 69. You won't believe what this jerk wrote."

"What does it say?"

I read it out loud.

"Mr. Big Shot 69?" She laughed derisively. "What -- is he a freshman in high school?"

"I can't believe he actually chose that email ID and added a 69. Is he a total asshole?"

"Must be."

I read it again in disbelief. "He thinks I'm an escort and wants me to attend a family event with him."

"He wants an *escort* to go to a *family* event with him?"

"He thinks I'm really high end and brainy." I wagged my eyebrows at her. "He's right, of course."

Candace laughed out loud at that. "But of course you are! You should play along. Pretend you're Sexy Lexi. Come on – you always wanted to be an actor. Write him back. Lead him on."

I glanced at her and bit my lip.

She was right about the always wanting to be an actor. I'd even enrolled in a Bachelor of Fine Arts degree when I first went to college in Oregon, but that was years ago in another life. Stuff happened that changed the course of my life and I decided to move across the country and start a new life completely different from the one I left behind.

Now, there's something you should know about Candace. She was the one who always got the two of us in trouble back when we were in high school. She was the instigator of all the bad things we did, from egging houses at Halloween (*Everyone does it, Alexa, honest!*) to driving around with boys who were older than us and who were drinking (*They can drive, Alexa, honest!*) to stealing cigarette packs from the display in the corner store (*Just stick it up your sleeve. No one will notice, Alexa, honest!*)

How many times had the girl gotten me in trouble? Luckily, I emerged from my teenage years alive, unscathed, and without a criminal record, but only barely.

So, I should have known to trust my own gut.

But I didn't...

"There must be a Lexi911 who's an escort. One tiny typo..."

I read over his email once more and considered. Should I play along, pretend to be the infamous Sexy Lexi? Part of me said no, because that would be unethical, but the other part said he was likely a real jerk to use an escort service. I mean, who pays women money to go out with them? Who *pays* for sex? It was unethical – immoral.

"Are you going to reply?"

I chewed a nail. "You think I should?"

"Do it." She moved closer, her chair almost crowding me out. "He's probably a real jackass."

"He deserves the best I can give." I smiled as I pressed reply. "The very best."

And so, I sealed my fate and started writing.

I mean – Mr. Big Shot 69?

What kind of lame email address was that? What kind of lame man thought up an email like that? It was arrogant and crass.

I tried to keep up.

To: mrbigshot69@icloud.com
Reply-To: Lexi911@yahoo.com
Re: Re: Emergency

Hey, big fella. Are you Mr. Big Shot with the emphasis on *big*? Or Mr. Big Shot with the emphasis on *shot*?

I know a lot of men named John, as you can imagine. Saturday is kinda short notice for a busy gal like me. I usually book two weeks in advance. Just so we're on the same page, how about you confirm the conditions and rates? They may have changed.

Later, SexyLexi911

I should have immediately sent him an email that he had the wrong address and left it at that, but there was something about his message that had me intrigued.

"There," I said. "Sent."

"Oh, my God." Candace and I stared at each other, huge grins on our faces. "Way to go!" She held up her hand for a high-five, and I dutifully responded, our palms slapping. "You did it!"

"I did, I did," I said but I didn't feel triumphant. I felt this vague sense of *Oh, my God what did I just do...*

I knew the moment I sent my response that I'd made a mistake but I had no idea how to recall an email sent through Yahoo and so I took in a deep breath and waited to see how he'd respond.

I turned back to the screen, wondering if he'd reply. I bit my lip and watched my screen, thinking he'd most likely catch on and realize he was being played. I actually hoped he'd reply in all seriousness. It could turn out to be a good laugh.

After about five minutes, Candace and I returned reluctantly to our books. I figured he backed out of responding, maybe realizing his mistake. Then my computer chimed once more and sure enough, an email appeared in my mailbox.

To: Lexi911@yahoo.com
    Reply-To: mrbigshot69@icloud.com
    Re: Re: Re: Emergency

Sorry about the short notice but I broke it off with my former girlfriend and I can't go alone or there'll be speculation about my ability to keep a woman interested in me. I realize that the very fact I'm contacting you suggests that's reality, but seriously, it isn't. I want to rub you in someone's face, so to speak. As to the terms, I understand that it's $1000 for the evening and more if I want any dessert. To be negotiated. I will likely not be asking for anything besides the date.

Oh, and emphasis on big. *EG*

I laughed out loud at his response. "I don't know how many times I can say Oh My God."

Candace rolled her chair back to my desk and read it, turning to me with the biggest grin on her face.

"Can you believe it? What a dick!"

"You can say that again." At the same time, my mind went to

more venal thoughts. *Mr. Big?* I'd watched practically every
episode of Sex and the City several times and Mr. Big had a
permanent place in my sexual fantasies.

MrBigShot69 was willing to pay some call girl $1000 to go to a
fundraiser with him so he could rub her in someone's face?

"Who *is* he? Whose face does he want to rub – me – in? The
ex-girlfriend? She must have broken his heart and not the other
way around."

"Must be the one who broke up with him. She's probably going
to be there and he wants to have some hot babe on his arm to make
her jealous. Typical male."

"He's probably some rich computer geek working on Wall
Street, most likely."

"Most likely..."

I should have stopped at that point, but it was too much fun so
I decided to keep playing along.

To: mrbigshot69@icloud.com
    Reply-To: Lexi911@yahoo.com
    Re: Re: Re: Re: Emergency

I like to know with whom I'm getting involved. You'll have
to reveal more about yourself before I rearrange my week
and say yes. Don't want to end up in the Hudson with
cement shoes. ;) Send me a pic and your real name, and your
cell number so I can text you. Email is so 90s and leaves too
much of a paper trail for a bright business woman like me.

Later, SexyLexi911

"I can't wait to see him," Candace said. "He's probably five feet nothing and weighs a hundred pounds, with a pencil neck, thick glasses and a pocket protector."

"You mean like every other geek we know?"

"Exactly." She patted me on the back. "We attract only the best."

I grinned at that and wondered what he looked like. I couldn't believe a truly handsome man would have to take an escort to a fundraiser. If he was a half-decent person, he'd probably have a friend or even his sister who could go with him in a pinch. The fact he was ready to hire an escort didn't speak too well of him as a person.

I waited to see if he was going to send me a photo of himself, give me his real name and his cell. If he did, I'd be shocked. He must be desperate if so. I felt bad for him, but seriously. He had to be more careful with personal security. Emailing some woman he didn't know out of the blue? Some high-priced call girl whose number he got from his friend?

My inbox dinged and I opened the email, noting several attachments.

"Oh. My. *God*... He's that desperate?" I turned to Candace. "Doesn't he have a female colleague he could ask to this function? I'm afraid to open the email, for fear of what I'll see."

I hesitated only briefly before I opened the email and clicked on the icon for the attachment. The software scanned the image and finding no virus, the image opened immediately. My jaw dropped to the floor when I saw what he sent.

A screen cap of his American Express Black Card beside a bill with the unlimited credit limit displayed...

At least *that* was gorgeous...

9

"What an asshole." I showed Candace. She peered at the image.

"He sent a credit limit pic?" She turned to me, a look of incredulity on her face. "That's an all-time new level of pretentiousness."

We both bent over with laughter. "What a dick..."

Then I opened the next image. It was a picture of a watch.

It was a Rolex Sea-Dweller. Black.

"The dick sent a picture of his watch." I showed it to Candace.

"A Sea-Dweller?" She frowned. "What's that?"

I opened a browser window and googled Rolex Sea-Dweller.

"It's a diving watch." My eyes bugged out when I saw the price. "Holy cow, it's worth $25,000."

She stared at me, her eyes wide, her mouth open. "Oh, my God, what a jerk!"

We both turned back to the screen to read his email.

To: Lexi911@yahoo.com
   Reply-To: mrbigshot69@icloud.com
   Re: Re: Re: Re: Re: Emergency

Real name is private until you sign a non-disclosure agreement, but you can call me Mr. Big Shot – just kidding. Text me at the number in my sig. That's a burner so don't try to trace it. Please, don't wear anything too revealing as far as dress for this event. In addition to my family, there will be an elite crowd of business and political people. I need you to smile, look pretty, be attentive, and not talk too much. John said you're smart, so the story will be that you're a student doing your masters in something or other. You can make up the rest, but nothing racy or scandalous.

I sat open-mouthed.

"He wants me to sign a non-disclosure agreement?"

I stared at the email and the pic of his Amex limit and Rolex. Then I responded.

To: mrbigshot69@icloud.com
    Reply-To: Lexi911@yahoo.com
    Re: Re: Re: Re: Re: Emergency

I'm pretty picky about my dates. How old are you and what do you look like? I'm not going to waste my time with a fat old loser no matter how high your Amex limit. As for your watch, my dad was an Air Force pilot and always said 'Big Watch, Small Cock' so that's not going to impress me. Show me something of your face or body, at least. You must have a pic that won't identify you or are you that much of a celebrity that I'd know who you are?

Later, SexyLexi911

Another email popped into my folder. I opened it and read the single line of text.

To: Lexi911@yahoo.com
   Reply-To: mrbigshot69@icloud.com
   Re: Re: Re: Re: Re: Re: Emergency

I've been told that I'm not hard on the eyes, if that's what you mean...

My jaw dropped yet again when I opened the attachment.

It was a pic of his naked six-pack abdomen, which was amazingly washboard. I saw a very pronounced hip cleft and the start of a noticeably bulging package beneath some black Joe Boxer briefs.

I sent a text to his cell number, using my Lexi911 alias.

Lexi911: Phew... I worried that you were a skinny geek with thick glasses. I don't send my photo to just anyone. We'll have to meet in person. One question – what happened to your date?

His response came right away.

MBS69: Geek, yes. Glasses, yes, sometimes when I have to read fine print. Skinny, no. As to what happened to my date? Suffice to say that both our expectations were off. She broke the rules, and I'm nothing if not a stickler for rules, so the relationship was off as well.

Lexi911: You are a stickler for rules for your women? My kind of man.

"Heartless jerk..." I said.

MBS69: I do not lead anyone on about my expectations, and I expect the same from the women I become involved with. I have rules. She had the wrong idea about how willing I'd be to break them.

Lexi911: Let me guess... you wanted sex but no strings, and she wanted you to tie her up with a big knot but not in the fun way.

MBS69: Let me put it this way – our relationship did not move to the next level on my part, but it did on hers. My family was interfering and trying to push things, but it wasn't working for me. So, I had to end it. That left me without a date on Saturday for this family dinner.

Lexi911: You could always go alone?

MBS69: *Not with this crowd. They're all married with trophy wives and expect the same of me and everyone in their circle. John said you were beautiful. If he thinks you're hot, I know you're perfect. Make sure you look classy and conservative. You have something appropriate, I hope? John said you were high end.*

Lexi911: *Oh, I'm very high end. The highest. I'd like to meet you in person before I go out with you. You like rules? That's one of mine. Hard and fast. Coffee would be fine. 1:00 Thursday. The food court at the Columbus Circle mall. Outside that sushi place. Wear something red so I know who you are. You can bring your Non-Disclosure Agreement and I'll sign. You're a stickler for rules? Same here.*

MBS69: *That's pretty short notice. I'm a business person and I am exceptionally busy.*

Lexi911: *Precisely. Me as well. See you then, Mr. Big. Shot.*

"You're really going to go meet him, right?" Candace's eyes were wide. It was something she would do, but not me.

"No." I was already hatching a plan to spy on him. "I'm going to go incognito and see what he looks like. I'll stand him up, let him go to this fundraiser alone. Serves him right."

"I wish I wasn't going to be in a meeting tomorrow afternoon with Professor Everly," Candace said, her voice sad, "but it's about my committee members and I have to go. I want to come, too..." She pouted.

I bit my bottom lip and considered, doubts creeping in about whether I should lead him on.

"Maybe I should send him an email and confess."

"No, no, *no*. You should go. This is a once-in-a-lifetime thing!"

"What if he's mad and starts to harass me?"

She shrugged, like that was nothing. "You could always block his cell if he starts to bother you. You could delete your old email. You don't use it anyway."

I made a face, struggling with my decision. I created my Lexi911 email when I worked as a 9-1-1 relief operator during the summers. After everything that happened with Blaine, I had initially planned on becoming a paramedic, but realized after answering calls that I couldn't face that kind of stress. So, I went into plain old social science instead. Something calm and non-stressful, like international relations. I did an undergrad in Portland, and then moved to Manhattan to do my MA at Columbia. Candace came with me, happy to leave the West Coast behind. I'd start my PhD next year, if all went well.

"He's obviously a real dickhead, so don't feel bad about leading him on." Candace moved back to her desk and flipped a page in her file. "What kind of guy has such rigid rules and breaks up with women over them? He sounds like he doesn't have a heart. He deserves some payback. Consider yourself Karma."

"What about *my* Karma?" I examined the pic of his abdomen again. "Will this be good Karma or bad Karma if I go through with it and stand him up?"

Candace shrugged. "Has a guy ever treated you badly?" She raised her eyebrows meaningfully.

She knew very well that a guy had treated me badly. One particular guy named Blaine who I only barely escaped with my life. I tried not to think of Blaine, because it was a very dark and

15

scary part of my life I'd rather forget, but that's the thing about trauma. You can't ever really forget it.

"Mr. Big Shot 69? Consider me Karma," I said and smiled.

CHAPTER 2

Luke

I met John at our favorite hot dog cart in Central Park West, relishing our weekly trip for some street meat.

It was a ritual we never failed to follow, the two of us going for a sausage slathered in mustard and heaped with sauerkraut. Although we were business partners, we had separate office space. John was CTO and in charge of the technology side of the business while I was CFO and in charge of the financial side. I spent my time on Wall Street and he spent his closer to the techies at Columbia. He wore jeans and a t-shirt and had a surfer-dude thing going on with the longish hair while I wore a business suit and tried to look like a banker. A competitive swimmer in college, John still swam for fitness and had the bleached-blond pool hair to show for it.

"So?" he asked, eyeing me as he paid for his dog. "What's the deal with Lexi?"

I shrugged, trying to appear nonchalant. "She agreed."

He raised his eyebrows, a crazy grin cracking his face, and gave me a playful cuff on the arm.

"I told you she would. Did she send you a photo? She's pretty, isn't she?"

I shook my head. "No, she didn't send one." I stood beside him at the hotdog cart, loading my sausage with sauerkraut.

"Well, she's beautiful," he said as he skillfully squirted mustard on the sausage. "I would have thought she'd send you a risqué picture at least. Believe me, she's hot." He turned to me, smiling like an idiot. His smile was infectious, and his excitement at my upcoming plan to teach my cheating bastard of a brother-in-law a lesson lifted my spirits. I'd been working like a dog for months, getting the financing in order to take our startup *Chatter* to the next level. It had paid off big time and soon, we'd be former owners, and richer each by a cool billion dollars.

The deal was the talk of Wall Street. The two of us were its darlings *du jour*. I'd been interviewed in the *Journal* and John had appeared on a segment CNBC about young entrepreneurs under thirty-five.

We were considered boy geniuses. Everyone loved a wildly successful success story and that was us.

"So, it's all set for Saturday?" John asked as he finished layering on mustard and sauerkraut in his meticulous way. "You're going to take Lexi to Cipriani's and scare the bejesus out of Eric?"

"It is and I am," I said as we walked to a bench and sat to eat our lunch. "I can't wait until Eric lays eyes on her."

"What do you think the bastard will do?"

I shrugged. "He's such a bullshitter, he'll probably smile and kiss her knuckles."

I took a bite and chewed thoughtfully for a moment. In truth, I had no idea what Eric would do. Once upon a time, I thought I knew the man, but I was wrong. Instead of a loyal husband and hard-working executive in my family's business, he was a cheating lying bastard. Whatever he did, it couldn't make me happy, but seeing fear in his eyes would be something.

"You got a lot of balls to do this," John said. "What if he punches your lights out?"

"Nah. He's more likely to slither off like the snake that he is."

"I'm surprised you didn't go over there and punch *his* lights out."

"Me?" I said, all innocent. "Resort to violence? I'm all about forgiveness."

John snorted and gave me an *I don't believe you* look. "Yeah, right."

I laughed ruefully. John was right. I wasn't all about forgiveness – not anymore. I usually could forgive a lot in a person, but cheating was the one thing I could never let go.

I had good reason to feel that way.

Since I discovered he cheated on my sister – my very pregnant sister – I'd come to know a different side of Eric with the help of a private eye I hired. He tailed Eric to see what he got up to on all those late afternoon meetings and out of town business trips. I came to know the Eric who spent lunch hours in the bar flirting with various women, or in the bathroom snorting coke, or getting blown by Lexi 911 when he was supposed to be out of town taking care of customer relations in my family's century-old investment business.

Eric was such a bastard, I doubted if anything could faze him. If he could cheat on my very pregnant sister, taking an escort to a trendy bar while his wife — my sister — was at home alone suffering from unrelenting morning sickness, he had no moral substance.

It made me so mad I could explode, but the marriage therapist

19

I'd contacted about how to handle the issue said my sister would not appreciate me being the one to tell her that her husband was cheating. That I should take Eric aside and tell him I knew and that he should tell my sister or I would.

I couldn't – *couldn't* – face being alone with the bastard for fear I would lose control and choke him to death so I decided to show him I knew. I'd take the very same escort to the dinner and shove her in his face. I wouldn't say anything, I wouldn't make a scene, but he'd get the message pretty damn quickly...

John took a bite of his dog and chewed, his eyes narrowed. "Do you want me to come?" he asked when he was finished.

I shook my head. "Better not," I said. "I don't want to get this girl in any trouble. When she sees Eric, she'll recognize him, but I'm sure she'll be discreet."

"He'll be shaking in his boots that you'll tell Dana and that'll be the end of his life posing as one of Manhattan's rich and famous."

I shoved down the last of my lunch. "As far as I'm concerned, he can fuck off right now, but I don't want to ruin Dana's whole experience of pregnancy and birth. Plus, new parents are totally jammed for a couple of months adjusting. After that? She can divorce the son of a bitch for all I care. In fact, I hope she does."

"It's hard being a single parent."

"She's all set up to live comfortably. They had a prenup. He'll get some cash, but not much because they've only been married for a couple of years."

We watched the pedestrians strolling through the park. It was still pretty hot in the last days of August.

John turned back to me. "How's the build coming?"

He meant the build of my new catamaran, on which we planned to sail around the world. A forty-two-foot beauty, The Phoenix as I dubbed her, was custom made and equipped with the latest technology and top of the line materials.

She was spectacular.

"Going really well. I'm looking forward to spending a few weekends at the beach house before the end of the season. Once the sale goes through, and as soon as the cat's finished, we can take it for a few test runs up and down the coast before heading out for The Bahamas."

"Can't wait."

Sailing around the world was what kept me going. The money from the sale of our business was nothing to me but freedom. It was a way to break completely free from the reach of my adoptive parents, and do what I really wanted. John and two of my buddies from Columbia were going to crew the cat with me. We'd worked hard for the past few years building up a social media app that would mean we'd be able to do whatever the fuck we wanted for the rest of our lives, each of us becoming New York's latest young billionaires under thirty-five. Hell, I was still under thirty.

I planned on getting into the space industry after we returned from our world tour, investing my money in the mission to Mars. I might even try to go on a one-way trip, become a modern explorer.

There was nothing on Earth keeping me there except my sister, so leaving on the journey of a lifetime and then the journey of a century? Hell yes, sign me up.

My agenda was completely free for the rest of my life once the deal went through. As soon as that happened and my cat was finished, I was *gone*.

But first – first I had to rub Lexi911 in Eric's smug face.

I could barely wait for Saturday to roll around...

We finished our dogs and walked back to my car in a parking garage a few blocks away. On the way, we talked about the deal and how the only snag was that one of the buyers was the brother of the woman everyone thought I was going to eventually marry.

Everyone was wrong.

Felicia Blake was sweet, and we did date on and off for the past few months, but she was not my type. Despite the machinations of my adoptive mother, Felicia's mother and practically everyone else in their close circle of friends, I couldn't be tempted out of my plans to leave. Felicia's brother Harrison was one of Chatter's prospective buyers, so I had to tread very lightly. I didn't want to lead Felicia or anyone else on about my intentions, but at the same time, I wanted Harrison's support for the deal. It shouldn't matter that Felicia and I were not going to tie the knot. I'd already had a very disastrous go at engagement and potential marriage. What should matter was that the deal was great and would make the new owners – and me – very rich.

I kept my fingers mentally crossed that nothing would happen to scupper the deal and that within a couple of weeks, the ink would be dry on the sale. Then, John and I would be casting off from the slip at Alpha Yachts in Patchogue, NY. Our first non-US destination? The Bahamas, followed by Jamaica and then a trip through the Panama Canal on our way to the Galapagos, French Polynesia, Fiji and then on to New Zealand and Australia before hitting Indonesia, Malaysia, South Africa, South America and back to the USA.

After that?

Whatever the fuck I felt like.

Which was space. I'd soon have a cool billion and I already had big dreams.

I only wished my parents had been alive to see my success, but they had both passed, killed in a car crash when Dana and I were only eight, leaving us orphans, raised by adoptive parents neither of us cared for.

On Thursday morning, John and I sat in my office and talked about the sale of our business, going over charts and balance sheets for our presentation. We had a big meeting coming up with the potential buyers in two weeks and we wanted to be on top of things. The time went by fast, and I was due to meet Lexi at 1:00 p.m. at the Columbia Circle food court. At twelve-fifteen, I closed my files and took my car, hoping to find a parking space somewhere near the mall. I brought along my red umbrella to identify myself to Lexi. In my pocket was a NDA that I'd get her to sign. Once she saw me, I figured she'd know who I was and so I didn't want her to go to the gossip rags and spill that I was hiring her as an escort. That was the last thing I needed, considering that I didn't, in fact, use escorts. I'd never used one and I never intended to.

Using Lexi was all just a means to an end.

I'd hire her for the night, parade her in front of Eric at the dinner, and then say goodbye. She'd play her part in my little family psychodrama, and then I'd never see her again. Hopefully, neither would Eric.

My PD continued to follow Eric after I found out he was cheating on Dana and discovered that he hadn't used her again or any another afterward, so perhaps the escort was just that one time. Still, Eric was on the edge, drinking too much, doing blow and generally acting like an idiot. I doubted he'd change when he discovered I knew about his cheating. If you could use an escort once while being married and your wife very pregnant with your first child, you could use one many times.

If he didn't use another escort or pick up a random woman in a bar for the rest of my sister's pregnancy and after the baby was born, I wouldn't tell her about his cheating ass. That would be my leverage. The carrot I would dangle in front of him to put him back on the straight and narrow. If he failed to heed my very generous warning, I'd use the stick. I'd tell her what he did, and the rest would be up to her.

So it was with a slight surge of adrenaline in my blood that I went to the food court and found a place at the front of the seating area, glancing around for a beautiful woman with long light brown hair, who John assured me, was attractive enough to be a model, even if she wasn't tall enough. John had seen her with Eric at a club in downtown Brooklyn on a weekend when Eric was supposed to be out of town on business.

I grabbed a tray of sushi and sat down, my red umbrella on the table beside me. There had been no rain for over a week, so she'd know who I was when she saw the red umbrella.

I planned on arriving early and watching the people come and go so I could catch a glimpse of her before she saw me. I liked to take whatever advantage I could when handling a business deal. I glanced around the food court, looking for someone who resembled the woman John described, but there was no one there who fit the bill.

I removed my cell and sent Lexi a message about five minutes before we were supposed to meet.

MrBigShot69: Hey, Lexi, I'm running late. I'll be there in about ten.

While I waited for her response, I ate my California rolls and pondered what I'd say to her, and whether I would tell her my evil plan or let her think I merely needed a date. In my texts and emails, I'd told her that I was dateless because of a recent breakup. I most likely could have gotten a date on short notice if I wanted one, but my goal was to teach Eric a lesson.

I hadn't had a serious relationship since my ex fiancée and I split over a year earlier, but Lexi would probably already know that once she realized who I was. My breakup with Jenna had made the local gossip columns, and was all that was talked about amongst my family and associates for a month after the wedding was cancelled at the last – and I mean last – minute.

Instead, I told her about my more recent breakup with Felicia just to satisfy her curiosity, not wanting to reveal the real reason I was hiring her or who I was until I had her sign the NDA.

Higher class escorts, so John told me, were familiar with them and were used to signing to protect the identities of their wealthier or more famous clients. As the adoptive son of one of Manhattan's most famous business moguls and partner in a deal that would crack over two billion, I would likely be immediately recognizable to Lexi.

I patted the NDA in my jacket pocket and took out my cell, wondering where Lexi was.

She finally responded about five minutes later.

Lexi911: I'm not waiting forever. I have places to go and people to see...

Was she already at the food court? I glanced around but didn't see anyone who fit her description. I responded right away, hoping to catch sight of her responding.

MrBigShot69: Are you there already?

ALEXA: No, but I'm on my way. Be there in five.

MRBIGSHOT69: Be right there. What are you wearing, so I'll know who you are?

Lexi911: Uh, uh, uh. I get to see you first and then YOU get to see me if I decide to do business with you. Sorry, but those are my rules.

MrBigShot69: Okay, be coy. I'll see you when you get here.

I watched the entrances for the next five minutes but she must still be on her way and didn't want to admit she was late.

I sat back and waited, wondering what Lexi of 9-1-1 Escorts looked like.

John assured me she was hot.

I hoped he was right...

CHAPTER 3

ALEXA

My stomach was all butterflies as I considered my approach to the food court at the Columbus Circle Mall, which was far enough away from my apartment that I likely wouldn't know anyone.

When I arrived, customers had filled almost every table. I got a plate of sushi, and sat at the back of the section so I could watch the entry and exit, as well as the tables outside the sushi joint. There were about twenty customers seated in the section as well as a handful getting sushi at the store.

I blended in with my hoodie and jeans, my hair pulled back into a ponytail. I even wore my Yankees ball cap, pulling it down low so that no one would look twice at me. I was as plain as plain could be.

My eyes darted everywhere, looking for a man in what I expected would be a business suit, with something obviously red on his person to signify who he was. Maybe a red tie, or a red kerchief tucked into his suit jacket breast pocket.

I checked my watch, and ate half-heartedly, my stomach not quite settled for fear he'd know who I was.

How *could* he know who I was? My cell number was private. All he'd get if he tried to track it down would be a provider and there were millions using the same service. He had no idea what I looked like.

The food court was busy with dozens of customers coming and going and almost every table was full. There were a few potential Mr. Big Shots in the seating area – men of his age dressed in expensive looking business suits, but I could only see the backs of their heads. I took in a deep breath and tried to relax, leaning back, deciding I was going to enjoy myself and stop worrying. This would be one of those stories I could tell my best friends forever.

Remember that jerk of a guy who was trying to hire an escort for a fundraiser? Yeah, what a total jerk!

About five minutes later, I got a text and was tempted to answer right away, but then, at the last second, I worried that he might be watching to see who answered their cell and would know who I was, so as much as I wanted to check my cell, I didn't.

I waited five minutes and ate my sushi. To amuse myself, I read the front page of the *New York Times* that had been left behind on the table, scanning the headlines absently, pretending to care. About five minutes later, I nonchalantly checked my cell, and saw that the text was from MrBigShot69 saying he'd be a few minutes late. I texted a response.

Lexi911: I'm not waiting forever. I have places to go and people to see...

I put my cell down and angled it so I could read any response without seeming to check. His reply came immediately.

MrBigShot69: Are you there already?

28

I didn't want him to know I was already there, so I lied.

ALEXA: No, but I'm on my way. Be there in five.

MRBIGSHOT69: Be right there. What are you wearing, so I'll know who you are?

Lexi911: Uh, uh, uh. I get to see you first and then YOU get to see me if I decide to do business with you. Sorry, but those are my rules.

MrBigShot69: Okay, be coy. I'll see you when you get here.

I relaxed and leaned back, glancing around to watch the doors, so I could see him as soon as he arrived. After a couple of minutes, one of the suits a few rows ahead of me stood up. He was facing the other way, so he couldn't see me. Tall, maybe six three. Well-built from the width of his shoulders under a very well-fitting and expensive looking black suit. Dark hair just a tad too long. When he glanced to his left, I saw a very sharp jaw and just enough scruff to be hot. Sharp regular features. His bangs fell into his eyes in a very sexy way.

God, now *he* was gorgeous, from what I could see. Armani gorgeous, Candace would say. Then, he picked up his tray and carried it over to the trash, emptying the used plates and plastic cutlery into the opening. When he turned back, I saw his face square on over the top of the *Times* and my *God...* Eyes so blue I could see them from where I sat about fifteen feet away. Regular features, square jaw, just the right amount of scruff. A white shirt under a black suit. A dark blue tie...

It wasn't Mr. Big Shot 69, sadly, for he wasn't wearing anything red that I could see.

He stood there, glancing around the food court with...

With a red umbrella in his hand.

His gaze passed over the other customers in the court but didn't even stop at me. He kept turning slowly in a circle as if trying to signal that he was there. He was obviously a liar, arriving early, probably hoping to figure out who Lexi911 was by watching who arrived and went to the sushi place.

Just like I had been doing.

He was there when I arrived. I'd seen him from the back, but couldn't tell if he had anything red on him. When he was looking away, I surreptitiously held up my cell and snapped a quick pic of him. Then, I ducked my head down and sent the pic in a text to Candace.

ALEXA: *This is MrBigShot69...*

Her text was almost immediate.

CANDYC: *OMGOMGOMG*

CANDYC: *DON'T YOU KNOW WHO HE IS???*

I frowned. No, I didn't know who he was. Sure, he was handsome, but I didn't recognize him and apparently, no one else at the mall did either.

ALEXA: *Who is he?*

CANDYC: *Just one of the hottest young soon-to-be billionaires!!! What cave have you been living in? No, wait... I take that back. I know what cave you've been living in... He's Luke Marshall of the Marshall banking fortune. Poor little rich boy whose parents both died when he and his twin sister were kids. They were orphaned and then adopted by the Marshall family. He owns Chatter!!! It's up for sale and will probably earn him a cool billion dollars.*

I raised my eyebrows and glanced back at him – at *Luke*. He went to the till at the sushi place and ordered something else. I watched as the clerk poured him a take-out cup of coffee. After he paid and exchanged a few words with the clerk, he stood there, glancing left and right, a distracted expression on his very handsome face. No doubt he was looking for someone beautiful, someone high class who would fit in at his fundraiser. Not someone dressed in sweats and a Yankees ball cap, her hair pulled back and no makeup on.

God. *Almighty...*

Mr. Big Shot 69 – *Luke Marshall* – was gorgeous...

I quickly texted Candace.

ALEXA: I had no idea who he is. What do I know about tech billionaires? I don't use Chatter. He's clearly gorgeous. What do I do now?

She didn't respond and I cursed myself. I could never go through with it. Despite my high school dream of being an actress, I could never pretend to be an escort and go out with him, despite how gorgeous he was.

CANDYC: Don't go up to him looking the way you do now or he'll laugh you out of the food court. His adoptive family is old money. His real family is old money. Besides being gorgeous and super rich, he's as blue blood as you can get. You look like a B Boy and certainly not date material for a swanky family dinner...

I almost laughed out loud at that, but she was right.

ALEXA: I know, I know... I won't go up to him now. But you're talking like I'm actually going to go to the dinner with him.

CANDYC: Are you craycray? Of course you're going to the dinner with him! OMG if you don't go, I will! I would hit that in a heartbeat. It's the opportunity of a lifetime. OMG Lexa. YOU MUST GO WITH HIM!

I bit my lip and considered. If he had asked me as a woman, as someone he knew socially, I'd be all over him like white on rice. But despite my background in theatre, I couldn't keep up that performance.

In fact, I felt incredibly guilty that I'd led him on this far. I couldn't lie to him and pretend to be an escort.

ALEXA: I'm not an escort.

CANDYC: Don't take his money. Do it as an act of charity. He needs a date. You're doing him a big favor. If you don't take any money, you're not technically a hooker. If you volunteer, you're just a date. If you don't volunteer, I WILL!

I chewed my lip. I'd be deceiving him if I went through with it. Did he care? He seemed to need someone to attend the family event with him – why I had no idea. He said he needed a date, but how could a soon-to-be billionaire who looked as hot as he did need a date?

ALEXA: *Why would he need a date? If he's as rich and famous as you say, I'd think women would be falling all over themselves to go out with him. Explain me that one...*

CANDYC: *I don't care why he needs a date. He needs a date. Honestly, Lexa. This is the chance of a lifetime. You're nuts if you don't do it. You can work those acting muscles that have gone to waste.*

I thought for a moment, wondering if I should, just to be charitable.

ALEXA: *I'll think about it...*

Then I chickened out. Instead of meeting him and confessing or sending him a text to tell him the truth, I left. I stood up and walked out of the mall. Before I went through the exit doors, I glanced back and saw he was standing beside his place at the table, his eyes scanning the crowded food court, red umbrella prominently displayed in his hand.

He was looking for some really high-end beautiful escort who charged a cool thousand dollars a night for a straight date, no sex.

He wasn't looking for me.

I hopped on a train back to my apartment near Columbia and took out my cell, hoping to see a response from Candace. There was nothing.

There *was* something from MrBigShot69. I hadn't heard the text because of the rumble of the train rolling into the station, but there it was.

MRBIGSHOT69: Hey, Lexi, where are you? I'm here waiting with bated breath to see how beautiful you are and how green with envy and jealousy someone will be when I turn up to the fundraiser with you on my arm.

I read his text over, read all his texts over, and felt incredible guilt that I was wasting his time.

LEXI911: Sorry, but I had a last-minute emergency. Have to cancel.

MRBIGSHOT69: Don't you pull out on me. I need you to attend with me on Saturday. It's far too late to find someone else. Please... I'll double your rate. I'll be a total gentleman.

LEXI911: Can't you use someone else at the agency?

MRBIGSHOT69: I trust John. He said you're the best. I'll triple your rate.

LEXI911: You haven't even seen me.

MRBIGSHOT69: John said you're beautiful and smart and that's as important as looks for this event. Trust me. I need you. Don't let me down. I'll quadruple your usual rate.

Four thousand dollars? Man, he was desperate. That just amped up my guilt, so I put my cell away and didn't look at it again until I got back to the apartment.

As I was climbing the stairs, Candace came running up behind me, take-out coffee in hand from the shop down the street.

"So, you're going to go to the dinner, right?" she asked, her face bright.

I shook my head sadly. "I can't."

"Why the hell not? He's like one of the most eligible bachelors in the entire country. He's also write-home-to-momma gorgeous. Armani Catwalk gorgeous."

"He is gorgeous. Why he's in need of a date I'll never know. He said he'd quadruple my usual fee."

"That's strange that he's so desperate to use you," she said and followed me into the living room after locking the door behind her — three locks and a chain. "You sure it was him? He was almost married last year but they called it off the week before. I wouldn't think someone like him would have to resort to an escort service."

I nodded. "He had a red umbrella with him. It's not raining today."

I handed her my cell and she read over his texts. "Aww," she said and shook her head. "That's sad. I kinda feel bad for him." Then she looked at me. "You should go anyway. If you don't, I will. Honestly, Alexa. You should go."

I frowned, unsurprised that she'd suggest it. Taking risks was how she rolled.

"You're seriously nuts and I'm even nuttier to listen to you," I said as I plopped down on the sofa. "What if he decides he wants some dessert?"

She sat beside me on the armrest. "What if *you* decide you want a few bites? He's a total babe. I'd do him. If you feel guilty, do it as an act of charity. The guy is clearly desperate."

"I couldn't," I said, although a jolt of adrenaline went through me as I considered going with him anyway. He was so gorgeous.

"He's filthy rich, Lexa. Have you ever been with a man who's filthy rich?"

I shook my head. "Nope."

"See? You'll get to check it off your bucket list." She grinned at me. "He has no credit card limit. It'll be a dinner. You'll wear something classy, and engage in small talk with rich people. He wants someone brainy. You're a brain. Talk to them about international treaties or the balance of power in the Middle East. Do it!"

34

I bit my bottom lip in doubt, but a smile came over my face. "Should I?"

"Yes!" she said and squeezed my shoulder in a hug. "Think of the story you can tell everyone when we meet for brunch on Sunday..."

I let out a huge sigh. "I don't have anything really classy to wear."

"Call Suzanne," she said. "She's got really nice clothes from when she worked for that designer. She must have something you could wear."

"What do you wear to an evening with family at Cipriani Wall Street?"

She shrugged. "A little black number with heels. A tiny silver purse. Your hair and makeup done. A red lace pushup bra and matching thong..." She wagged her eyebrows.

"I can't believe I'm actually considering it," I said with a laugh, considering it seriously. "I could always confess to him that I'm not really an escort, and tell him the whole truth."

"Of course you could," she said. "This is an opportunity of a lifetime. To help out a fellow human being, even if he is a dickhead rich boy. He's a hella good looking dickhead rich boy. You'll get to go to a classy dinner, drink champagne with the rich and opulent. Practice your acting skills."

"You're first rate crazy," I said and made a face. "And I must be to even consider it."

"I am first rate crazy. You love me anyway," she said with a mischievous grin.

"I do."

I took out my cell and decided to text him back, still torn but determined to follow through despite my reluctance. I didn't have to accept any money. It would be just me doing it so he had a date. A simple act of paying it forward.

A good deed.

"Come over here," Candace said, sitting at her computer. "Let's check him out."

She googled Luke Marshall, and for the next hour, we read everything we could get our hands on about him. His Wikipedia page detailed his family, the death of his parents and adoption by the Marshalls, his education and his startup, Chatter. It even had a link to his ex — Jenna Cornwall. We googled her name and there were dozens of images of her, taken by various gossip columnists.

She was stunning. Dark hair, perfect features, classy clothes... In every picture, she looked beautiful. There were a few of her with Luke, before their breakup.

There were a few articles about the wedding being called off due to mutual agreement.

Luke looked so happy in those pictures...

After we'd had our fill of snooping about Luke Marshall, I went to my own computer and read over his emails and then I re-read his texts.

I thought – *what the fuck are you doing, Alexandria? What would your father think?*

My father, the upright law-abiding honest-as-the-day-is-long father, Air Force officer who valued truth and honesty above everything else. What would he think if he knew I was masquerading as a high-class hooker so I could go on a date with a newly-minted soon-to-be billionaire?

He'd give me a withering look that said everything I'd need to know.

LEXI911: *Look I really must say no. I'm so booked this weekend that I can't make the time you want. I've got a client earlier in the day and then one after you. I need some down time...*

MRBIGSHOT69: *Cancel your other appointments. I'll pay*

you whatever you would have earned from them plus what you'll earn from me. It will be the easiest night you've ever had.

LEXI911: I don't know... I don't like cancelling on clients. Especially repeat clients. If I piss them off, I could lose business long-term.

MRBIGSHOT69: Just this once, please! I'm desperate. I need someone with me at the function.

ALEXA: I could fix you up with another escort at the agency. Candy. You'd really like her.

MRBIGSHOT69: No, no, please! It has to be you. John described you and I want you. No one else will do. Period. I'll quintuple your usual pay plus add in what you would have earned from the other two clients... I'm desperate, Lexi.

I read over his texts and could sense his desperation. He really did need someone to come with him on Saturday and he seemed set on Lexi. I felt bad that I'd strung him along for as long as I had. To string him along even more and then not show up would be really mean.

He probably deserved it, considering he was hiring an escort and all, but at the same time, I felt sorry for him. He obviously needed a date for Saturday night.

LEXI911: Okay. I'll meet you at the event. Tell me the time and place. We can sign the NDA before it starts. And since I'm squeezing you in, there'll be no dessert. Just a straight up date. Is that acceptable?

MRBIGSHOT69: PHEW... Thank you. Yes, certainly. If you insist. I'm not using you for sex. I really just need a date for this function. Believe me, you won't regret it. Cipriani on Wall Street. We can meet before at Club 55, on the upstairs terrace so we can sign the NDA. Seven sharp. How will I know you?

LEXI911: I'll be wearing a jade Mala bead bracelet with a white-gold tree of life bangle.

MRBIGSHOT69: Cool. See you then.

"Welp, I did it." I looked up at Candace, who had a huge grin on her face and forced a nervous smile back at her. "I just agreed to be an escort to a rich jerk who calls himself Mr. Big Shot 69."

"A rich *gorgeous* jerk and soon-to-be billionaire who calls himself Mr. Big Shot 69," Candace corrected me. "What can go wrong?"

What *indeed...*

Friday went fast since I had a seminar to attend and lots of work finishing up edits on a paper. I was honestly too busy to think very deep or hard about Mr. Big Shot and my date with him, but on Friday night before I went to bed, I did google him just to check him out. As Candace said, he'd been engaged but called he wedding off only a week before. His bride-to-be was from one of Manhattan's wealthiest families. The google search turned up a blind item on gossip page that other people said was about Luke Marshall's failed engagement.

...A little birdie told this reporter that a recent society wedding featuring the most eligible bachelor and bachelorette was called off because a he cheated and she found out...

What a dick. For a moment, I almost changed my mind. If he cheated on his soon-to-be wife, and he hired escorts, I could see why he couldn't get a date...

Despite what I read, when Saturday came, I woke up with these annoying butterflies in my stomach that lasted all morning as I tried to focus on studying for my comp, but it was no use. I was a basket case.

"Did you know the wedding was called off because he cheated on his fiancée?"

"No," Candace said, frowning over her cup of coffee. "He really is a dick, if that's the case."

"Maybe I won't go," I said, doubting my decision to be a mercy-date for him. "If he's that much of a jerk, he should suffer."

"Go," she said. "It's the chance of a lifetime. You'll get to see how the one-percent lives."

"*Ha*," I said with a sardonic laugh. "More like the zero-point one percent..."

"Even more reason to go."

Later that afternoon, determined to go through with it, I went to Suzanne's apartment in Chelsea to find a dress good enough to wear to Cipriani's on Wall Street. Suzanne was an assistant to a fashion designer in Chelsea and had immigrated to Manhattan from London after she won a competition. We went through her closet, looking for something classy and sexy at the same time, so I could fit in with the rich bastards crowd. I tried on several dresses, discarding a red silk dress with a high neck and pleated skirt, as well as a floral dress that seemed more in line with a summer cocktail party on a patio than in an expensive restaurant venue.

"What about this?" she said and held out a black sleeveless dress with a low-cut V neck and cinched waist. It fell just above the knee. "This is classy enough but it also shows a bit of cleavage, which you have in abundance."

I tried it on and it emphasized my very round butt and bust line, but also my narrow waist, for which I thanked my mother's good genes.

"What do you think?" I said and turned in a circle.

Suzanne stood with her head tilted and examined me from head to foot. She was almost my size, except her curves weren't quite as full as mine, so the dress was a bit tight. Not too tight that I couldn't breathe or sit, but almost.

"With your blonde hair, it looks smashing. You look a lot better in it than I do, so I'd say it's the one."

I stood in front of her mirror and examined my reflection. I did look classy. With heels and some work on the face and hair, I might be good enough to count as arm candy for an evening with family and business associates.

"This is the one," I said, smiling.

I left Suzanne's place with a pair of heels, which she said were the most desirable shoes available at the moment. I didn't know heels, since I never wore them, being more of a Brainiac than a Fashionista. I took her word for it.

Finally home, I had a shower and washed my hair. I put on a robe and sat at the kitchen table while Candace blew out my hair and then hot ironed it so that it was long, straight and shiny. Then, she applied a coat of makeup.

I slipped on the dress and hose, then the heels. In the end, I had to admit I looked the part. Candace had mad makeup skills and she highlighted my features with some extra mascara and lipstick. It made me look much more glamorous than I could have accomplished on my own.

"You sure the lipstick is the right shade?" I asked, noting the plum-pink color that matched my own lips.

"It's perfect. You look high end, not cheap. Exquisite, actually. He'll be really happy."

"Worth four grand?"

She laughed. "I thought you weren't going to take the money."

"I'm not, but when he sees me, I want him to think he's getting his money's worth at least. I haven't been dressed up for over a year..."

"It's time you get out and circulate again," she said. "Meet someone good." She squeezed my shoulders, knowing the troubles I'd escaped over two years earlier. Troubles that I wanted to leave behind in the past where they belonged.

"I highly doubt Mr. Big Shot 69 is my man," I said with a sour expression. "He's rich and gorgeous, but what kind of asshole calls himself Mr. Big Shot 69 and cheats on his fiancée?"

"A very rich asshole. Hopefully with a big dick to match his credit limit. And if you want to sample the appetizers, or eat a cocktail sausage, who'd blame you?"

"Eat a cocktail sausage," I said and made a face of disgust. "Where do you come up with this stuff?"

"I'm here every night," she said with a laugh. "You're going to stand there looking beautiful, drink champagne, eat *canapés* and make polite small talk to rich assholes, occasionally wowing them with some political science. It'll be fun."

"Yeah, sure," I said and grimaced.

"You just wait," she said while I spritzed on some perfume. "I bet you'll have so much fun that you'll go on an actual date with him once you tell him the truth. He won't be able to resist you, now that he's girlfriendless."

"Always the optimist," I said with a sigh. "He'd have to have repented from his cheating ways before that would happen."

"Look, your life is good, now," she said and nodded. "Try to enjoy it for a change. You've holed yourself up in this apartment for almost two years surrounded by books. The bad stuff is behind you."

The bad stuff...

Candace understood. She knew everything about Blaine, having gone through it with me. It was nice having someone who knew my deepest darkest secrets and didn't care.

She gave me the look – a look designed to chide me for being so pessimistic about everything. I had more than enough reason to be that way, but I was trying hard to overcome my nature. Be more like CandyC.

Candy Cane — my nickname for her.

"I'll try but I doubt tonight will be fun. The best I can hope to get out of it is the food and champagne. With my luck, it'll be boring and a flop."

"Stop!" she said and shook my shoulders. "Go with a positive attitude at least. Think of this night as your good deed for the year that will build up some good Karma for you. You deserve it, of all people."

I forced a smile at her and glanced at my butt in the mirror. "Does this dress make me look fat?"

I caught her giving me the look again. "Baby got back, so flaunt it," she said and smacked me in the butt.

"Hopefully, there won't be any dancing or baby'll get sore butt when I fall in these heels," I said with a laugh, finally relaxing a bit. I grabbed my coat and bag and air kissed Candy's cheek before leaving the apartment.

CHAPTER 4

Luke

Usually, I could barely stand the thought of spending another night in the company of my adoptive parents and their crew of Manhattan elites and would politely give my regrets, but this was our annual family dinner with our business partners and so I had to go. The only thing that made me look forward to the night was enacting my little plan for teaching my cheating brother-in-law Eric a lesson.

Of course, he was there, standing like a peacock in his three-thousand-dollar suit – bought with the Marshall family's money of course – a drink in his hand, my sister at his side looking up at him with a mix of adoration and awe. A beauty, with long brown hair and a face that graced many gossip magazine covers, Dana was better than him. She had one hand on her very pregnant belly, and the other clasped tightly in Eric's hand, listening raptly as he expounded on his latest exploits over in Abu Dhabi.

The bastard...

I used to like Eric. I thought he'd be good for my sister when she started talking about him and then when they started dating. Little did I know...

Now, I was no prude and I had no plans on getting married myself, but I did believe in monogamy. If you made the vows, keep them. That was at a minimum what I expected from any husband of my sister, and any brother-in-law, and especially any top executive in my family's corporation.

My anger at him burned in me as I stood and made small talk, forcing a smile I didn't feel while I listened to him boast about his latest conquests half way across the globe in our Middle East office. By all rights, he should have been fired as soon as I learned about his cheating but I couldn't.

I couldn't break my sister's heart. She finally had what she thought she could never have – a baby. She had a rare disorder that made her almost incapable of becoming pregnant without extreme measures and a lot of money. Luckily, our family had that, but it took months and months of effort. When she announced that she was pregnant, I was shocked because they had almost given up and were planning to adopt. Now, she'd have her own child and I hoped she'd be happy but then I found out Eric had been fucking cheating on her?

What – couldn't he use his hand in the last few weeks of Dana's pregnancy for fuck sake?

I seethed while Eric bleated on and missed his question entirely.

"What?" I said, glancing up from my watch, checking to see what time it was, anxious for Lexi to arrive so we could get the show on the road.

"I asked you what you're working on now?"

"Oh, yeah, right. Sorry. I'm expecting my date any minute and was just checking to see what time it was."

"Who?" Dana asked, genuinely curious. "Is it someone I know?"

I hadn't had a date since I ended things with Felicia and so I knew Dana would be insanely curious.

"You'll meet her soon enough," I said and smiled. "She's someone I met at Columbia. You'll love her."

"I'm surprised you invited her," Dana said, raising her eyebrows and tilting her head to the side. "You know, with Mother here and Felicia as well..."

"I'm brave," I said with a laugh, knowing exactly what she meant. "I want to discourage Mother as much as I can. And although Felicia's a lovely woman, she's just not my type."

"That's an understatement," Dana said, smiling.

We were twins, Dana and I. We were *sympatico* on most things, and our dispositions very similar. One thing we agreed on was that our adoptive mother, Dragon Lady as we called her, was far too much of a busybody for either of our tastes. And of course, our adoptive father was a first-class letch...

"Tell us who the lucky girl is," Eric said, wagging his eyebrows at me. "You haven't brought anyone to family events since you and Felicia split. Everyone's starting to gossip about you giving up and going to the other team."

"Eric," Dana said, poking him angrily.

"Well, it's true. When you fall off a horse, you're supposed to get right back up on the saddle or you'll never ride again. Isn't that true?"

He was referring to my failed engagement.

I had, at one time, believed in love, but that was last year. I was no longer into the whole marriage scene or the whole engagement scene, despite my adoptive mother's best intentions.

"I'll get back into the saddle again on my own schedule," I said, through gritted teeth, trying to control my anger.

"You will and you'll be snapped up in no time," Dana said and smiled at me affectionately. "After all, you're a single man with a soon-to-be personal fortune," she said, taking a sip from her soda.

"And not in need of a wife," I replied, knowing the *Pride and Prejudice* opening line very well, having been through an English lit class with Dana, who was wild about Jane Austen. "At least, not this single man with a soon-to-be personal fortune."

"How is the deal going, anyway?" Eric asked. "Have you closed it yet?"

I shook my head. "Still in negotiations," I replied and checked my watch once more.

My real mother would be proud about my success with *Chatter* and it wasn't the first time that day I'd thought about her. It was her family's money — my inheritance — along with my own savings, that helped get *Chatter* its start. I wished she was alive to see the deal finally signed.

"Let's hope it goes through," he replied and swirled his drink. "Then, you'll be your own man."

"I've always been my own man, Eric," I said with a wry smile, although I would have preferred to punch him in the grin. "Now, I'll have my own money."

"When are you guys leaving?" Dana asked, rubbing her belly.

"Soon as the ink's dry and the build is done."

"It sounds wonderful. Maybe someday, I can do that. But not for a few years," Dana said and smiled.

"Not for a few years," I replied. "You're going to be busy parents for the next few years, I expect. Now, if you'll excuse me, I have to go find my date."

"You go ahead," Dana said and leaned in. "Bring your date over and introduce us."

46

I gave her a kiss on the cheek. "I plan on it," I said with a smile.

Then, I left the two of them at the bar and went upstairs to the terrace where I would meet Lexi and get her to sign the NDA my lawyer had drawn up. The last thing I wanted was for an escort to start blabbing around town that I, Lucas Marshall, son of the Marshall Family, and soon-to-be former CEO of a billion-dollar tech startup, used an escort service.

I couldn't wait for Lexi to show up so I could rub Eric's smug self-satisfied and cheating face in it.

CHAPTER 5

ALEXA

The taxi took me to Cipriani's on Wall Street – the famous Club 55. Not that I knew what Club 55 was until I googled it earlier in the day. It was way out of my league.

Mr. Big Shot 69 was way out of my league.

I'd spent most of my life traveling with my dad to bases around the USA, living in base housing, and communing with the other military kids. We were firmly lower middle class. Before he retired and took a job teaching flying at a local flight school near Portland, my father drove an old Ford Country Squire station wagon and we pulled a trailer behind us when we went on vacation. He drank beer, liked to barbecue steaks over coals and wore a Timex.

So, I wasn't used to expensive men. I was only attending Columbia on scholarship and could never have afforded it on my own or based on my father's income or pension.

I paid the cabbie and then got out, standing in front, taking in the building with its impressive façade. Even the entry was gilded, shiny brass fixtures and glass. I didn't belong there but had to admit it was fun to get the chance to go inside.

I took in a deep breath and opened the door, clutching my bag and wondering what kind of evening I'd have.

The interior of Cipriani's ballroom was amazing. It was a huge venue with several large rooms used for meetings and receptions, as well as a restaurant and several bars. I had no idea where the terrace was, and in fact, had no idea that there were so many separate rooms, but the place was big. It looked like something you'd see in Italy. I went to the main bar in the ballroom and stood there, wondering where the terrace was. The venue was dim with sparkling lights that made the vaulted ceilings look like something out of Rome or Florence.

A tray of glasses sat on a linen-covered table. A small card at the bottom read "Bellini" which was a cocktail made with peach nectar and Prosecco – a sparkling wine like champagne. I took a glass and turned around to check out the crowd of people in the hall. I sipped the Bellini, enjoying the Italian cocktail's sweetness.

I glanced down at myself, straightening my dress, checking that my jade Mala bead bracelet was on display, with my tree of life pendant. I wanted to watch to see if Mr. Big Shot 69 saw me and how he'd respond so I scanned the crowd.

Then, my cell dinged. A text.

I removed my cell from my bag and read it. Of course, it was from Candace.

CandyC: So, how's it going? I'm dying of jealousy here...

Alexa: I'm here, Bellini in hand, waiting. No sign of Mr. Big Shot yet.

CandyC: Text me as soon as you can with all the gory details...

Alexa: I will.

I was going to put my cell back into my bag, but then I got

another text and read it, thinking it was Candace, adding some snide or cheerleading comment.

Instead, it was MrBigShot69 himself. Luke Marshall. Cheating bastard with a huge fortune.

MrBigShot69: Come up to the terrace and meet me at the south end. I'll be sitting at a table in the alcove so we can do some business before pleasure.

I swallowed hard at the pleasure part. He was the kind of man who might populate my sexual fantasies. Scratch that — he *was* the kind of man who most definitely populated my recent sexual fantasies, although he'd never be someone I'd want to get close to.

I sent him a text.

Lexi911: I'll be there in five.

I drank down my Bellini for courage and then found the closest washroom so I could check myself over. I'd have to walk up to him while he watched, and I didn't want anything between my teeth. Satisfied that I was as presentable as I could possibly get, I left the washroom and found a sign that gave directions to the terrace.

I took the huge marble stairs leading to the balcony, which was a narrow room with huge high windows overlooking Wall Street. Linen-covered tables lined the terrace and at the far end sat Mr. Big Shot himself, all alone. He was checking out his cellphone, and was sprawled on the chair, his legs spread like he owned the world. His dark bangs fell into his eyes in this really sexy way.

I took in a deep breath, and started to thread my way along the tables towards him, my heart beating a little faster.

Was I really going to do this?

I kept walking. I was really going to do this.

On his part, Mr. Big Shot was wearing some fashionable dark framed glasses and was dressed in a very sober black suit with a silky black tie and crisp white shirt. A red kerchief was tucked into

51

his suit jacket pocket and I smiled to myself despite my nerves. It was his way of signaling who he was.

When he glanced up from his cell, I saw how gorgeous he was, even with the glasses. In fact, they made him even more gorgeous, because they gave him this air of nerd wrapped up in a very non-nerdy desirable package.

He removed his glasses when he saw me, tucking them in his pocket. Then, he stood, buttoning his jacket, blinking when our eyes met. Well, that was a good sign, right?

He stood straighter, a smile finally spreading on his lips. He looked pleased, at least.

When I arrived, he stepped closer to meet me, and bent down to kiss me softly on my cheek, one hand squeezing my arm.

"Lexi, I presume," he said, his voice deep and warm. He met my eyes and his smile seemed truly pleased.

"Alexandria, to be precise," I replied firmly, trying hard to be professional when what I really felt was sick to my stomach. "Apparently, that's where I was conceived."

"Alexandria, Virginia?"

I shook my head. "No, Egypt."

He made a face of surprise. "Exotic."

"Not really. My father was an air force pilot stationed in Germany. He took my mother to Alexandria on their honeymoon and I was the happy result. Hence, the name." I smiled, then kicked myself mentally. I was telling him about *me* – the real Alexa – not Lexi911. I wanted to come off as a sophisticated escort, not a nerdy college student. "You must be Mr. Big Shot 69."

He bent down and kissed my other cheek, a smile on his nicely-full lips. I could swear he inhaled when he pulled back, as if he were trying to smell my perfume.

"The very man," he said with a chuckle. "You can call me Luke." He pulled out a chair and pointed to it. "Please, have a seat.

We have some business to take care of first. But I'm truly interested in your story. John didn't tell me anything, so I'm all ears on how a girl with a family like yours ends up being an escort."

I sat down and he helped move my chair closer. I laid my bag on the table and waited while he sat back down beside me.

"Tuition is expensive." I left it at that.

"Well, I'm pleased regardless," he said, pushing the sheet of paper and a very ornate fountain pen towards me, a cocky grin on his face. "Very pleased. John said you were hot in addition to being a brain, and he was right about the first part and if you're at Columbia, probably the second as well. That dress..."

I smiled to myself and leaned slightly forward, knowing full well that it would afford him a peek down my cleavage, which even I had to admit looked nice. I read over the legal document in front of me.

This Nondisclosure Agreement is entered into by and between Lucas John Marshall of Marshall Windsor Investments Inc. ("Disclosing Party") and _____, of Manhattan ("Receiving Party") for the purpose of preventing the unauthorized disclosure of Confidential Information as defined below. The parties agree to enter into a confidential relationship with respect to the disclosure of certain proprietary and confidential information ("Confidential Information").

I'd never signed, let alone seen, an NDA so it was all new to me. I read it over, pretending that this was all routine to me, and when I had finished, I wrote my name on the line and signed the bottom, dating it as well. Then, I handed it back to him with a smile.

"There you are, Mr. Lucas John Marshall. Signed, sealed and delivered."

He took it from me and folded it up, tucking it into his jacket interior pocket and slipping his fountain pen in as well.

"Wonderful," he said and then sat there for a moment, taking me in, his eyes roving over me in a very lascivious manner. "I hope you don't mind me asking once again, but why is such a beautiful woman like you selling yourself as an escort? You could be a model, with your looks."

I scoffed at that. "You flatter me. I'm far too short, my curves are too big for standard modeling and not big enough for plus-size." I shrugged.

"You look perfect to me. I personally love short women. I like to be able to pick them up and carry them to my bed." He grinned widely at that. "Place them on top of me and let them ride me like a bucking bronco."

My eyes would have usually widened at a statement like that, but I had to catch myself. I was an escort. Who knew what kind of whacky and perverted things I must have done in my time servicing rich men? Instead, I kept my cool.

"Then I'm your girl," I said and smiled. "Short, eminently carry-able, and in addition to being a budding political scientist, I'm a very skilled bronc rider."

"Political Science?" he said, his mouth open. "He said you were smart, but I had no idea it was Poli Sci."

I had no idea what I was doing, revealing true tidbits about myself, but I decided to just go with the flow.

"Yes, I was going to study medicine, be a paramedic, but it was far too stressful. International Relations is far more sedate. You know, nuclear weapons treaties. International conventions on chemical weapons. That sort of thing."

His eyes narrowed in response and he kept watching my mouth as I talked.

"I can see why he likes you," he said softly.

"Who? John?" I replied, remembering the story of how he got my name. Of course, it was all a lie, but I wasn't going to fess up at that point. Maybe later, when I saw how the night went, if he wanted some extra delicacies instead of just a straight date. At that point, I'd confess that I wasn't Lexi911. Then, I'd go home with a fantastic story to tell at our weekly brunch the next day.

"Who?" he asked, his expression blank as if his mind was elsewhere. Then, he shook his head as if he'd made a mistake. "Oh, yes. John, of course. That's how I got your name. Through John."

"Yes," I replied, a weird sense that we were both lying. "Through John." Then, I got nervous. What if John was at the function? I had no idea who he was. As soon as Luke introduced us, the jig would be up and I'd have to confess.

All of a sudden, I got this feeling – the feeling that I should stop listening to Candace and start thinking for myself. I thought because I was older that she would no longer be able to lead me down the path to hooliganism, as my mother called it back when we were in high school. Apparently, I hadn't grown up yet. Candace had a real rebellious streak due to a bad family life, and it was only finding her calling in life – the study of rocks, of all things – that kept her from ending up in Juvenile Hall. I had no such excuse.

"Is John coming tonight?"

"No, unfortunately," Luke said and frowned. "I don't think he can come. Sorry to disappoint. All you've got is me tonight."

I smiled. "That's fine. I just thought..."

He nodded. "You just thought since we were business partners that he'd be here at the dinner. No," he said and leaned back in his chair. "He was invited but had other plans. This is all family and their business colleagues. My family. A pack of wolves if there ever was one."

I frowned. "Really?"

"You don't know much about my family, do you?"

I felt really stupid for other than my google search on his failed engagement, I hadn't done much reading up on Luke Marshall and his family fortune, relying on Candace to fill me in. I knew Marshall was a big name in the business world, but I wasn't much into the local business scene. I was studying treaties. What did I know about business?

"Sorry," I said. "I'm not from Manhattan. I'm pulling a blank."

"You know Er--," he said and then stopped and frowned, adjusting his tie. "I mean, you met John, though."

I had to think fast. "We didn't do a lot of talking..." I raised my eyebrows suggestively, hoping that would shut him up.

He grinned and laughed nervously. "Of course not. It's just that I've never done this before," he said and pointed to me, and then to himself. "I've never hired anyone before, to, you know. Go on a date. Or have sex. I've never really needed one."

I nodded, trying to appear sympathetic but he sounded like an arrogant dick.

Never needed one...

"Of course you never needed an escort," I said, and rested my chin on my hand, trying to look at him adoringly, when I was really thinking he was a spoiled brat. "I can't imagine you'd be single for very long – or have to pay for sex."

"I haven't been and I don't." Then he took in a breath, like he was steeling himself for something unpleasant. "Let's go downstairs. I hope you can put on the performance of your lifetime. Pretend we're old friends from college. I went to Columbia for my undergrad so we can say we met then. We started to see each other only recently, but are very much in love. How does that sound?"

He raised his eyebrows, waiting for my response.

"It sounds like a good story," I said. "I happen to be a student at Columbia and while I was never in any business classes, maybe we met at the pub. It could have happened. I can fake it with the best of them."

He stood up and held out his hand. "It totally could have happened. But," he said and pulled me close, holding my body against him with a hand on my lower back. "No faking it with me if we get into any extra-curricular activities later. Okay?"

"I won't unless I need to," I replied, narrowing my eyes suggestively.

"You won't need to," he said, his voice sounding husky, like he was already getting ideas.

Who was I kidding? I was already getting ideas...

Then he kissed me, a full-on lip lock, and it wasn't just a friendly kiss. It was enough to set my heart racing, and my traitorous body responded like Pavlov's Dog to a bell, swelling and wet and ready.

When he let me go and grabbed my hand, it took a few seconds for me to recover and I couldn't help but smile to myself. When I saw his own smile, it made my back stiffen. He was *not* going to control me so easily.

Mr. Big Shot 69, arrogant cheater on his fiancée...

I took in a deep breath and tried to get ahold of myself. It had been a loooong while since I was with a man and I was not going to just fold up like a chair at the first handsome, sexy, wealthy, alpha male billionaire that kissed me.

At least I'd try not to...

We walked past the empty tables to the marble staircase.

"Here goes everything," he said and took in a deep breath. Together, we made our entrance to the event.

I felt eyes turn to see us as we emerged from the staircase to the main ballroom and several people pointed. It made me feel a bit like Cinderella at the ball with her Prince, except Luke wasn't charming. Well, he was, superficially, but he was still a jerk. He was totally a business man, doing business, an exchange of money for services rendered, and was trying to make someone jealous.

Okay, I had to stop kidding myself. He *was* charming and gorgeous. Let's face it, a man who looked as good as Luke didn't have to be too charming. You could shut off your ears for a while, forget he was a cad, and just look at him...

Was it a recent girlfriend he was trying to make jealous? Would she be here? I hadn't thought to ask about who he was trying to make jealous.

"I forgot. Who are you're trying to make jealous?"

"Don't you worry about the why," he said quickly. "Just look beautiful and sound smart when you talk to my family and any colleagues we meet."

I nodded and together, we walked out into the throng of people, who looked like all the rich and famous of Manhattan's business elite. Not that I personally would know what any of them looked like, but if I could imagine it, they would look like these people, polished, rested, rich.

Who was this Lucas Marshall?

I'd never heard of him until this whole business, but that wasn't saying anything since money and commerce were not my things. More like politics and sociology.

Once upon a time when I was in High School, I had a dream to become an actress and move to Hollywood. I was my drama teacher's star pupil and was hopeful. Then I got mixed up in an intrigue that took me on a one-hundred and eighty degree turn from that and changed my life.

So, even though I had no idea who this bunch of rich people were, I knew how to act.

I'd pretend.

CHAPTER 6

I could see why Eric picked her.

She was gorgeous, with long fair hair and perfect skin, blue eyes and a brilliant smile. Her curves made my dick twitch, her waist tiny and her ample breasts and hips were nice and round. Her dress was formal but just a little bit sexy, with the v-neck showing a touch of her very ample bosom. Just perfect. Sexy, beautiful, and yet classy. Smart as well, from our text messages, which I enjoyed far too much.

I stood, taking in a deep breath. It wasn't often I was struck by a woman's looks, but Lexi had it all – at least according to my tastes. She walked up, a confident smile on her face, her full lips very kissable. Right away, my mind went to where I'd like those lips to go and despite my determination not to use any of her unadvertised services, I couldn't help but imagine her on her knees before me, with that delicious mouth wrapped firmly around my cock

After some introductions and the signing of the NDA, we walked down the stairs and into the fray. I introduced her to my colleagues who were attending the event, and Lexi was gracious, smart and well-spoken. I had to admire the ease with which she met perfect strangers and made polite conversation. When it came time to finally meet my brother-in-law and sister, I had to take in a deep breath and calm myself. I didn't want to ruin the night with a big scene, so I wanted it to go just right. I couldn't wait to see Eric's face when he saw me with Lexi.

I'd talk about marriage and sacred vows and how being a parent was a huge responsibility. I'd even mention how volatile the business world was and how one could never count on a job for life anymore.

It would make him think.

We walked up to Dana and Eric but if he was surprised when he saw Lexi on my arm, he said and did nothing to show it. Instead, he raised his eyebrows like he was admiring her instead of being totally shocked that she, of all women, was my date for the night. The bastard even wagged his eyebrows at me and smiled, his expression full of lewd suggestion.

Of course, I didn't think about how Lexi would react when she saw Eric was my brother-in-law. I didn't get that far, because I was too focused on how Eric would respond. At that moment, I was hit by a sense of guilt that I hadn't thought about how awkward it would be for Lexi. I had nothing against her. She was smart and beautiful. It was too bad she felt she had to sell herself to pay for college. I wasn't trying to hurt her. It was Eric I wanted to cause pain.

Neither of them did what I expected.

Eric was smiling like a Cheshire Cat and Lexi looked as cool as a cucumber.

"Well, hello," Dana said when we walked up. "Please introduce us to your date, brother."

I could tell by the way Dana was looking at Lexi that she approved of my choice of dates. It made me burn with anger at the thought that her bastard of a husband had actually fucked Lexi. I turned to Lexi and smiled.

"This is Alexandria, or Lexi, for short," I said, emphasizing the Lexi. I gestured to Dana and Eric. "Lexi, this is my sister Dana and her husband, Eric. Dana and Eric have been married for two years and are finally going to become parents for the first time. Isn't that amazing?"

Lexi smiled at my sister. "Hello," she said in a soft voice. "Nice to meet you. Luke has told me so much about you. He's so happy you're having a baby."

"I know," Dana said and smiled, leaning in closer to Lexi. "He's been so excited about it and I know he'll be a fantastic uncle."

Then Lexi turned to Eric, but she didn't seem to recognize him or at least, she put on a great performance. "You must be very excited. To be a father for the first time. I can't imagine."

"Oh, very," Eric said and took Lexi's hand, kissing her knuckles gallantly. "I'm extremely pleased. So, tell us how you two met?" he said, looking between Lexi and me. "Luke doesn't bring many dates to these functions, so we're very curious."

"Luke and I share a love of politics," Lexi said and turned to glance at me, an expression of fondness on her face that despite it all, I wished was real instead of fake. "You should hear the discussions we get into about foreign trade rules and whether the Chinese are really currency manipulators." Lexi winked at me.

"Oh, they most definitely are," I said, winking back at her. "And you know it, no matter how hard you try to deny it."

She laughed. "But you're wrong. It was me who convinced you they are."

"Not the way I remember it," I replied, watching Eric's face. He seemed unaffected by Lexi's presence, his gaze moving between the two of us, like he was watching a tennis match, smiling the whole time. He was obviously not a man who showed any remorse.

The man had zero morals or conscience, apparently.

I pulled Lexi closer and kissed her forehead, putting on a show of affection. Those two were the consummate actors, to be pretending they had no idea who the other person was. I couldn't imagine Lexi didn't recognize Eric, and I knew that Eric sure as hell would remember Lexi. There was no way on earth that a man would fuck Lexi and not remember doing it. She was beautiful and definitely sexy. Sexy Lexi was right. She was friendly, at ease with my family full of rich Manhattanites. She was a consummate actress, not showing a moment's hesitation when speaking with Eric.

Eric was also a man you couldn't forget once you met him. He had that upper crust British accent that had impressed Dana when he came over to take a job in our New York office.

I expected to see him sweat, stutter, get red-faced or cough.

Nothing.

The four of us made small talk for a while and it was then that John showed up.

I hadn't expected him to come, and in fact, didn't want him to. It was John who followed Eric and Lexi to the club in Brooklyn where they danced and drank. Then, it was John who tracked her down for me, finding out who she was after Eric had drunkenly blabbed to someone her name and how one could hire beautiful women for the night if they had the right connections and enough cash.

It was John who found 9-1-1 Escorts and told me her email.

It was John who suggested that I hire her and show up with her on my arm. We agreed and that was that.

My little cover story about John giving me Lexi's email address was great, because he did.

John smiled at me and at Lexi when I introduced them. On her part, Lexi choked on her drink and seemed to freeze, her eyes widening like she was shocked. On his part, John said a round of hellos to Eric and Dana and then grabbed my arm.

"Can we talk for a moment?" he said, giving me the eye.

"I'm kind of busy," I said, tilting my head to the side. "Chatting with Dana and Eric."

"It'll just take a moment."

"Can't it wait?" I said, frustrated that he wanted to leave.

"Now, Luke."

I finally gave in. "Will you excuse us?" I said to Lexi and then to my sister and Eric, who looked like everything was just hunky dory.

That was definitely *not* at all the effect I was hoping to have.

When we got out of ear shot, and were standing at the bar a dozen or more feet away from them, John turned to me.

"That's *not* Lexi."

"What?" I frowned and turned to glance at her. She'd been looking at me and quickly looked away -- almost guiltily.

"I don't know who she is, but she's not the Lexi I saw get into Eric's car. Not the Lexi I saw dancing with Eric, nor the one whose email I gave you."

I was at a loss for words, standing there with my mouth hanging open.

"Are you sure?" I asked, leaning in closer. "She passed herself off as Lexi, whoever she is."

"Maybe the real Lexi was busy and she sent someone else in her place?" John offered. "But then, why not just admit it?"

"Lexi, or whomever I texted, did say she was really busy tonight and couldn't do it but I coaxed her until she said yes. I even offered to pay four times her usual rate."

I glanced back at whoever it was standing with my sister and her cheating husband and who obviously wasn't Lexi of 9-1-1 Escorts.

"Well, that's definitely not the woman Eric was with at the club. She wasn't as short and not a blonde. She was attractive, like I said – hot in this classy hookerish sort of way. Smart, too. That's not Lexi. What email did you send to?"

"The one you said." I spelled it out. "Lexi911 at yahoo dot com."

John frowned. "Wait – it was supposed to be *Lexxi911* at yahoo dot com. You know – with two X's like in X-rated. The porn thing."

Now it was my turn to be confused. I pulled out my cell and checked my email sent folder.

"Oh, *God*, I sent it to Lexi911 with *one* X."

I glanced up at John and we stared at each other for a few seconds.

Then we both burst out laughing.

John laughed so hard, he snorted. After we calmed down and he wiped his eyes, he looked at me, his brow furrowed, and spoke in a more serious tone. "If she isn't Lexxi, who the hell is she?"

I shook my head and turned to stare at her, standing with my very pregnant sister and cheating bastard of a brother-in-law.

She was beautiful. I'd even considered asking for something more than just a date, despite the fact I didn't approve of escorts.

Who the hell indeed?

CHAPTER 7

ALEXA

When a handsome blond-haired man who looked like a surfer in a suit walked up to us, I turned to him, wondering who he was. When Luke identified him as his best friend John, I almost choked on my Bellini from shock.

John was there?

Luke said John wasn't coming. He'd know I wasn't the Lexi that Luke was supposed to have hired. He'd tell Luke and the jig would be up.

I'd be outed as an impostor.

What would Luke do? What *could* he do? I hadn't broken any law, as far as I could tell, but I was impersonating someone. Could you impersonate a stage name? I was sure she wasn't really named Lexi. That was an obvious made-up name that was probably used on the promotional website.

Finally, the two of them walked over, and Luke stood close to my side. When I glanced up in his face, he smiled at me but there was this look in his eyes... It was a look that told me my little game was over. Now, how would he handle it?

"How are you doing, Lexi?" John asked, smiling at me. "Long time no see."

"Oh, ah," I stuttered, "I'm doing fine. And you?"

"Never better. You're looking good. Different from the last time I saw you. What is it – did you do something to your hair?"

What was he doing? Was he pretending that I really was Lexi?

I touched my hair, trying to make it look like I'd done something to make me look different.

"My hair was a bit darker before," I said, my voice wavering from nerves. "I got highlights."

"That must be it," he said and made a clicking sound with is tongue, pointing his finger at me like it was a gun. "Because, I only saw you a week ago." Then, John turned to Luke. "That's right, isn't it?" Then he turned to Eric. "Have you met her? Lexi?"

"Who?" Eric said, his face changing. He glanced at me. "You mean Alexandria?"

"Lexi, Alexandria, whatever. I mean Luke's new date. Quite the *looker*, isn't she?"

Eric seemed upset and nodded quickly. "Yes, we met. Luke introduced us earlier." Then, he changed the subject. "How are you John? How's business been treating you?"

He had a nervous smile and I wondered what the heck was going on between the three men. Dana turned to me and smiled. "Don't you hate it when men talk about us like we're not actually here?"

"Oh, really?" I said, laughing nervously myself. "I didn't notice."

"Well, what if I said something like, gee, doesn't Luke have nice pecs? He's quite buff, don't you think? Do you think these guys would like it?"

I frowned, not really wanting to get into any kind of controversial discussion.

"Oh, sorry, Dana," John said, a hand over his heart. "My bad. I was just so taken with Luke's new escort for the night that I lost my mind."

A really super weird vibe passed through the guys. Was John deliberately trying to out me as an escort? Why did he mention the word escort? Why was Eric's face so white and why was he pulling Dana closer?

"We really must mingle," Eric said quietly and started to lead Dana away from us. "Come along, darling," he said and leaned down to kiss Dana on the cheek. "We should go say hello to your mother."

Dana smiled at me before she left. "Nice to meet you Alexandria. That's such a pretty name. Very exotic."

"You can call me Alexa," I said.

"I hope we see you again," Dana said, eyeing Luke, narrowing her eyes. "Luke, you should bring Alexa to the beach house some weekend. Remember, we're having our annual family meeting in two weeks and there'll be lots of people there. I'm sure everyone would be glad to meet her."

"I plan on it," Luke said and squeezed me, his arm slipping around my waist. "As long as Lexi's free. She has exams, so..."

Then, Dana and Eric walked off, leaving me alone with Luke and John.

"So, what's the deal, *Alexandria*," John said, putting emphasis on my name, his blue eyes narrowed. "Tell us who you really are. You're not Lexi. Are you one of the other escorts at the agency?"

"I, I..." I stuttered, unsure of what to say. "I'm not from the agency."

"What?"

I looked at them both and took a step back. "I'm so sorry. I got your email by mistake and, well," I said to Luke, shrugging. "I went along just to see who you were. Then, I got too far in and couldn't find a way to bow out gracefully."

Luke glanced away, and I could see a muscle in his jaw twitch.

"Who the *hell* are you, then?" John said.

"I'm Alexandria Dixon. I'm an MA student in Political Science at Columbia."

"How did you get Lexxi911's email?"

I made a face. "I got Luke's message in an old email mailbox I used when I worked for 9-1-1 as a relief operator. My friend and I, we thought it would be fun to play along. See who it was with an alias like Mr. Big Shot 69." I glanced at Luke who wasn't looking at me. Instead, he was clearly angry, his face dark. "I mean, what grown-up uses an email ID like Mr. Big Shot 69?"

"Oh, that?" John said with a laugh. "Let me tell you about Mr. Big Shot. He's been in business practically since kindergarten."

"John..." Luke said, giving John a deathly look.

John wasn't fazed. "No, I swear. He used to get all these comic books that he didn't like. You know – Archie and Veronica, Scooby Doo. He sold them in public school. Then, he moved up to graphic novels. He had enough money saved up from selling used stuff that he started an online business when we were in high school. We called him Mr. Big Shot because he bought a really cool car when he turned sixteen with his own money made from his business. The name stuck."

John clapped Luke on the back, smiling at him. "Isn't that right, Mr. Big Shot?" John turned back to me. "As to the 69 part? Well," he said and grinned. "I'll leave that to your imagination."

He smiled so broadly I couldn't help but smile to myself. I turned to Luke, who was frowning.

"I thought your family was really rich. Why were you selling used comics?"

Luke finally glanced my way, our eyes meeting. "I wanted my own money. So, I went out and made it."

"That's admirable," I said, wondering what it must have been like to grow up in such a wealthy family. "I'm surprised you felt that way. Most kids would just enjoy their family's money."

"I have a very independent streak. John and I started *Chatter* to break free of our families. John's family is almost but not quite as bad as mine."

"That's right," John said and wrapped an arm around Luke's shoulder. "We're brothers in arms. Tackling Wall Street together. Casting off the bonds of our families together. And, if our deal goes through, we'll be free. Free of the old money and finally our own men."

"I'm already my own man," Luke said, laughing finally, his mood lightening. "If only Dragon Queen would get the message."

I turned to Luke. "Why did you have to hire an escort if you're so wealthy? I'd think you'd have to fight off the women wanting to date you..."

Luke glanced at me almost guiltily and bit his bottom lip. "I haven't been honest with you either. You see that slimly worm of a man with my sister?" He gestured with his head to where Eric and Dana were standing, talking to some other people at the function. "He's been cheating on my sister with Sexy Lexxi of 9-1-1 Escorts. I wanted to hire her and bring her to the event tonight to rub her in his cheating face. Give him a message that he'd better get clean or I'd expose him."

My mouth dropped open in shock. "That's what you meant?" I shook my head. "I thought you wanted to rub me in your ex's face."

"Nope," Luke said, shaking his head. "Eric's cheating face."

"Maybe you should just tell your sister the truth?"

"What?" He frowned. "And break her heart? She's going to have a baby."

I shrugged, thinking to myself that I'd want to know if my husband was cheating on me.

"If he's been cheating on her with an escort service while she's pregnant, their marriage is doomed. Better to know now than later when she's been with him longer."

"She'd be a single mom before her baby's even born."

"Better a hard truth than a comfortable delusion," I replied.

"Well, that's easy for you to say. You're not in her shoes. I've talked to her before. She said she didn't think she could survive as a single parent. I don't want to force that on her, so I thought I'd send a message to Eric instead. If he doesn't wise up and clean up his act, then I'll let her know. But only if he doesn't stop. If he does, maybe they can stay together and things will improve."

"I doubt it," I said, thinking about my own experience with cheating bastards. "Better to have a clean break than stay with someone who's clearly not monogamous."

He shrugged. "Well, that's your opinion, I guess."

"It is," I said and the two of us stood our ground, both of our arms crossed, turning slightly away from each other.

"Look," I said and took in a deep breath. "I didn't mean for things to go this far, but it was fun and my best friend and I were going along for a laugh. When I told you no, that I couldn't attend tonight, you sounded so desperate. I didn't want to let you down. I never planned to take your money." I looked him in the eyes and he finally nodded. "I told you I couldn't do anything more than just a date, and so I figured I was doing a good deed. Getting some good karma by helping a stranger. I had no idea you were going to use me as a threat to your brother-in-law. If I had, I would never have agreed to come tonight."

"What do you mean, you never would have come tonight?" a

woman's voice from behind us said. "Lucas, John, so glad to see you both here." She smiled at Luke and John then she turned to me, frowning. "Lucas, you must introduce me to your date. I'm so surprised you brought someone. You never do."

At that, Luke turned and then extended his arm, gesturing to a woman who was approaching us and who must have overhead my last sentence. She was in her fifties and looked like she'd been spray-painted into existence, her makeup thick and professional, her hair bouffant with every single hair lacquered in place like she used Gorilla Glue.

"Mother," he said, his voice flat. "May I introduce Alexandria Dixon. She's a friend from Columbia. We've been seeing each other for a while and I invited her tonight." He turned to me. "Alexandria, this is my mother, Janet Marshall."

"Alexandria?" Mrs. Marshall said, turning to me. "You've never mentioned her before. My dear, why do you keep your... girlfriends... secret? We had no idea you were bringing someone..."

Mrs. Marshall smiled at me, but it was the least friendly smile I had ever experienced. She didn't extend her hand and simply pressed her coral lips together in a smile that didn't reach her eyes.

"You can call me Alexa, Mrs. Marshall," I said, nodding my head. "Pleased to meet you. Luke's told me so much about you."

"All of it good, I hope," Mrs. Marshall said, giving Luke the evil eye. "Lucas is such a closed book, it's hard to know what's going on with him at times. He never comes by for dinner or just a visit. It's terrible for a son to be so negligent."

"Mother, you know I'm currently busy working with John to finalize the sale," Luke said, his voice sounding tired, like he'd had this argument with his adoptive mother forever. "That's taken up all my time. Father knows that I'm planning to spend time at the beach house as soon as it goes through."

"He knows, but he misses you, darling. Are you coming to the party in two weeks? I know there'll be many people who will want to congratulate you on the deal. Felicia will be there. She'll be happy to see you. You've been so busy lately..."

"I'm bringing Alexandria with me to the party, Mother."

"But I told you that Felicia and her family were coming."

I caught the frown that passed between her and Luke. Apparently, Mrs. Marshall wanted to push Luke together with Felicia and Luke didn't appreciate it. He was using me as an excuse to avoid her.

"Alexa's coming," Luke said, his voice firm.

"But Felicia will be so upset..."

"Alexa and I are seeing each other exclusively," Luke said, raising his eyebrows at me, pulling me even more tightly against him. "I wouldn't want to go without her. Felicia and I are friends, nothing else."

Mrs. Marshall harrumphed. She visibly pouted, her back stiff like she was preparing to do battle.

"But I—"

"*Mother*," Luke said, his voice acid. "I'm seeing Alexa. I'm not interested in Felicia. We're just friends."

"So, you invited Alicia, did you?" she asked, peering at me closely, assessing me from head to foot.

"Alexa," Luke corrected.

Mrs. Marshall glanced at me. "I imagine you'll look quite scandalous in a bikini, with that figure. For heaven's sake, don't wear one or we'll probably have to provide you with bodyguards to protect you from the young hounds who will be there and defibrillators for the older men."

I felt immediately naked and exposed at that, and wished I could pull down my skirt's hem a bit and maybe pull together the neck of my dress to hide my cleavage. I hated when people commented on my too-full curves.

"*Mother*," Luke said, frowning. "How can you be so crass?"

"Well, it's the truth," Mrs. Marshall said, eyeing me disapprovingly. "She's quite the full-figured girl."

"She's not full-figured," Luke said and raised his eyebrows at me. "She's beautiful." Luke regarded me with clear approval in his eyes, which made me feel a little bit better. He must hate his adoptive mother so much that he was starting to defend me against her, when only a few moments earlier I could swear he hated me.

"Well, whatever you say, darling," Mrs. Marshall said and sighed. "But I know Felicia will be very disappointed that you'll be bringing Alana and won't spend time with her."

"It's *Alexa*, Mother. Besides, Felicia understands," Luke said dryly. "It's you and Mrs. Blake who don't."

She gave me one last glance from head to toe. "Well, I must be off and circulate."

At that, Mrs. Marshall turned away, giving us an acid smile before she left.

Luke turned to me, his eyes meeting mine, a softer expression in them than he had earlier.

"I'm sorry about that. My adoptive mother's a bit of a witch."

"A bit?" I laughed nervously, surprised that he was so open about it. "She's certainly forthright in expressing her views on things."

"You always know where you stand with Mrs. M," John said with a grin.

"I need another drink," Luke said and exhaled. He glanced at me. "Can I get you another one as well?"

I nodded. "I better have something non-alcoholic. I have to study tomorrow for my comp."

"Comprehensive exam?"

I nodded. "Yes. I start doing thesis work as soon as I finish."

"What's your thesis area?"

"Globalization."

Luke nodded and then pointed to the bar. "I'll be right back. John, what can I get for you?"

"Whatever you're having."

"Probably should be hemlock, but I'll have a beer instead." Luke said and left me standing with John.

I turned to him, feeling like the three of us had just survived a battle. "So, I take it Luke and his adoptive mother don't quite see eye to eye."

"That's the understatement of the millennium. She wants him to marry Felicia Blake and he most definitely doesn't want to. Well, she really wanted him to marry this woman called Jenna, but that's a whole other story."

"This is the 21st Century," I said. "People find their own partners when they get married."

"I know that and Luke knows that, but apparently, Mrs. M didn't get the memo. She's not one to take no for an answer though. I see sabers at dawn in Luke's future."

"Really?" I said. "I'm surprised that there'd be such a big fight over who Luke marries."

"Old money wants to keep it all in the right families, and Felicia comes from only the very oldest money. We're talking cousins of the founding families of Manhattan's banking class. They do things differently than the rest of us."

"I wouldn't know," I said with a shrug. "I come from good old working class stock. Dad was a pilot in the Air Force."

John shrugged. "That's pretty decent stock."

"We're definitely lower middle class, but only just. My dad happens to be skilled with hand-eye coordination and cool under pressure. My grandfather worked on the docks. My other grandfather worked on the railroad as an engineer."

John nodded. "Good red-blooded American working class. Nothing to be ashamed of."

"I'm not," I said with a smile. "I'm really proud, actually."

"What are you proud of?" Luke asked when he joined us, a couple of beers in one hand and a bottle of 7-Up for me. I took it from him and the three of us clinked bottles.

"She's proud of her working-class family background," John said.

"Oh, yeah?" Luke said and turned to me. "How did you get into Columbia? Scholarship?"

I nodded. "Scholarship all the way. My father's working but his income isn't enough to really help with tuition to a good college."

"Columbia's great. You're doing an MA so that means you have brains as well as beauty."

"Your adoptive mother didn't seem to think I'm very attractive."

"She's just jealous," Luke said and leaned closer. "She's measuring you up against Felicia Blake, and realizes that there's no competition."

Luke smiled, his eyes playful.

I didn't know what to think of him. He knew I wasn't an escort, and that I was a grad student. I wasn't going to sleep with him so why was he being so nice?

Then, for the next hour, we circulated, John in tow, and the three of us met and talked to various family friends and business associates. Luke introduced me as his girlfriend and luckily, no one seemed interested in asking me anything in detail.

Then, Luke stopped up suddenly and held out his arm to stop John.

"Oh, crap," he said. "Look who showed up."

I glanced over and saw an incredibly handsome man with dark hair walk into the ballroom from the main entrance. On his arm was a woman my age, tall, slim and very elegant looking.

"Who's that?" I asked, wondering why Luke would be so alarmed.

"Heckle and Jeckle," John said with a sour face. "Heckle is Felicia's brother Harrison. He's a big wheel on Wall Street. He's taking over from his father at the helm of this big investment banking company. He really likes Luke for Felicia's husband and is one of our investors. Jeckle is his girlfriend, one of the recent debutantes of the rich and famous named Jessica. We don't like her much."

"If Harrison's here, Felicia and her mother won't be far behind them." Luke took a long swig of his beer like he was trying to get courage up to face them.

"You don't like him?" I asked, noting how Luke stood straighter like he was steeling himself for battle.

"He's friends with Eric," Luke said. "In fact, he introduced Eric to Dana. He's also involved in the acquisition so I have to walk a very fine line with him."

"Should I leave?" I asked, thinking a quick exit would be best.

Luke shook his head. "Nope. He has to get the message that Felicia and I are not a couple and are never going to be one."

"I just hope he doesn't do anything to hurt the deal," John said, making a face. "I didn't think the Blakes were coming tonight."

"Neither did I," Luke replied, his brow furrowed. "My mother's doing. She takes every opportunity she can to push Felicia and I together."

"Attention," John said and cleared his throat. "Here he comes."

Luke stood a little straighter and I could tell he wasn't looking forward to speaking with Harrison and his girlfriend.

"Well hello there, stranger," Harrison said as he reached us. "Luke. John."

"Hello, Harrison," Luke said dryly. "How are you? Nice to see you again, Jessica."

"Harrison," John said. "Jess. Great to see you, as always."

She gave Luke a cutesy smile and nodded at John. "You, too."

"Who do we have here?" Harrison asked, giving me the once-over.

"This is Alexa," Luke said and pulled me against him. "She's a good friend from Columbia."

"Oh, really?" Harrison said and eyed me. "Columbia? What are you studying?"

"Political Science."

"Hmm," Harrison said and glanced from me to Luke and back. "Have you seen Felicia and my mother? They should be here already."

"No, we haven't," Luke said. "I didn't realize you were coming tonight."

"We were a late invite," Harrison said, smiling icily. "For some reason, we were left off the invitation list, but your mother assured us it was an oversight and wasn't intentional."

"I'm sure," Luke said.

I was shocked at the level of tension between Luke and Harrison. Both men smiled at each other but I could tell they disliked each other intensely. Harrison glanced over me like I was some kind of eyesore.

"You haven't spoken about Alexa before," Harrison said.

"She's a friend from college who I've been seeing for a while. We have a lot in common."

"Oh, yes? Such as? I'm really curious that we haven't heard any hint about some girlfriend from your mother."

"You wouldn't. I like to keep my private life private."

"From your own mother?"

Luke shrugged. "She has her own ideas about my future. I have mine."

"Apparently," Harrison said. "Is your family from New York?" he asked me, his eyebrows raised.

"No," I said. "We're from Oregon."

"Oregon?" he said with a blatant look of disgust. "Who's from Oregon? How did you end up in Manhattan?"

I shrugged. "I got a scholarship to Columbia and NYU as well as several other colleges. I wanted to live in Manhattan. Columbia won out."

"Hmm," he said and glanced away like I was some bug he wanted to crush under his foot. "Well, we better mingle. Great to see you again, Luke. John."

He said nothing else to me, pulling his girlfriend along with him. I noted that she said nothing at all. She did, however, smile at me many times but every one of them seemed totally condescending.

"Wow, some great friends you have," I said tartly. "Am I wrong or was he really rude to me in an offhanded way?"

"He was really rude to you. He's a blue blood and thinks anyone who isn't of his kin are the dregs of society. I mean, who *is* from Oregon?" Luke said with a sardonic laugh. Then he turned to me, his expression curious. "So, you're from Oregon? How did your people end up there?"

"My people are still *in* Oregon." I shrugged. "My people came from Ireland to New York during the potato famine and then made the trek over to the West Coast during the gold rush days. They stayed. My great grandfather worked on the railway and then my grandfather after him. My father wanted to be a pilot and so he joined the Air Force back in the day."

"Salt of the earth," Luke said and held up his beer bottle. I tapped it with my bottle of 7-Up.

"The best."

"No, seriously," Luke said. "I mean it. I admire anyone who

has a dream and follows it. Especially people who start from scratch or have some huge talent or smarts. Obviously, your father had some serious flying skills to make it into the Air Force as a fighter pilot. You're obviously really smart to get a scholarship to Columbia and be working on an MA in Political Science."

"And you excelled in selling comic books from a young age."

Luke laughed, genuinely pleased. "I can sell more than comic books, I hope. I've got a business I hope to sell to a big buyer next week."

God, he was so cute and handsome at the same time, with a hunk of a body and a boyish grin. Those blue eyes...

It was too bad he was a cheater on top of it.

"You could sell oil to the Saudis," John replied.

"Hopefully, I can sell Chatter to our investors."

"You will." John held up his bottle of beer. "I have faith in your mad skills, Luke. If you can't sell Chatter, no one can."

Luke shrugged, smiling like he was embarrassed at the praise. "I do my best."

"If you'll excuse me, I have to make a trip to the washroom," I said, deciding to take a break and freshen up.

"Okay," Luke said, but he grabbed my arm. "As long as you're not running off in order to escape my family, especially not when Felicia Blake is on her way..."

"No, honestly," I said and smiled. "I really do have to use the ladies."

He nodded. "We'll be here."

Then I left the two of them and made my way to the washrooms, which were located at the far corner of the ballroom. I went inside the ladies and got in line to wait for my turn when Luke's sister walked in, her hand on her belly.

"Oh, hi," she said and came right over. "How are you holding up? Our family events aren't all that fun. A lot of stuffed shirts and silver-spoons, if you ask me."

I laughed, surprised that she seemed so honest. "Well, it does seem to be the cream of the Wall Street crop, from what Luke tells me."

"Bankers and more bankers. You'd think we had no imagination. I mean, who other than Neumann grows up and wants to be a banker?"

I laughed at her Seinfeld reference. "It sounds a bit dry, but that's maybe just me."

"No, it's dry. Believe me, it's dry. I've grown up surrounded by men talking banking and finance all my life. Dryer than the Sahara."

I smiled and looked at her very prominent belly, unable to resist. "So, congratulations. You must be very excited. When are you due?"

"Oh, thank you. We're over the moon. I'm due in about eight weeks. I've heard they let first time mothers go ten days past their due dates, so it could be almost nine weeks. I hope not. God, it's getting harder and harder to sleep at night."

"I've heard it's preparation for when you have sleepless nights after the baby's born," I said.

"Well, I'll be ready, if that's the case. I practically sleep sitting up. Luke's really excited about becoming an uncle. It's funny – he never said anything about you. When did you two meet? Are you seeing each other exclusively? Luke seemed to suggest it, but that's so unlike him. Not that I'm complaining, mind you. We're all so happy to see him finally find someone more permanent after everything."

After everything... she must have meant his breakup with his fiancée.

"We don't know each other really well," I said, feeling bad

about lying, but I didn't want to tell her the truth, of course. "He's not the type to be exclusive."

"You got that right. At least, not anymore. Not since last year." I nodded, trying to appear more in the know than I really was.

"Luke never brings anyone to these functions anymore, so I'm surprised he did tonight. He must really like you – or he really hates you and wants to torture you with our highly un-entertaining family."

She gave this delightfully sarcastic laugh, her eyes twinkling. I felt like she was the kind of person I'd like to be friends with. I felt bad that her husband was cheating on her. I could see how Luke would want to punch Eric in the face. Dana was delightful and bubbly.

"You and Luke are twins, right?"

She nodded. "Yes, we were inseparable when we were kids, until we both discovered that we were supposed to hate each other. Until our parents died, we had no idea. They let us be best friends but our adoptive parents didn't. So, we stopped playing together at that point and went our own ways, but we're really close still. Now more than ever."

The stall opened and so I offered it to her. "You go. I'm sure you need it more than me."

"Oh, thank you!" she said and squeezed my arm. "The baby seems to like sleeping on my bladder so I'm always in and out of the bathroom." She went into the stall and I waited for the next one to open. Being in the stall didn't seem to stop her chatty ways and she kept talking to me over her very loud stream of pee.

"So, what has Luke told you about his past?" she asked.

"Not much," I said, wondering if she'd shed more light on the mystery surrounding the breakup. "What should he have told me?" The stall next to hers opened and so I took it and sat down myself.

"He didn't tell you about his ex?"

"You mean his fiancée?"

"Yes. You know they were childhood sweethearts, and he only found out a week before the wedding that she was cheating on him with her ex. You were at Columbia with him. He was dating her that whole time."

"I'd read it was him who cheated on her," I said.

"No, that was the cover story. He let that story out to protect her reputation. I mean, when a woman cheats, it's like the worst thing. When a man does, at least everyone already expects it. He was being gallant, taking the fall."

I took that in, totally surprised at the news.

Luke took the fall? It was his ex who cheated?

I had to re-evaluate everything I thought about him.

"He seems really closed up about his past relationships," I said quickly, trying to cover my mistake. "I can see why he wouldn't want to talk about it. This happened a year ago, right?"

"Yes," Dana said and I heard her flush. "He's still recovering. He and Felicia went out a few times, but he wasn't into her. So when I saw you with him, I though he was finally over it. You must have met him after they split."

"Yeah, that must be it," I said, trying to come up with a story on the fly. "We did only meet before the end of the semester last year."

"What was he doing at Columbia? He graduated before that," she asked.

"I thought he was taking classes, but I guess he was visiting someone? We met at the pub."

"Well, I hope he's finally over everything. Being with you tonight is a good sign. We were all really surprised to see him with someone tonight. I mean, you're the first other than Felicia since they broke up. It was really nasty."

"He never said a thing," I said, feeling like I'd have to really wing it. "We hadn't seen each other for a while and then just bumped into each other, so... When I asked about whether he was seeing anyone, he said no. He never filled me in on the details."

"He really turned sour on marriage after the breakup, as you can imagine. It was hard for him to be betrayed like that considering they were together since high school. She'd been fucking this guy all through their relationship but he didn't want to get married so she stuck with Luke, who did."

"He said he was so dead set against marriage," I said, remembering his comments from earlier.

"Well, the truth is our adoptive father cheated on our adoptive mother. There was this huge secret in our family while we were growing up. They put on happy faces but we found out later that he was a hound dog. I guess Luke finds it hard to trust. He decided to take a chance after he saw how happy Eric and I are and became engaged to Jenna and of course, the rest is history," she said and left the stall. "I keep hoping he'll find someone and fall in love. Get over his hurt, but it's probably too soon. Maybe with you, but I'm a big romantic and just want to see him happy like I am."

I cringed inwardly at her confidence in her marriage. How hard must it be for poor Luke to listen to her talk about her own happiness and how great things are for her, while knowing her husband has been cheating? It must drive him crazy, feeling like he can't tell her the truth.

I finished and left the stall, standing beside her at the mirror while I washed my hands and she checked her makeup. I couldn't help but feel an immense sense of sympathy for her, so happy, so positive and so wrong about her cheating bastard of a husband.

"I hope you and he work out," she said and looked me over, smiling. "I like you. You're beautiful and you seem really nice."

"Thank you," I said, my cheeks heating. "We're not serious. We're just convenient, I guess."

"That's too bad. The fact he brought you here made me think

you two were more serious than that, but I guess it's still too soon for him. Oh, well." She shrugged and smiled. "You never know about these things."

Then she squeezed my arm and together, we left the washroom. "It was nice to meet you," she said when she got a few feet away. "Don't give up on Luke, even if he is a bit stuffy at times. He's a good guy. And I'm not just saying that because I'm his sister. He really is one of the good ones."

I smiled and went the other way, a sick feeling in my gut that she had no idea her husband had been one of the bad ones, and had been cheating on her while she was pregnant.

What a horrible truth to learn. I could see why Luke didn't want to tell her.

I arrived back at the bar where Luke and John were standing. Luke turned to me and put his hand on my arm. I saw him now with completely different eyes. Everything he'd said and done was now filled with a different meaning.

"Hey, we've spent enough time here," he said and smiled. "How about we go out and find a place that's less stuffy."

John laughed. "You mean with fewer of your family present?"

"Exactly. We could go to Gibson's down the street. They have music all night. Good dance music." He looked in my eyes. "Feel like dancing? I'm all energized and can't imagine sticking around this place."

I was torn. I really should go home early, but the prospect of dancing sounded like a good way to top off the evening of tension between Luke and his wacky family. I felt so sorry for him now, after learning about his broken engagement and betrayal. The truth was that I admired him for taking the blame.

"You're trying to escape before Felicia arrives?" John

commented.

"You read my mind, wise Sir," Luke said. "The sooner we ditch, the better. Alexa?" He held out his arm. "Come with me and dance a bit, salvage some of this awful night?"

"I really should go home. I'm no longer of any use to you, as far as teaching your brother-in-law a lesson so..."

"No, please, don't feel that way. You were a good sport, and were acting out of charity. I owe you a good time."

"I don't know..."

"Please," he said and took my hand, squeezing it. "Just come out for one drink, dance a bit. I'll have my driver take you home whenever you want. Besides, I really do want you to come to the family weekend at the beach house. If you don't mind being my excuse not to get shoved together with Felicia..."

"You really want me to come?"

"I really do."

I finally relented. "I guess it won't hurt to stay for another half an hour or so..."

"Thank you," he said, his voice soft, his eyes soft as well. "Being around my family usually ruins my night. This will at least make it somewhat better."

I placed my arm in his, and John offered his arm and so the three of us walked across the ball room to the front entrance. We were just about there, when of course, we were stopped.

"Great," Luke said under his breath when he saw the two women who approached us. I heard him take in a deep breath and then he met my eyes. "Be prepared for a second inquisition."

"That bad?" I whispered.

"Worse," he said.

"Who is it?"

"The woman who wants to be my future mother-in-law and her daughter."

CHAPTER 8

Luke

I stopped in the entry way because there was no way I could escape Mrs. Blake and Felicia.

It was ridiculous that I couldn't avoid her, given I was a full-fledged adult with my own business startup that was going to make me and my partner a cool billion each if the deal went through.

I had to be nice — as nice as possible without being rude — because everyone and everything in Manhattan was tied in some way to the Blakes. They practically ran Wall Street through their influence. They had tentacles into banking and investment. Harrison was one of the execs of the investment firm that wanted to buy Chatter.

It would be hard, but I'd have to finesse my way with Mrs. B if I didn't want to risk the deal.

When Felicia saw me with someone, her face fell. It wasn't that Felicia was unattractive or unpleasant. She'd be a good catch for someone who wanted to get married but I was no longer the marrying type and she was just not my type anyway. I knew men who would be very pleased to be matched up with her. But she was everything that Alexa was not. Her dress was ostentatious. Something that looked like it belonged on a bridesmaid instead of at a family function. She was lean while Alexa was petite and curvaceous. She was quiet and shy, while Alexa was smart and witty, even sarcastic.

Felicia was sweet but she wasn't for me.

I couldn't resist sarcastic for some reason, perhaps because it felt truthful and I was through with nice if deceitful.

As for Mrs. Blake, she wore a suit, looking every inch the matron of the family. She and my mother were tight, and probably planned on marrying me to Felicia after things fell through with Jenna. I told my mother to stop with the matchmaking, but Felicia seemed passive in the face of our parental machinations.

"Lucas," Mrs. Blake called out when she saw us. "There you are. Felicia and I are sorry we're so late."

She scowled when she saw me pull Alexa closer and plant a quick kiss on her lips. Luckily, Alexa was just fast enough that she got my intent and smiled at me when I pulled away, wiping lipstick off my lips like we were an old familiar couple.

"You're a tease," she whispered, winking at me very surreptitiously.

"Thanks for playing along," I whispered back.

Mrs. Blake reached us, and gave Alexa the once over.

"Who's this?" she asked, her hands on her hips.

"Mrs. Blake, may I introduce my girlfriend Alexa Dixon."

"What?" Mrs. Blake gave Alexa the twice-over, her face shocked. "We never heard that you had a girlfriend, and especially so soon after, well," she said and her eyes widened. "After. When did you get a girlfriend?"

"She's a friend from Columbia. We've been seeing each other for a while."

She made a sour face. "Your mother never said anything..."

"Mother didn't know," I said. "But I was able to introduce Alexa to her a few moments ago." I turned to Felicia. "Nice to see you again, Felicia."

"Nice to see you as well, Luke."

Felicia looked shy and awkward, as usual.

I turned back to Mrs. Blake. "Sorry to run, but we've got other plans."

"Going so soon?" Mrs. Blake said, glancing at John like she was already thinking he might be a good second-choice for Felicia. "We haven't even had a chance to talk to you. This must be John."

"Yes," I said and turned to him. "This is John, my partner and CTO at Chatter."

"Nice to meet you," John said and smiled winningly at Felicia.

"Nice to meet you as well. It's good to see you again, Luke." Felicia smiled politely but she looked as if she felt completely awkward. "I hear good things about Chatter's future. Good luck with the deal."

"Thanks," I said and then pulled Alexa with me. "We really have to go..."

Felicia nodded, and I could see in her face that she was mortified as usual with her mother's behavior.

The three of us left and I felt incredible relief.

"If you need me to take her off your hands, you can encourage her mother to try to marry me off," John said, turning around and walking backwards so he could catch another glimpse of Felicia. "Her family's the Blake family of the Blake Fortune. I could get into marrying money."

"You're going to *be* money, bro. You don't need to marry it."

"Then we'd both be money, and she wouldn't be after me for mine."

"Well, whatever. My adoptive mother's been itching to get us together and was really excited when we started dating. She must be crushed that I'm with someone else."

John laughed. "You'd think we were back in Victorian times."

I didn't blame Felicia for her mother's and my adoptive mother's follies. She was probably expecting to find me alone at the event and would spend time with me – maybe to satisfy her mother – maybe because she really did hope we ended up together, although I never gave her the idea I'd go along with it.

Sure, I humored my adoptive mother, and although I had taken Felicia out to a few events, I had never once given Felicia any idea that I was interested beyond being polite in social situations and going out a couple of times for dinner and to see a movie.

Only a few weeks ago, Felicia pulled me aside and apologized for her mother's behavior.

"I'm sorry," she'd said, looking really mortified at how gleeful her mother had been at the prospect of us eating our dinner side by side. "She's a bit delusional and doesn't understand that you were really hurt by what happened. It's not like you want to just jump right up in the saddle again."

"It's okay," I said, glad that Felicia wasn't going along with the whole plan to get us married in place of Jenna. "I just don't want to give anyone the wrong impression. You should tell your mother I plan on being a permanent bachelor and living in sin my entire life."

She smiled at that, and it endeared her a bit to me, but only because it meant I didn't have to worry about her getting the wrong idea. She understood how I felt and was just going along with her mother to avoid conflict. Mrs. Blake had a very big personality to match her stature and size.

That night, I imagined Felicia merely felt even more mortified than usual because I had an actual date with me, which was something I never did – not since Jenna and I split. I hadn't brought along a date to these functions since we broke up.

So, when I watched Felicia walk away with her mother, I felt sure that Mrs. Blake would finally get a clue that I wasn't into her daughter and leave the poor girl – and me – alone for once.

I held out hope that my own meddling adoptive mother would get the same clue, but she'd shown no evidence of it and even now, I felt her eyes on me and Alexa, no doubt watching as I turned down yet another attempt to match make me with Felicia.

The three of us left Cipriani's and made our way down the street to the venue, glad to be free of my family with its craziness.

The club was crowded and the electronic dance music was at full blast. All the tables were taken so we found a spot at the bar and ordered drinks.

"Come on, have something," I said to Alexa, who ordered a soda. "Live a little. It's Sunday tomorrow. Can't you take Sunday off?"

"No rest for the wicked," she said and shook her head sadly. "I have to meet my friends for brunch and then it's time to hit the books."

"All work and no play makes for a dull girl," John said and held up his beer.

"All play and no work will keep me from getting my scholarship renewed and that would mean no Columbia for me," Alexa replied and held up her bottle of soda.

The three of us clinked bottles once more and I took a long draw on mine. Then, I turned to the dance floor and watched the people move. I was glad to have left Cipriani's and felt like having fun, and pretty, vivacious Alexa was just the right company. I turned to her.

"Care to dance?"

She made a face. "Usually, I'd say yes, but I'm wearing these. They're like stilts. I'm not used to heels so high. I usually wear high tops or Blundstones."

"Take them off," I said. "I promise I won't step on your toes."

She watched the dance floor for a moment and then shrugged. "Oh, what the heck. If you promise to catch me if I fall, I'll give these a try. I don't really want to walk on that floor in bare feet."

"I'm your man. Promise to catch you before you hit the floor." I grinned and took her hand.

"Later, bro," I said to John, who nodded and held up his beer graciously. It wouldn't take him long to find some pretty thing and ask her to dance.

The music blared and people danced around us on the small dance floor to the left of the bar as we crossed it and found a place in the middle of all the writhing bodies. We started to dance and I saw right away that she was uncomfortable in the heels, but she still looked sexy, moving her hips in a gentle sway that send my mind imagining what it would be like to have those hips riding me.

"I haven't been dancing in ages, " Alexa said. "Do you come here often?"

I couldn't help but smile at her lame line. "Do you always use that pick-up?"

She grimaced and then laughed. "Oh, God, I've been so focused on my comp, I think I've forgotten how to talk to people. I should ask you something else, more personal. Like, what the heck is going on in your family? So much intrigue..."

"Don't ask," I replied, making a face of disgust. "Suffice to say that my family is not really my family. My real parents died when my sister and I were very small. So, technically, we're orphans and they're our adoptive parents. They adopted us, because they were business partners with my parents. We don't like either of them."

"You don't like your adoptive parents? Either of them?"

"Nope." I shook my head. "Unfortunately, he's a blowhard cheater and she's a meddler."

"I'm sorry to hear that. It must be really tense at family gatherings."

"It is. My sister and I tend to avoid them as much as possible. So, you can see why I wanted to send my brother-in-law a message about using an escort service. It's just my adoptive father all over again. I don't want Dana to go through a divorce, especially with a baby on the way."

"You couldn't just talk to Eric?"

I shook my head. "I'd be afraid I'd punch his lights out."

Alexa didn't say anything for a moment, and the two of us danced for a while in silence. She couldn't move much on those heels, but when she did, she was very sexy, wiggling her hips more than she could do many complicated steps. I glanced over her from head to toes. She was so damn sexy. Of course, my man brain wanted to take her home with me and try her on for size. I figured she'd be a great fit and I remembered her joking texts when I was trying to sound all alpha and mentioned bronc riding. She had a great sense of humor, which I highly valued.

"We should sit down," I said and pointed to her heels. "Your ankles look like they could collapse at any time and I don't want to be responsible for any long-term injuries."

She wiped her brow dramatically. "Whew," she said and smiled. "I was hoping you'd say that. These heels are killing my feet."

I took her arm and led her off the dance floor to the bar where

John was busy talking up a pretty young thing. "We're going to find a table," I shouted to him over the blaring music.

"You go ahead," he said and gestured to the young woman beside him. "Mia and I are going to dance."

I nodded and then Alexa and I grabbed our drinks. I took Alexa's hand and scanned the tables for a place to sit. I found one off in the corner that was a bit out of the way and then led her there. I pulled out her chair and then sat next to her, moving my chair closer so I could hear her speak.

"So, tell me about Alexa. I know your father was in the Air Force and that you're a military brat. You're a poli science MA student, and you're from the great state of Oregon. What else should I know?"

She shrugged. "I don't know... I have an older brother, John, who's also in the Air Force and is training to be a fighter pilot. My parents live in Oregon, in a bedroom community outside Portland. My father teaches at a local flight school. That's it, really."

"Your family sounds great. Sounds like a real family."

"It is. They are."

I watched her face. "No boyfriend?"

She shook her head. "Not recently, no. I've," she said and lifted her shoulder. "I've been focusing on school instead of a social life, I guess."

"Any past serious relationships?"

She frowned. "Why do you ask?"

"I just wondered why you're single. You're hot. You're smart."

"Why are you single?" she asked, raising her eyebrows.

"I was almost married," I said finally. I didn't really want to talk about my failed engagement but she should know. "Things didn't work out."

"I'm sorry," she said and gave me a sympathetic look.

"Plus, I saw a bad marriage close up with my adoptive

parents. Now with my sister's marriage to that slimy bastard of an Eric being in question, I've decided that relationships are not my thing. I like to have fun, but I have no plans for anything long-term."

She looked at me for a moment and shook her head. "It's sad that you've given up on a meaningful relationship. I think they're what really makes people happy. Not money or fame. Close personal relationships."

"If they make people happy, I haven't seen it." I shrugged, not wanting to get into a big debate about it. "Maybe someday. You say you've been focused on school? I've been focused on building my business. Now that our deal looks like it'll go through, I'm planning a year off so I can sail around the world."

"You sail?" Her eyes widened in interest.

"I do," I said and held up my watch. "There's a reason I wear this. I did some diving and spent a few summers on a yacht. I'm having a catamaran built and John and I plan to sail to the South Pacific with a couple of college buddies. Go to the Galapagos and see the iguanas. Sail to Australia and then to Cape Town, South Africa and back. We'll see."

"You and John?"

I nodded. "The cat's almost done. We'll sail through the Panama Canal, and then make the crossing. When I come back, I want to start something new. Maybe join the space race."

"Wow," she said and took in a deep breath. "That's amazing. How wonderful to be able to take a year off and just sail around the world. Do anything you want."

"Money is freedom. I know a lot of men who work 12 hour days six days a week and have no life. They have big fancy apartments on Fifth Avenue but spend no time there or with their wives and children. They live at the office. I don't want that. I want a *life* and I want work to be part of that life. My dad died so young and never got to do what he really wanted, which was to sail around the world."

"That's sad," Alexa said. "My dad got to fly planes all his life. He loves it. He always told me that I should find my passion and pursue that and never settle for less. That I would eventually make a living doing it."

"So, your passion is politics?"

She nodded. "I want to get my PhD and teach somewhere in Europe. Maybe do some work for the UN. Who can say? Definitely in Europe, though."

"Not good old USA?"

"No." Then she laughed. "I was conceived in Alexandria and I think I have wanderlust. I want to go back there, and live outside of the US if I can. Life's too short not to go after what you want."

"I agree." I watched her face as she talked some more about her father and how he lived his dream, flying planes in the military. She was animated and really seemed passionate about what she was doing, envisioning a future teaching at a university somewhere in Europe or doing international relations.

I *liked* this woman. She wasn't your ordinary run-of-the-mill girl I would meet at a club dancing on Saturday night. She seemed smart and centered, despite doing something as crazy as agreeing to go out with me and masquerading as an escort.

I realized she did it first on a dare, never intending to follow through, but then when I had pleaded and begged, seemingly desperate, she agreed out of sympathy. She was the kind of woman that I would want to become involved with – if I was that kind of man.

But I wasn't.

Not anymore, at least. I had plans and they didn't include a woman – other than as a fuck buddy. Not for the next few years, at least, if ever.

Women, yes. I had my needs as much as any other red-blooded American guy. I liked sex, but with no strings.

Alexa was the type of woman men wanted to have to themselves. I could see that by the way other men at the club watched her when we were dancing and how they glanced her way now. She was beautiful. Voluptuous with a body that just wouldn't stop with all its curves.

"So, you want to be like all the other billionaires and go to Mars?"

I laughed. "Something like that. I want to do things with my money that will live after I'm gone. Chatter was just a way to make money. Mars? That's something real. It's the new frontier. The only thing big enough to satisfy me is a mission to Mars. Everything else will get swallowed up in history."

She rested her chin on a hand. "So, would you go?"

"To Mars?"

She nodded. "It would be a one-way trip, if I remember what I read about it."

"I'd go in a heartbeat."

"Really?" she said, wide eyed. "Leave everything behind? You feel so disconnected to everything here?"

I took a sip of my beer. "Once I do my round-the-world sailing trip, I'd go happily. It would be a once in a lifetime experience."

"It would be dangerous."

I shrugged. "Life is dangerous. Sailing around the world is dangerous. Hell, walking across the street in Manhattan is dangerous. It doesn't matter how you die. It matters how you live. I want to really *live*. That means taking risks."

"But you won't risk a relationship with someone?" she said, her eyes narrow. "You won't risk marriage?"

I stiffened. "Marriage is a trap," I said. "People get married, have kids and then their lives are over because of responsibility.

Or, their partner cheats on them and leaves them for someone else. I want to really *live* my life and not be held back by a wife and children."

She glanced away and her expression suggested that she didn't agree and thought I was being immature. I'd gotten that response before when I talked about my plans to leave the corporate world, sail across the oceans, and get involved in the space race. I couldn't expect other people to understand.

"There are already too many people on the planet," I said and sipped my beer. "I don't need to add any more. My line will end with me, I'm afraid."

She frowned. "But your children would have a real chance to do something with their lives. They'd be wealthy enough to go anywhere and do anything they wanted just like you're able to. It seems like a waste of your circumstances not to have children. What about your sister? Should she not have become pregnant?"

"No, that's not what I think. She wants kids more than anything. I'm glad she's going to have a child. But look at what happened to her – she finally gets pregnant but it's with a cheating bastard." I took another sip of my beer, trying to calm down. Just talking about Eric made me angry. "No, it's not for me."

I shrugged, because I knew she wouldn't understand. That's just the way I was. I'd seen enough of bad marriages and cheating partners in my life to want one myself. Maybe her parents were happy, but mine sure as hell weren't.

"You never know what's going on in someone else's mind. I used to like Eric, before I discovered he was a bastard."

"You can't let the bad people in your life make you think there aren't still good people," she said. "What kind of life will you have if you don't have a family? You'll be lonely when you get old if you don't have family."

"I'll have friends. I'll have people who choose to be with me, not those who are forced to be with me out of blood ties."

She glanced away and I could see this was one of those issues that we could not see eye to eye on. I could tell she was upset, and didn't want her to start having second thoughts about going with me to my family retreat.

"I hope this doesn't put you off from being my plus-one at the beach house in two weeks..."

She glanced back at me. "You really can't just say to Mrs. Blake that you're not the marrying type and you're not interested in Felicia? Why not be direct? That way, you can go on your own and not have to worry about bringing anyone along."

I shook my head. "I need a pretend girlfriend so that I can go without worrying about being pushed together all the time with Felicia."

"You don't need me," she said, drinking her soda. "I'm sure you have other women you could bring along just for the sake of appearances."

"I said I was bringing you. I concocted this whole story about how we met at Columbia and are now serious."

"Look," she said met my gaze. "I get that you're not the marrying type, especially after what happened. You're not into a relationship. Really, at this point in my life, neither am I, but I'm just not interested in spending time at your beach house with a bunch of strangers, so I'm probably better off just spending the weekend studying."

"I take it that's a firm no?" I said, feeling strangely let down that she was pulling out. "I can't convince you with tales of the great food and surfing, and of the fabulous company?"

She shook her head and smiled, but I could see it was forced. "Nah, let's just chalk this night up to a comedy of errors and leave it at that. And now," she said and glanced at her watch. "I really should get home. I'm meeting the girls for brunch and then I have all these journal articles to read..."

"I'll pay you what I said I would."

"What?" she said and made a face of disgust. "Are you kidding me? I'm not an escort. I'm not impressed by your money or your family. I did this because I thought you were truly in need of a date because you must be such a loser that you had no one who wanted to be with you. I did this to help a stranger – who, I might add – came off as a real jerk. I don't want your money."

"Ow," I said and winced. "Why don't you tell me what you really think?"

She shrugged and I could see how angry she was.

"Let me take you home," I said, standing up when she did. "That's the least I can do if you don't want my money."

"I know my way around the trains," she said and boy, what a change of atmosphere from earlier. I must have said something that bothered her.

"I'd feel better if I could at least pay for a cab so I know you got home safely, if you won't let me take you."

"I'm a big girl," she said and waved me off, not meeting my eyes. "I've been taking the trains for the past couple of years. You stay." She glanced around. "There are lots of girls around who would probably love a one-night stand with you. I have a life to live."

Then, she walked away on those heels and out of my life.

As I watched her leave, still appreciating the sway of her nicely rounded ass, and the way her long pale hair fell to her waist, I wished she had stayed. I wanted to be taking her home with me.

She was right – I could probably find someone and take them home tonight. There were a lot of attractive young women at the club, and I'd seen a few turn my way.

But I felt a deep sadness that I couldn't quite place.

No matter. I glanced over at the bar where John was still talking to his sweet thing and buttoned my jacket. When I went over to stand beside him, ordering another beer, he put his arm around my shoulder.

"Hey, there, Luke, meet Lena," John said, raising his eyebrows.

"Lena," I said and smiled. Then I turned to John. "Are you going to stay? I think I'll head home."

"Don't go," John said and grabbed my arm. "Lena here has a best friend who's in the washroom right now. Stick around. You'll love her."

A young woman walked towards us and when she saw me, her eyes lit up.

"Hi, there," she said when she got to us. She came to my side and gave me the once over.

"Luke, meet Cherise," John said and gestured to the woman, who was attractive enough, with brown hair and eyes and a decent figure. On any other night, I might have found her attractive enough to consider hooking up. But I felt tired because of the whole business with Eric and Alexa and Felicia and forced a smile.

John pointed to me. "Cherise, this is Luke Marshall."

"*The* Lucas Marshall needs no introduction," Cherise said, smiling at me. "I've been reading about you and your deal to sell Chatter in the *Journal*."

"Nice to meet you," I said. "Sorry but I have to leave." I turned to John. "Catch you later."

"You're going?" John said and made a face. Cherise made a face as well. I guess the three of them had already put me with Cherise for the evening after Alexa left.

I was so damn sick of other people trying to arrange my love life.

"Yeah, I'm not really up to partying. We'll catch up tomorrow. Call me."

Then I left.

My evening had been a total flop.

Alexa was not Lexxi911 and so I'd been unable to teach Eric a lesson, although I think John and I laid down a big enough clue for him that we knew of his cheating ways. Hopefully, he'd wise up and be loyal to my sister, at least long enough for her to get used to the new parent thing before she sued his sorry ass for divorce.

Alexa was beautiful and smart and I wanted to fuck her brains out, but apparently, she didn't feel the same. In fact, she thought I was a heartless jerk for not wanting a real relationship.

The night had not gone at all like I planned...

CHAPTER 9

ALEXA

I left the club and walked down the street to the subway, regretting that I'd even bothered to go out with Luke. What a stupid move – who does that? Who goes out with a perfect stranger they met through an email that wasn't intended for them?

Who pretends to be an escort?

I really had to stop listening to Candace. She always got me in trouble.

Not that I was in any kind of trouble. I'd had fun enough with Luke and John, after getting over the whole business about my identity. It was kind of exciting. But it was a flop, in the end. Luke thought he could use me to teach his brother-in-law a lesson, but I wasn't who he thought I was. We had fun for a while, dancing and talking, but I realized after talking to Dana in the washroom that Luke was still hurting over his failed engagement. He was on the rebound and those men were to be avoided at all costs. He had decided he wasn't the kind of guy who had relationships, or even considered marriage and family in the future.

What kind of guy wants to go to Mars?

Someone who does not want to fall in love and get married.

So, he wasn't the kind of guy I should spend any more than a few moments of time thinking about. No matter how gorgeous he was, no matter how smart and successful, he was not a long-term guy. That's what I wanted and needed.

My parents had the best marriage ever. I wanted one like they had – a partnership where they loved each other and were each other's best friend.

Luke seemed to turn sour on women and love after his bad experiences. Now, he viewed women only as fuck partners. So, it was best that I say goodbye early and get the heck out of the club.

I sat on the subway car, glancing around at the other commuters, and wished I could find someone real, but I'd rather be single than be with just anyone. I wanted someone who was going to love me, support me, want to be with me and only me.

If that meant I had to wait until my degrees were finished and I had a job somewhere and was living somewhere I really wanted to be – like Zurich or Copenhagen or Florence, so be it. I'd rather be single than waste my time with men who were only out for a good fuck and nothing deeper.

I got off at my stop and walked the couple of blocks to the old brownstone in which I lived with Candace. She was in her pajamas and was watching SNL when I arrived home.

"There you are," she said and moved over on the sofa. "How did it go?"

"It was okay, I guess," I said and plopped down beside her. I removed the straps from the high heels and rubbed my feet. "He wasn't a serial killer luring me out to kill me so there's that."

"So tell me everything," she said, impatient for the details.

"I can't tell you," I said and shrugged. "Remember? The NDA?"

"Oh, come on – you can tell me. I'm your bestie. There's no way I'm going to spill."

"I really shouldn't..."

"Come on, Alexandria Marie Dixon. You better tell me. Who was it who moved all the way across the country with you to go to Columbia? Who was it who kept you at my apartment after your insane ex came after you?"

"You."

"Exactly. If you can't trust me with details, how can you trust me with your life?"

I sighed. She was right. "He hired me to rub me in his brother-in-law Eric's face because Eric cheated with Lexxi911. That's it."

"What?" She moved closer, her eyes wide.

"Yeah. His brother-in-law Eric hired this escort named Lexxi from 9-1-1 Escorts. It's spelled *Lexxi* with two x's. Eric's married to Luke's very pregnant sister."

"Wow. What a story."

"You have no idea."

"What's he like? Tell me! I already know he's gorgeous and rich."

"His heart was broken by his ex-fiancée and he has a really awful family."

"Oh, that's right," she said, her eyes wide. "I read about him in one of the gossip mags online. They were engaged like, forever, and then they broke it off, apparently because he cheated on her."

"Other way around."

"What?" Candace said, her mouth open wide. "She cheated on him?"

I nodded. "I guess she'd been cheating on him for years with this other guy but the other guy didn't want to get married. She wanted to get married and Luke was an easy mark, I guess."

"That's horrible," she said and made a face. "I can understand why he might be a bit down on relationships."

"Tell me about it," I said and she knew exactly what I meant. I was down on relationships, too, but unlike Luke, I did want one.

"So, Luke hired me because he wanted to bring Lexxi to the family function as a warning to Eric that if he didn't shape up, Luke would tell his sister."

"Unbelievable... The lifestyles of the rich and famous."

"I know," I said and leaned back, taking in a deep breath, then I filled her in on the rest of the evening's events.

"That sounds so fucked up," she said and crossed her legs. "I thought rich people would be happy and have these fantastic lives. It sounds like they have just as many problems as we poor folk do."

"Maybe more. I bet people are always trying to use them because they're rich. It must be hard to know who likes you for who you really are and those who like you because you have money."

"Yeah, I guess," she said and twirled her hair for a moment. "Still, I'd rather be unhappy and rich than unhappy and poor."

"I don't know if it really helps."

I didn't know. Luke seemed really injured by his fiancée's betrayal. He'd soured on marriage as a result. He'd soured on relationships, too. His money didn't stop that betrayal. In fact, it was probably because he was so rich that his fiancée stuck with him even though she was really in love with the poor guy.

What a mess...

"He wants me to come to some big family function in Westhampton."

"Really?"

I told her all about Felicia and why Luke wanted me to go to the beach house for the weekend.

"Are you going?"

I shook my head. "No, I don't want to waste my time pretending to be someone I'm not. If I'm going to spend time smiling at strangers at a weekend party, I want it to be because I'm in love with my boyfriend, not because some stranger wants to avoid being matched up with the daughter of an old family friend."

"He's pretty hot, though. You have to admit it."

I pictured Luke in my mind's eye. "He's incredibly hot, but he's also way out of my league. Besides, he's planning on going to Mars so he's not going to be around for the long haul."

"He's going to *Mars?*" She gave me this comical look of disbelief.

"That's his plan after he sails around the world, and communes with the iguanas of the Galapagos. So, he's serious about not getting married or even having a long-term relationship."

"Aw, that's too bad. He sounds really sad."

"He's actually kinda fun, though, so it's a serious loss to womankind. His sister said he was really broken-hearted after the breakup."

"How long has it been since they called off the engagement?"

"Less than a year."

"Oh, he's still in mourning then," she said. "Give him time. He'll get over it, especially if he meets someone and falls. Men are the biggest saps when it comes to love. They fall so easily. It's us women who have to be convinced."

I gave her a frown. "What are you talking about? It's the other way around. It's men who don't want to fall in love and women who do."

"No, you're wrong. Men *say* they don't want to fall in love, but they fall the hardest. It's their hormones. They got it bad. In comparison, women are much more selective. We expect more from our guys than just looks, whereas men will fall for a woman solely based on how pretty they are and how much they smile. Seriously."

"You're a geology major," I said with a snort. "You know rocks, not men. Believe me, men want lots of sex, yes, but they don't really want to commit. Or when they do, it's the whacko control freak variety."

"Not every guy is like Blaine," she said and reached over, squeezing my arm. "There are good ones out there. You'll find one someday."

I shrugged, not wanting to discuss Blaine or my chances of finding a real relationship. Maybe I was as jaded as Luke, but wasn't as honest as he was. I had little hope that I'd find someone and have as good a relationship as my parents had. It was my hope, but that was pretty much it – hope. It wasn't my experience.

Blaine had been a nightmare from which I only recently woken up. I still had these sensations like he was watching me from a distance, spying on me, even though he was three thousand miles away. I was still in fight or flight mode when it came to Blaine, always fearing he'd show up and try to take me back.

And when I mean take, I mean take, as in abduct.

I turned down Harvard and moved to Manhattan to get as far away from Portland as I could and as far away from Blaine as I could. I figured New York City was big enough that he could never find me.

The next day, Candy and I went to meet our friends from Columbia for a girl's brunch at Luigi's, a deli in the upper east side. It was busy as usual and we managed to snag a table in the corner so we could talk without any interruption as the servers practically ran down the aisles to deliver plates of food to hungry patrons. We all had our usual meals and each one of us related the latest horror to befall us in terms of romance. When my turn came, I had the best story, of course, but couldn't really tell anyone any specifics because of the non-disclosure agreement.

"Who is he?" Mara asked, punching me lightly on the arm. "You can tell us. We won't spill, right?" She glanced at Jan and Jan shook her head vehemently.

"Of course we won't tell," Jan said. "Spill, sister. Who is this hunk of a billionaire who hired you as an escort to send a message to his cheating brother-in-law?"

"I honestly can't say more," I said, shaking my head. "I signed an NDA. There's no way I want this story to get out and get sued because of it."

"Aww," Mara said, pouting. "I want to know who this guy is. He's really rich?"

"Super-rich," Candy said, and made a face. "Like billionaire rich. Comes from a rich family. Big fortune."

"Wow," Jan said, her eyes dreamy. "How come nothing exciting ever happens to me?"

"Believe me," I said and shrugged. "It's not like it was anything great. I mean, the guy isn't into relationships, and I spent about an hour meeting his creepy family and their wealthy friends. The rich really are different," I said with a nod.

"Do you have a pic of him?" Mara asked, ever hopeful.

"You might recognize him if I showed you."

"Take my word, he's gorgeous," Candace said.

"*You* saw him?" Mara asked, glancing at me with a look of disapproval. "How come she gets to see a pic of him and we don't?"

"That was before I signed the NDA," I said and shrugged helplessly. "Sorry."

"If Candy gets to see him, we should in all fairness."

"Sorry," I said again, and shook my head firmly. "No can do.

But he's about six foot three, built, with a great body and dark brown hair, blue eyes, square alpha male jaw."

"He's totally drool-worthy," Candace said, excitedly. "I told Alexa to sleep with him, but she's being old-fashioned."

"Are you going to see him again?" Mara asked, leaning forward, eager for more.

"He wants her to come out to their family beach house in Westhampton for a weekend," Candy answered for me, "but she said no."

"What?" she asked and looked at me. "Why not?"

I exhaled in frustration. "Because he's got this really fucked-up family and there's all this tension between them. I liked his sister and his friend John, but the rest of them are kind of hoity-toity."

"Hoity-toity? What are you – from Jolly Old England?"

We all laughed.

"Seriously, though, he's really down on relationships. I don't blame him, but he has no interest in getting serious about anyone so it would be a waste of my time."

"But if he's hot, why not? Get some. You deserve it, girl."

I smiled at Mara. She always felt bad for me that I had to escape a potential – or should I say – actual nutcase of an ex.

Then I thought maybe Luke and I were two peas in a pod. Both of us had been hurt by exes. He was betrayed by a cheat, and I was threatened by a creep.

Two suckers, in other words.

We all said goodbye and then Candy and I went home, resigning ourselves to a couple of hours of studying because of upcoming exams. I had my comp to study for and would be swamped with reading until the Wednesday night before the exam. I spent the rest of the day in my room with my headphones on and a journal article or textbook open in front of me. I only broke for supper, which consisted of a bowl of noodles with some added vegetables in a minimal stab at eating healthy.

The two of us spent the next few days quiet except for brief bouts of television during meals. The rest of the time, we hit the books and were silent.

About eight o'clock on the night before my comp, I got a text.

From Luke.

It wasn't from his MBS69 account so I'd moved up in the world from secret call girl to real live person.

LUKE: Hey, Alexa, I was just thinking of you.

I read it over and wondered whether I should respond. If I let it go, I'd never have to talk to him again.

Given his aversion to real relationships and his desire to live on Mars, I let it go, turning back to my paper on international treaties. About thirty minutes later, I got another text.

LUKE: I realize you probably never want to see or hear from me again. I just wanted to say I'm sorry I put you through the hell that is my family. I really appreciate what you did, even if my plans for teaching my bastard of a brother-in-law a lesson fell through. John managed to throw in your name and the word 'escort' enough that I think Eric finally got the message. What can I do to repay you? Your comp is this week, right?

I was steadfast in my intention to ignore him and let the whole Sexy Lexi business go into the forgotten past, but I could see Luke's handsome face as he bent over his phone and texted me hopefully.

LUKE: So yeah... I guess you don't want to come to Westhampton next weekend for fun and sun and great BBQ? The regular cast of characters will be there and it would be nice if I could have someone sane to talk to besides my sister.

I smiled at that.

ALEXA: You think I'm sane? ;)

He texted back right away, and I could almost feel his relief that I wasn't going to totally ignore him.

LUKE: Oh, I know it. Crazy maybe, but not insane. :)

I laughed and couldn't wipe a silly smile off my face. I felt bad for him, having to face his family alone, especially if Felicia would be there and Mrs. B would be pushing them together because he was alone.

And then, without any coaxing from Candace, I decided to take a chance. Live dangerously.

ALEXA: Will Felicia and Mrs. B be in attendance?

LUKE: You can count on it. I need you, Alexa. I need you as a decoy and diversion. Pretty please?

ALEXA: If I agree, you accept that it's purely a platonic weekend. We can pretend to be all kissy-kissy, but there will be no spit-swapping or any other bodily fluids.

LUKE: Aww, shucks! No spit??? But okay, I get it. I agree. No bodily-fluid-swapping involved.

I smiled, remembering kissing him. I hadn't realized it affected me so much and felt quite a lot of regret, but I had standards.

LUKE: ...but what if you're drowning in the surf and I need to lock lips with you to administer CPR, and some of my saliva accidentally gets on your mouth?

ALEXA: GROSS!

LUKE: Ha ha! Welcome back to public school. :)

ALEXA: I will perform as your girlfriend. I will let you hold my hand and put your arm around me, and you can even kiss me in public and show simple PDAs, but no tongue, okay? And if we sleep in the same room, no funny business.

LUKE: I'll have you know that none of my business is funny. Only the most serious kind of business. Sober. Grey flannel kind of business so boring you'll fall asleep before you know it.

ALEXA: I'm serious!

LUKE: I promise. No funny business. Not even a joke. >:-(

ALEXA: Good. Okay then. I'll go out with you for the weekend to the beach house as long as you pinkie swear.

LUKE: Pinkie swear??!!

ALEXA: Since we're back in public school and all...

LUKE: Okay. Pinkie swear. I promised no funny business and I mean it. We'll do some surfing, and lie on the beach, work on our tans. Eat fresh fish and drink cold beer. You'll enjoy it after your comp, am I right?

ALEXA: It sounds great. What kind of stuff do I need to bring? I want to fit in with all your wealthy family members... Will I need formal evening dress and gloves? A tiara, mayhap?

LUKE: Just bring a bathing suit, a sundress and sandals, and you'll be fine.

ALEXA: I note you didn't mention a nightgown...

LUKE: Oh, DARN. Busted. ;) Bring a nightgown. The tiara is optional. My adoptive mother might like it, but I prefer something less ostentatious.

ALEXA: Okay. When will you pick me up?

LUKE: Friday, as soon as I'm free. I'll probably work until six, so I can pick you up at seven if that's okay.

ALEXA: Sounds good. See you then.

LUKE: Thanks a bunch, Alexa. I mean it. You'll be my sanity and I'll make sure you won't regret it. I'll be the perfect fake boyfriend. No hanky-panky. Just lots of PDAs to keep the wolves at bay.

ALEXA: I'll hold you to that promise.

LUKE: You can hold me to anything, especially you. ;)

LUKE: Okay, now you know I had to take that opening. The world would not be right if I left it hanging...

ALEXA: Bye...

LUKE: See you Friday.

I put down my phone and smiled. Then, I forced the smile off my face. I really shouldn't have agreed to go with him, but I'd be done with my comps by then and it would be kind of nice to spend a weekend in Westhampton. I'd only been to the Hamptons once before with Candace the previous summer and always planned on going back. Now was the perfect time. It was late in the season, but the weather was warm enough so it would likely be a fantastic weekend.

The Marshalls most likely had a fantastic house, and the food would be good. I'd spend the time with Luke, fending off his family. We could get some surfing in – or at least, I could try. The fresh seafood and cold beer sounded so good, plus the beach and the sun. I'd been working like a dog for so long, it would be wonderful to escape Manhattan for a weekend.

Spending it with one of the best-looking men I'd seen in a long time, with those blue eyes, and those bangs that fell into his eyes in that incredibly sexy way...

Hell, who was I kidding? He was the best-looking man I'd ever seen up close.

Or from a distance.

A weekend spent pretending to be in love with him, staying at his family's beach house in Westhampton? Lounging around on the beach with him beside me in a pair of swim trunks, that delicious washboard abdomen on display? That smile and those eyes...

Yeah, I could handle a weekend like that.

My only fear was that I'd enjoy it too much and end up being just another notch on his very committed bachelor's belt.

I left my bedroom and found Candace in the kitchen rummaging through the refrigerator.

"What's up?" she asked when she saw me, a carrot stick in her hand. "You finished for the night?"

"What's that orange thing in your hand? I don't recognize it." I went to her and bent closer to peer at the carrot. "That's not a Cheeto..."

"I went to the corner store, okay? Don't make a big deal."

I laughed. Then, I realized I had to tell Candace that I'd be going to the beach house after all.

"I just agreed to go to Westhampton with Luke."

"What?" She came over and gave me a hug. "You go, girl. Finally. You really deserve this, Alexa. Of all the people I know, you deserve to spend a nice weekend with a hunk of man like Luke. Seriously."

I smiled, agreeing with her. "I do deserve to have some fun with a hunk of a man. He promised to be good and not try anything."

"And if you want him to try anything, you can always encourage him."

"I'm not going to," I said and shook my head. "I'm just doing this because he's actually pretty nice and he needs an excuse to keep his adoptive mother and her best friend from setting him up with the best friend's daughter. They dated a few times and now they want to marry him off to her."

"You're such a philanthropist," Candace said with a snort. "Talk about a sacrifice. I'd go with him if you decided to turn him down. Seriously. He's amazingly hot, amazingly rich, and sounds like a decent guy."

"He's also amazingly dead-set against a long-term relationship, so there's that. It's a game changer, in my opinion. The only reason I'm spending time with him is because he probably has a really great beach house and the food will be good."

"Not to mention the view."

"That too," I said, wondering where the beach house was located. "I should google the beach house and see where it is."

"I didn't mean that kind of view, silly," she said and elbowed me playfully. "I mean, who would want to miss Luke in bathing suit?"

"Oh, yeah, *that* view." I took in a deep breath. "That view's pretty nice, too."

Then, I did google the family, and searched for a beach house address in Westhampton and sure enough, I found one. It was a huge home with a security fence surrounding it, and it was beach front.

"You're going to live the lifestyle of the rich and famous for a weekend," Candace said with a sigh. "Too bad you couldn't bring me along. I'd kill to go in your place. Couldn't you take me with you in an extra-large suitcase? I could sneak out and pretend to be a beachcomber..."

"Sorry, sister," I said and shrugged. "It's just me. He's picking me up at seven on Friday. I'll stay for the weekend and be back Sunday night."

"You are one lucky girl."

I smiled, hoping she was right. It sounded good on paper – a weekend spent with a fabulously rich hunk of a man pretending to be his girlfriend. I'd learned my lesson about that things that were too good to be true.

They usually were.

CHAPTER 10

LUKE

The following Wednesday, John and I had sausages and eggs at Barney's Deli down the street from my apartment. He'd been out of town for two days, working with a client in Silicon Valley and flew back that morning and so we met for lunch to catch up.

"So, you talked to Alexa? She's coming with you after all?"

I forked a sausage and chewed for a moment. "Yeah. She caved to my manly charms."

"Probably more like the prospect of a weekend a the beach with all the trimmings. It's great this happened, in a way. Better than if she'd been the real Lexxi."

"One wrong letter in an email. That'll teach me to rely on my memory."

"It's so bizarre," John said and bit a piece of toast. He chewed for a moment. "It's one of those fate moments, I guess. You know, when wires get crossed and your life changes."

I frowned and watched him dig into his home fries. "What do you mean?"

"I saw you with her. You *like* her."

"She's nice," I said and thought about Alexa. "She's beautiful and smart. But she wants a real relationship."

"Like every other woman in existence, Luke," John said, narrowing his eyes at me. "Get used to it."

I sat up straighter. "I happen to know several women who are only interested in a good time."

"Yeah, sure...That's what they tell you, but deep down? They want you to put a ring on it. Don't kid yourself."

"No, really," I said and thought about the three women I'd been seeing on and off for the past couple of months. "None of the women I've been hooking up with want anything more than a good hard fuck now and then. They're too busy trying to slay dragons in the business world to get tangled up in a marriage."

"That'll change once they hit thirty and they hear that tick tick tick," John said. "Then, you'll have a harder and harder time finding women your age who don't want a commitment."

"I made a commitment last year – to never get serious about anyone. I am very faithful to my commitment."

"But you liked Alexa," John said. "I could tell."

"I like a lot of women," I said and sipped my coffee. "I like women. I just don't plan on getting married. Ever."

"Tell me another one. You were all ready to get married last year to she who must not be named."

I failed to hold back a grimace. "That was clearly a mistake. No, I'm dead serious. I plan on dying a crusty old bachelor living alone in my lonely old mansion by the ocean, cared for by a bevy of beautiful young nurses. Now that I've tried it, I like being independent."

"Independence is good," John said. "But the love of a good woman is better."

"To independence." I held up my cup of coffee, unwilling to give in to him.

John made a face. "To love," John said and held up his.

"To having a fucking good time with beautiful women."

"Now, *that* I can toast to as long as there's love at the end of it."

"You are a total romantic. You must have never had your heart broken."

We clinked coffee mugs and went on with our meal.

While we ate, my thoughts returned to Alexa, and how pretty and smart and funny she was. What a good sport she was to go along with everything that night. She was someone I would like to see again, and see naked, but that was the extent of it.

"Really, though. What made her change her mind?" John asked, his eyes wide.

Around us, the other customers were talking and eating, and the noise level was high. Barney's was a busy deli and so I had to lean in closer to John so he could hear over the din.

"She was won over by my promise of fresh seafood and cold beer. She's going to continue the pretense of being my girlfriend. That way, Mrs. B will set her sights on someone else."

"Why not me? I'm going to be super rich soon, too," John said, winking.

"If you want to come along, do. I'm sure Felicia would love to have someone to talk to."

"She's beautiful. I'll take her off your hands no problem."

"I'll put in a good word for you with Mother. She'll be pleased to be able to match you up with someone."

Just then, my cell rang. I had the sound setting on cluck, denoting my adoptive mother was calling.

"Oh, great, speak of the devil. It's Dragon Lady," I said and answered. "Hello, Mother," I said, trying to sound pleased to hear from her.

"Hello, dear," she said, her voice sounding flustered. "I was just speaking to Eloise Blake about Saturday night. That girl Alana that you brought along?"

"It's *Alexa*, Mother..."

"Why are you bringing her? We invited the Blakes because we thought you and Felicia were a great pair. Why didn't you tell me you had a steady girlfriend?"

"Mother, I don't tell you every intimate detail of my private life," I said. "I'm a fully-grown man. I look after my own relationships. I don't need any matchmakers."

"I understand that, but you haven't been serious about anyone so far since last year. I was just surprised to meet this Alicia girl. She's pretty, if you like full-figured girls, but really..."

"She's not full-figured. She's curvaceous. She's not a girl either, Mother. She's a woman. She's a Master's student at Columbia studying International Relations. She's very smart. And her name is *ALEXA*."

"Well, whatever," my adoptive mother said and I could hear the impatience and disapproval in her voice. "We're inviting the Blakes to the beach house. I hope you're bringing along John at least. The Blakes have made plans to spend the entire weekend and so I don't want poor Felicia to be all alone."

"Don't worry," I replied dryly. "John is coming and he's very eager to get to know the lovely Ms. Blake better."

"He is? Oh, *good*," she replied, sounding pleased. "That's one thing I can cross off my to-do list then."

"Was there anything else?" I asked. "My eggs are getting cold. We're at Barney's for lunch."

"No, that's all, dear. See you on Friday night."

"See you then," I replied and ended the call.

"Evil Dragon Lady problems?" John asked with a grin.

"As usual, meddling in everyone's affairs. She's glad you're coming, though. She was worried that poor Felicia would be without a dinner companion at the table. You don't mind?"

"Not at all," John said and smiled eagerly. "Count me in. The Blakes are a great old family. My mother will be so pleased to hear I spent the weekend with her."

"Your mother," I said with a laugh. "So different from Dragon Lady. No meddling."

"Ever," John said. "Just polite questions and patient waiting for me to meet Ms. Right. Unlike you, I want to get married. Start my own dynasty."

"You'll have no problems, if that's your goal in life. I'm sure there'll be dozens of women lined up eager to be your princess."

"One of my goals," John said. "Marital bliss like my parents had."

I nodded. John's parents were like Alexa's. Happily married for three dozen years. Then Mr. Andrews kicked off after a massive heart attack and left Mrs. Andrews alone. I liked John's family. A lot more than mine.

But John was a romantic. Always falling in love with every tall woman he met. At barely six feet, he was shorter than me, and he had a preference for tall dark-haired women.

"I like to see them eye to eye," he said one day when we were sitting in the park during lunch watching the people go by.

I preferred petite women.

Night and day, the two of us, but we'd been friends forever.

I left John and went back to my office, spending the afternoon working on several reports, trying to distract myself from the upcoming meeting about the deal. It kept me busy for a while, but soon, my stomach growled and I decided to take a few reports home so I could read them over that night after supper.

When I got back to my apartment, I felt at a loss. I didn't know what to do with myself when I wasn't at work or working out. I paced my apartment, listening with half an ear to the game on television, thinking about the upcoming meeting with JL Investments, the parent company of the tech giant that wanted to buy Chatter. We'd already met once and discussed options, and this meeting coming up would be the clincher. We'd either have a deal or it would be off, but I was sure it was on.

Still, I was tense, wondering whether the deal would go through. I wanted to do something with my life, not just live idly off the money my family's money created and passed on from one generation to the next. When the money from the Chatter deal came through, I wanted tó invest as much of it as possible in ethical stocks and investments.

Then I thought about Alexa.

She was a political type, and I figured she'd know about things like human rights and labor laws.

It was something I could talk to her about. She was a student in international relations and would know her way around that kind of issue.

So, I took out my cell and texted her.

LUKE: Hey, what do you know about ethical investing?"

I sent the text and sat back on my sofa, half my concentration on the game and the other on my cell, hoping that Alexa would respond. I wanted to talk to her about ethical investments.

Hell, who was I kidding? I wanted to talk to her.

Period.

She texted back in a few minutes while I was flipping through an edition of the *Wall Street Journal*.

ALEXA: *I know next to nothing. Are there investments that are ethical?*

LUKE: *Haha. You're not serious are you? If so, you must think I'm a total creep because I plan on being an angel investor.*

ALEXA: *No, it's not that. I wish I had money to invest. Honestly, I don't have any money for investments and I can barely afford tuition and the cost of living. There's nothing left over. A beer or three on the weekend. Maybe someday when I'm older and I'm actually working, I'll have time to think of what I could invest in and what might be ethical. Right now, not so much.*

I smiled when I saw her text. Of course, she was a student. She barely could afford to spend money on entertainment, let alone investments. I'd been lucky all my life and had never been without money. I was lucky that my father and then adoptive father ingrained in me a respect for creating a budget and sticking to it, even if it was a pretty generous budget. I loved playing the stock market when I was growing up, and had a practice account when I turned fourteen under his tutelage, and when I turned eighteen, I invested one hundred grand, which turned into two hundred, and then half a million.

What can I say? I inherited a fortune and a knack for numbers. From the time I was a kid, I loved math, computers and coding. I loved buying and selling stocks. I loved to watch investments grow and then reinvest to build a bigger better portfolio.

LUKE: *Do you know about anything international labor legislation? Trade?*

ALEXA: *Zip. Zilch. Nada. I specialize in war and peace rather than international trade. Although the two are connected, but that's a very long discussion.*

LUKE: *I have time.*

ALEXA: *LOL Maybe for another night. Right now, my eyes are almost crossed from studying. My comp is tomorrow.*

LUKE: *Oh, yeah. I won't bother you. We can talk when you come to Westhampton with me. We can sit on the beach and drink beer and talk international relations.*

ALEXA: *Sounds riveting. ;)*

LUKE: *You know you want to...*

ALEXA: *You really want me to come?*

LUKE: *I need you to come. Mrs. B and Felicia will be there. If I don't have you at my side, Dragon Lady and Mrs. B will conspire to push poor Felicia next to me every opportunity they can find. It would be hell. You must rescue me.*

There was a pause and I wondered if she'd pull out or still agree to come with me.

ALEXA: *If you really think you need me there, okay. But it's all a performance. No a la carte ordering.*

LUKE: *I'll be the perfect gentleman. Scout's Honor.*

ALEXA: *Okay. I'll probably really need the escape after my comp is done. I've been studying straight for weeks now.*

LUKE: *You deserve a break. Our beach house is nice, very comfortable, the ocean is right there, a nice beach, all the amenities.*

ALEXA: *Sounds wonderful. Welp, I gotta go and finish reading my journal article on the ICBM Treaty and the Iran Deal.*

LUKE: *SNORE...*

ALEXA: *No, seriously, it's very good. Very exciting.*

LUKE: *ZZZZzzzz*

ALEXA: *Goodbye, sir.*

LUKE: *Later. ;)*

I read over our texts, smiling to myself. She was smart but she was also playful. I liked that in a woman. She could be serious, but she could also have fun. I couldn't stand people who were uptight or couldn't take or tell a joke.

The truth was I actually *liked* Alexa. I looked forward to spending time with her, just talking. Well, I'd really like to fuck her brains out, but afterwards, I'd like to pick her brain about politics so I could check out that angle for ethical investing.

Plus, she was really easy on the eyes. She was pretty. She had a great smile. She was smart. She had a hot body that I wanted very much to explore.

I should have known better than to keep seeing her.

But I didn't.

CHAPTER 11

ALEXA

Thursday came and along with it came my comprehensive exam. It went fine, I was well prepared, and when it was all over and I spoke with my advisor, noting how easy it seemed.

She laughed.

"You have to remember that you're the expert in this area now. We've all read in the area in a general sense, but you've gone in depth."

"I never thought of it like that."

She smiled and patted me on the back. "Now, it's a tradition that your advisor takes you and the other MA students for a drink, so I hope you're willing to come with us to the pub this afternoon. We're going to a place downtown called *Valencia*. Five o'clock until seven."

"I'll be there."

"Good. Drinks are on me."

I went home and of course had to report to Candace how my comp had gone and that I'd passed. She hugged me and brought out a bottle of champagne that she'd been storing in the back of the refrigerator.

"Let's toast to your continued success. It's onward and upward to your thesis research."

We had a glass of champagne and I told her about having drinks with my advisor and the other students in my year.

"Sounds like fun," she said.

"Yeah, but Ichabod is going to be there," I said and made a face of disgust.

Ian Crane, aka Ichabod, was a PhD student who couldn't seem to get the picture that I was not interested in his long-winded talks about the US election. He'd corner me in the hallways at Columbia and lean in close, droning on and on about the president or the FBI and it was all I could do to not run away. Although I was a political junkie, I had enough of US politics and the election. I was focused on my studies, not on what was happening outside my door. That may sound small, but I was tired of getting into arguments with people about it.

"You can survive one night with dear old Ichabod. You have to do this – commune with your fellow grad students. Besides, I'll be there to cheer you on."

"Thank God for that," I said and gave her a hug.

We dressed in our best causal clothes, with me in a pretty sundress with tiny straps that showed off my assets, and Candace wore her little black dress. Most of the time, my fellow grad students saw me in jeans and a t-shirt, Blundstones, and a backpack. I didn't want to get too dressed up, but at the same time, this was a celebration so a little extra effort was warranted.

We trooped down to *Valencia* for a drink and supposedly to celebrate my successful comp, but apparently, people in my course didn't really know how to have fun. An hour in and the evening had grown almost too dull for words and so I excused myself and went the washroom, happy to have a reason to leave the table. Ichabod, aka Ian, had been hitting on me, and I found it difficult to be polite when he thrust his face close to mine and made that face, his eyebrows wagging suggestively

I really didn't have to go, but was hoping to find a way to extricate myself from Ichabod's attentions. I checked my cell, trying to distract myself from thoughts of him making the moves on me, and discovered that Luke had texted me.

LUKE: Save me.

I frowned. What the hell?

ALEXA: Save you from what?

LUKE: Terminal boredom.

That made me smile. I could see him in my mind's eye, sitting in a meeting, yawning behind a hand, his blue eyes wide with frustration. Maybe those sexy dark rimmed glasses on that made him look so brainy.

ALEXA: I was going to ask you to save me.

LUKE: Oh, yeah? From what? Whatever it is can't be as bad as the current hell I'm in...Quarterly financial reports... *yawn*

ALEXA: You'd be wrong about that. I'm at a supposed party at Valencia to celebrate my successful comp, and I'm practically falling asleep with my eyes open it's so dull. And then, there's this guy...

There was a pause.

LUKE: What guy? *takes on a fighting stance* Doesn't he know you're my fake girlfriend???

I smiled.

ALEXA: I was thinking of pretending there was a family emergency or something like that. Ichabod won't leave me alone and I can't be mean to him because he's my advisor's star teaching assistant.

LUKE: Ichabod?

ALEXA: Ian Crane, a PhD student. He has this really skinny face and red hair. He reminds me of Ichabod Crane in this book I read as a kid. If he gets any closer to me, I'll scream. When he talks, I swear I can see his uvula.

LUKE: His uvula? GROSS

I laughed.

LUKE: You have to learn to give men a big hint because many of us – not me, of course – can't catch a clue. Tell him you have a boyfriend. You can use me as an excuse. I mean, since I used you. Turnabout is fair play and all...

ALEXA: I can't do that. Everyone knows I'm a total nerd and don't have a boyfriend. I haven't had one for a year at least.

LUKE: YOU. ARE. NOT. A. NERD. You're a geek. Lie. Everyone does it...

There was a pause as I thought of how to respond.

LUKE: A YEAR??? HOLY SHIT. Not to pry, but you haven't had sex for a whole year?

ALEXA: One typically needs a partner to have sex so, yes, over a year, actually. Don't make fun or I won't be nice and go to Westhampton with you.

*LUKE: Sorry but I can't imagine you *cough* being single for over a whole year. My God, don't you go crazy? I mean, more than a year? How much more?*

ALEXA: None of your business. Some of us have control over our biological functions.

LUKE: Nuns and priests, maybe...

ALEXA: I'm no nun. There are alternatives to actual sex with another human being, you know.

LUKE: Hmmm. Tell me more... Not that I'm slavering to imagine you doing all kinds of nasty things to yourself in the absence of a proper man with proper man parts...

ALEXA: Ha! Wouldn't you like to know.

LUKE: I would, I would. Tell me everything.

ALEXA: Not on your life. I'll leave it to your imagination.

LUKE: OH GOD...

LUKE: How am I going to get to sleep tonight? You vixen...

I smiled and read back our texts. What would he think of me admitting I took matters into my own hand? I knew the mere suggestion would send his man brain into apoplexy. That was my desired effect.

Yeah, I could be a tease.

ALEXA: Maybe I'll come down with a headache. But the party's for me and we reserved the back room and have food and everything. I can't skip out on my own party.

LUKE: Yes, that's right – your comp. I know it went well. You don't even have to tell me. As to Ichabod, I could come and rescue you, riding in on a white charger. Or Black Mercedes SUV. Whatever works for you.

ALEXA: No, that's all right. I'm a big girl. But thanks for the offer.

Candace must have come looking for me because she stuck her head in the washroom and called out.

"Hey, Alexa are you in there?"

"Yes," I said and glanced up from my phone.

"Did you fall in?"

"No, I'll be right out."

ALEXA: Gotta go. I'm being summoned.

LUKE: Okay. Talk later. And congrats again for the successful comp exam. But I hold you totally responsible for a great deal of current discomfort and probably a lot more later tonight when I'm in bed and I think of you all alone with no man parts to help out...

ALEXA: Simple. Don't think of me.

LUKE: Yeah, tell me another one. Not gonna happen.

ALEXA: I'm sure you can take matters into your own hand.

LUKE: I'd rather you take them into your own hand.

ALEXA: Good night, Mr. Marshall.

*LUKE: *sigh**

I grinned widely and ended the conversation, slipping my phone into my bag. I washed my hands while looking in the mirror. There were bags under my eyes due to too many late nights studying, poring over research articles and reading reports. Luke was a flatterer, but he probably wouldn't find me all that alluring tonight if he saw me looking as tired as I was.

I didn't mind putting in so many late nights studying. It was what I loved. I'd rather do it than spend my time socializing with the rest of my fellow students. Especially Ichabod, who had this annoying habit of leaning in close enough that I could count the nose hairs poking out of his very large nostrils.

I smoothed my hair and then left the washroom, making my way back to the table. I sat down, but unfortunately, I had to sit beside Ichabod once more. I wondered how long it would take for him to try to monopolize my time, hoping that I could excuse myself sooner than later and get the hell out of there with Candace.

Sure enough, Ichabod leaned in and began talking to me, taking off from the conversation about his new paper on Iran's nuclear program and the threat to Israel. I tried to smile, but it felt forced and all I could think of was *RESCUE ME CANDACE!* But she was sitting across the table from me, talking to someone else, blissfully unaware of how much pain I was in.

The monologue from Ichabod went on and on, his voice droning in a monotone that threatened to put me to sleep. I tried to catch Candace's eye, signaling with mental telepathy to come to my rescue. Her eyes widened as she watched something behind me.

Just as I was turning to check it out, I felt someone lean in even closer than Ichabod, kissing me on the cheek before I could do or say anything.

Luke.

"Hey there, beautiful," he said and knelt between me and Ichabod, his arm around the back of my chair. "I'm sorry I'm late. I got hung up in a meeting and couldn't get here sooner to help celebrate."

I sat there with my mouth hanging open for a moment before getting on top of things.

"No," I said and cleared my throat. "That's okay. You got here really quickly."

He smiled. "My office is just a few blocks away."

I sat mute, unable to think of what else to say. Candace made a face at me, her eyes wider than saucers.

"Alexa, why don't you introduce us to your *friend*?"

"Oh, oh, yes," I said, stuttering. "Luke, this is Candace, my best friend and these are my colleagues. Everyone, this is Luke."

Luke reached out and extended his hand across the table to Candace. "Hey, Candace," he said. "Nice to meet you. Alexa told me so much about you."

"All of it good, no doubt," Candace said and blushed. Luke kissed her knuckles gallantly. Then he turned to Ichabod.

"Ian, right?" he said and pointed to Ichabod. "Nice to meet you. Alexa told me about *you* as well."

Ian extended his hand and the two men shook. It was when Luke reached to Ian that I saw the tattoo extending down below

135

his shirt cuff to wrap around his wrist. Something tribal, in dark blue ink.

It was so unlike what I thought of Luke. He didn't seem the tattoo kind of guy. It made me want to take off his shirt and inspect the tattoo. See what else he had on his body besides that wonderful washboard abdomen. And of course, our conversation while I was in the washroom came back to me, and I couldn't help but imagine his hands on me.

"Alexa, you never told us about a boyfriend," Ian said. He smiled at Luke but I could see it wasn't a truly friendly smile. "How long have you known each other?"

How would I explain him to everyone?

If I was at a loss for words, Luke wasn't, improvising on the spot.

"I used to go to Columbia, and we met at the pub last year when I was there for a reunion. We lost contact for a while and reconnected recently."

Luke grinned at me, winking slightly.

"How nice," Ian replied, his voice low. He looked rather upset. The other female students were a bit wide-eyed, no doubt impressed with Luke as any woman would be. He was gorgeous and looked high end, in his dark grey suit, white shirt and black tie. Plus, that obviously expensive black watch.

He was, quite simply, Armani gorgeous.

I took in a deep breath and calmed myself. Seeing him again, I realized that Luke was a hunk of man like I hadn't seen in a loooong time. Tall, built, handsome... Even I was excited. I pasted the most alluring smile on my face and prepared myself to play his new girlfriend. It would solve the problem of Ichabod so it was worth having to deceive my colleagues. I put my hand on Luke's bicep and squeezed, enjoying the feel of the hard muscle underneath my fingers.

"Yes, I met Luke last year at Columbia. It was nice to see him again after he left for the business world and well, we just couldn't stop seeing each other."

Luke and I looked at each other, smiling like a couple deeply in love. I could see the gleam in his eye. He was enjoying this little charade.

He took my hand and kissed my knuckles.

What a change from the other guys at Columbia. He was a slick charmer, for sure. I could see Candace almost bursting with glee across the table, her grin ridiculously big. She loved the game as well.

"You're *the* Luke Marshall?" one of my fellow students asked, leaning forward. "The Luke Marshall of the Chatter app? The deal that's rumored to be worth two billion?"

"The very one, but *shh*," he said and held a finger to his lips. "We don't want that number repeated too many times. Just in case it falls through. The deal's still in the works."

"How did that number get out, anyway?" I asked. "Shouldn't it be a secret?"

Luke shook his head. "Sometimes, it's good to have a few rumors floating around. Increases buzz around a deal and might attract a higher bid by someone who wants to win the deal."

Luke pulled up a chair and the group moved on to some other discussion. When their attention was focused elsewhere, I leaned closer to him.

"I know your family's rich, but that's still a lot of money," I whispered, barely able to believe it.

Luke leaned closer and smiled back. "It is a lot of money, but I can then be my own man, with no money from the family."

"What are you going to do next?" I asked, unable to imagine what a cool billion could do to a person's life.

"Like I said, it's money that'll let me sail to the Galapagos."

"But after that? The Mars mission?"

He put an arm around my shoulder. "Something like that. Maybe build an orbital platform. Or a mission to the asteroid belt, to mine rare minerals and gold."

"That's visionary thinking."

"I want to do something with my wealth. Something that moves us forward as a civilization."

"Why not feed the poor? Or fight global warming?"

"I can do that, too."

I nodded and watched him while he took a drink of the beer a waitress brought over for him. He turned to me and smiled when he caught me looking at him.

"What?"

I glanced away, realizing that despite the charade we were playing, he was most definitely out of my league. He came from a wealthy family, and money was no object to him, and yet...

And yet he seemed to fit right in with the group, talking to someone about the most recent baseball win.

We sat with the group and Candace peppered Luke with questions about his business, and what he planned to do when the sale went through. Finally, Luke glanced at his watch. Then he leaned in to me, his lips beside my ear.

"Have you eaten?"

I shook my head. "Just nachos." I pointed to the basket of tortilla chips in the center of the table.

"Want to get out of here? Go get some real food?"

He met my eyes and how could I refuse him? He was so damn gorgeous...

"Sure," I said. "I'm hungry."

I glanced at Candace, who was watching the two of us, her expression pleased.

"We're going for supper," I said and stood. "Thanks to everyone for coming for a drink and to help me celebrate."

There was a round of congrats and Candace nodded, smiling.

I thanked my advisor, then said goodbye. Luke took my hand, leading me out of the bar to the street. A half a block down sat his SUV, all black and shiny.

"Where to?" he asked, leading it to me.

"Wherever you want to go."

"What do you feel like? What kind of food?"

"At this point, I'll eat practically anything," I said with a laugh.

"Okay," Luke said and opened the passenger door for me when we got to the vehicle. "How about Italian? There's a fantastic restaurant down a few blocks from my office."

I glanced down at my dress. "Am I dressed appropriately?"

"You look beautiful. You're dressed more than appropriately," he said and looked over at me, smiling approvingly. "John and I go there all the time for great pasta and meatballs. It's a family restaurant. Authentic Italian."

I smiled, relieved that I'd fit in. "Sounds delicious."

We drove down 105th and then made our way along the side streets until we came to a small restaurant in an old brownstone building, the storefront with a table in the window. It was quaint, all in red brick and black trim, and looked like a family business, white tablecloths and empty bottles of Chianti with candles lit in them.

The music was Italian and the smell inside was wonderful.

A waitress greeted us and pointed to the entire restaurant, which had only a few customers.

"Let's sit in the window," Luke said and so we sat at the tiny table, the candle lit between us, and examined the menu. The waitress took our drink order, and I turned down anything but ice water. Luke did the same.

I had to admit that my stomach was filled with butterflies because this felt like a real date. We didn't have to come out for supper. He could have taken me home and gone his separate way, but he asked me to go to dinner with him.

That was kind of a date, right?

I checked over the menu and when the waitress took our order, I settled on some spaghetti with meatballs, which was the house specialty. Luke ordered the same and then when the waitress left, we turned to each other.

"So," Luke said and smiled at me, his blue eyes twinkling with humor. "How did I do as your fake boyfriend?"

"You were fabulous," I said, grinning back. "Can I use you anytime I need you to fend off my fellow students who can't find a clue?"

"Anytime," he said and took a sip of ice water. "I excel at empty meaningless relationships. Usually, there's lots of empty meaningless but very enjoyable sex involved, but I can do straight fake boyfriend if needed. However, I expect you to do the same for me, next weekend. Remember?"

"I remember. I'll be the very best fake girlfriend you ever had. I'll smile and gaze lovingly in your eyes, listen raptly to everything you say and I'll never disagree with anything."

"Oh, no," he said and mock-frowned. "You must disagree. Disagreements are key to a good fake relationship. Makes the fake sex spicier."

He grinned at that, and I couldn't help but smile back. He was such a cute man, plus very handsome in a boyishly devilish way, with that tiny hint of evil in his eye. Mischievous, like he was holding back in order to pretend he was nice.

I wondered if he really was a bit kinky like he said when we first texted, and what that meant. It made me a little breathless to imagine what empty meaningless but very enjoyable sex would be like with him. I couldn't help but think about riding him like he was a bucking bronco and squirmed a bit in my chair.

Down, girl...

I told myself that he was not for me. He was going to be sailing around the world for a year, and then wanted to go to frickin Mars or the Moon or something. He did not want to spend his time being married to me and living in Zurich or Copenhagen.

Still, I couldn't help but imagine it. Maybe I could do meaningless sex. I'd done very bad sex. I'd done loveless sex. Maybe good but meaningless sex would be a whole lot better.

"So, about the weekend," I said, after our food was brought to us and we dug in. "What's expected of me? What will we be doing?"

"We'll be hanging out with the family at our beach house. It's right on the beach, so I intend to spend as much time as possible lounging around on beach chairs, drinking beer and catching the sun. We could surf. We could get some great fresh seafood. We'll have bonfires. We'll talk with those members of my family that I don't hate, like my sister."

I thought about his pregnant sister and her cheating husband. "It must be hard for you to be around Eric."

He took in a deep breath and shook his head. "You don't know how hard. I want to plough him every time I think about it but I don't want to ruin her experience of childbirth and being a new mom."

"That might take a year, from what I hear."

He shrugged and twirled some pasta on his fork. "That's okay. She can live in ignorance for a while. I'll see what Eric does in the meantime."

"Will you tell her eventually?"

"What do you think I should do? You're a woman. Would you

want to know if your husband cheated on your when you were pregnant?"

"Oh, God, I don't know..." I took a drink of water and considered. My parents had such a great relationship. I couldn't imagine how my mom would have felt if she learned my dad cheated on her. "I'm not one to talk about relationships," I said and shrugged. "But I do think it's important to know the truth."

"I might wait until I think she's capable of dealing with it or until Eric convinces me he's repented. But if he doesn't, if I catch him straying again, I'll bring the hammer down. It won't be pretty."

"You're close with your sister?" I asked but I already knew they were.

"Very close," he said and popped a meatball into his mouth. He chewed thoughtfully for a moment. "It was hard when my adoptive parents moved us to separate schools. They thought it was bad for us to be too close. Like they were afraid we'd become incestuous but that was nuts. I think both of us were traumatized by it."

"It must have been hard. I can't imagine. My parents are still married and they've been together for thirty years. I'm sure they're still in love. They say they're each other's best friend. That's what I want in a relationship. In a marriage," I added.

"They're one of a kind, if that's the case," Luke said. "Half of all marriages end in divorce. Even second ones. It's a wasteland of broken hearts. I honestly don't know how people keep hoping one will stick."

I watched him while he sopped up some sauce with a piece of bread. He was really closed to the idea of a happy marriage whereas it was high on my list of must-haves in life. As easily as we got along with each other, as attracted as I was to him, I knew that there would never be anything between us. I'd have to protect myself from feeling anything but lust for him because he was out of reach for anything else.

"That's a very sad way to look at love," I said finally, turning back to my own meal. "You must be lonely."

"Not at all," he said and sat up a bit straighter. "I'm too busy to feel lonely. I have good friends. I have an amazingly successful business and am soon to be a bona-fide tycoon." He gave me a wicked grin. "And I'm going to be on my yacht on my way to the Galapagos with my best buds in the world as soon as I can get it built. Who's lonely?"

"I guess," I said and sighed. Maybe it was me who was lonely, but I didn't feel it. "I'm too busy to be lonely as well," I said, "with my classes and studying and part time job as a teaching assistant. There's barely any time in the day that I can just flake out and do nothing."

"So what are your future plans?"

I shrugged and picked up a piece of meatball. "Get my PhD and get on the tenure track. Maybe work for a think tank in Washington or New York, for the UN. I won't consider settling down until I'm firmly ensconced in a good job in Europe."

"Europe?" he said and made a face. "Why not the good old USA?"

"I could say the same to you," I said and smiled. "Why Mars?"

"*Touché*," he replied.

We finished our meal, talking about *Chatter* and the pending deal, how he and John started the business and how successful it became – beyond any of their expectations.

When we were finished, he checked his watch then paid the bill with his credit card. When the waitress brought back the receipt he looked in my eyes. "Well, I guess I better go. I have another hour of work to do before I go home."

"You're going back to the office at this time of night?"

"It's only eight," he said with a laugh. "I usually work until ten. I'll be slacking off if I go home at nine. Plus we have a meeting about the deal, so..."

"What a life," I said and we got up to leave. "I'm done with work until next month when I start my research for my thesis."

"What are you going to do in between then and now?"

I shrugged. "Well, I'm going to be going to Westhampton for a weekend of performance art."

He grinned. "After that," he said and opened the door for me. We walked to the vehicle.

"I am a free woman," I said. "Two weeks of glorious doing nothing at all. Maybe I'll binge watch some House of Cards."

"Would you take a trip back to Oregon and see your parental units?"

"Parental units," I said with a laugh. "No, not likely."

"Why not?" he asked and opened my door. We got inside and he started the car.

I didn't answer right away. I didn't want to get into the whole bad relationship that I was trying to escape back in Oregon.

"Reasons," I said and made a face. "Reasons I don't really want to talk about."

He frowned. "Are you a wanted criminal back in Oregon?"

"It has nothing to do with me being a criminal. Someone else, but let's not talk about it, okay?"

Even thinking about it made my body tense and my heart rate increase.

"Sorry," he said and held up his hand. "Say no more. I won't pry."

We drove off.

"I'd love to go and see my mom and dad but I can't. Maybe they'll come out East for a visit."

"You're lucky you actually want to be around your family. Me?

144

I can't wait to escape their company, with the exception of my sister."

We stopped at a light and I watched him. He rubbed his chin, which was covered with just the right amount of scruff.

"I would love to be around my mother and father, but it's not possible."

He nodded and finally, we arrived at my building. He stopped the car and got out, quickly opening my door before I could.

"You're pretty gallant for someone who doesn't believe in romance," I said and stepped out, taking his hand.

"I believe in being extremely courteous." He helped me out, then offered me his arm. "To make up for being a heartless rake." He wagged his eyebrows at me.

I laughed at his expression. We walked up the eight steps to the front entry to the building and stopped as I got out my key.

"Well, thanks again for rescuing me," I said and let out a sigh. "I don't think Ichabod will be bothering me again after your stellar performance."

"No more seeing his uvula, I hope?"

"I hope," I said and smiled. I felt a bit awkward because usually, if I remembered dating at all and I barely did, this would be the time when he'd lean in and kiss me or I'd invite him up for coffee.

"Well, I'd invite you up for coffee," I said, and tilted my head when I looked at him, "but I don't drink coffee after three o'clock in the afternoon and you've got work. Besides, I'm not into the whole empty meaningless but very enjoyable sex thing."

He leaned in closer, our eyes meeting. "That's too bad," he said, his voice sounding a bit gruff. "I'd throw over my extra hour of work in a heartbeat if you were."

We stood like that, our faces just inches away from each other and the moment seemed to stretch. Finally, I turned and slipped my key in the slot and went inside, kicking myself for not just kissing him. I should have. It's not like he wouldn't have kissed me back, but I wasn't sure I wanted to let myself get too close.

I turned when I got to the inside door and waved at him. He was still standing on the doorstep, watching me.

"If you change your mind, you can text me. I'll be right over..." He raised his eyebrows at that. When I shook my head, he laughed. "Just kidding. I know you're not into meaningless if incredibly enjoyable sex. My loss."

"Good night," I said and as I closed the door ad went to the stairs, almost running up them. I couldn't wipe the smile off my face.

I really enjoyed being with Luke. He was very, well...likeable. Let's face it. He was very fuckable, too, except for the part about leaving in a short time to sail around the world and his plans to leave the Earth for Mars or the asteroid belt.

I planned on staying put on Mother Earth and didn't want my heart broken again.

Once was more than enough.

CHAPTER 12

LUKE

The next day, I spent the time in meetings with Andy, one of Chatter's lawyers who was there to talk about the deal. We discussed our meeting with the investment company that wanted to buy us out. We talked strategy and tactics, and then what we'd do once the deal went through.

John leaned back in his chair, his hands behind his head.

"Me and Mr. Big Shot here are going to sail around the world."

Randy Andy, as we called him, turned to me.

"After you get back, you're pulling a rich boy going into space?"

"Something like that," I replied. "Maybe John will join me on a one-way trip to Mars."

"Not on your life." John shook his head and held out a hand. "I'm sticking to the good old planet Earth with its oxygen and living soil and protective atmosphere and geomagnetic protection from harmful cosmic radiation. Once we're back from the trip, I'm going to find me a rich blue blood woman and start my family dynasty. Do everything right."

I laughed at that. "Seriously, what are your plans? You're going to have a billion dollars. What are you going to do with it?"

"Make another billion."

"No philanthropy? No fulfilling a life-long dream?"

"After finding me a good woman to make me an honest man, I'm going to make another billion will be fulfilling a life-long dream so I'm good."

I turned to Andy. "You and Shana getting married?"

"Probably," Andy said, his hands folded. "She's getting antsy about getting pregnant before she's too old."

I nodded, but felt strange. "I guess I'm the odd man out," I said. "Not getting married or starting a dynasty. I want to create a legacy that will outlive me. Space. That's my life-long dream."

"You would have been singing a different tune if this happened a year ago," Andy said, his eyebrows raised suggestively. Of course, I knew what he meant. Before I found out Jenna had been cheating on me.

"You're right, of course," I said. "I would have been planning the biggest wedding of the year. But that was then. This is now."

"You're the last man in your family. If you don't procreate, there will be no one to keep the family name going."

"I'll donate my sperm. Someone will carry on the genes, if not the name."

"A name is everything, man," Andy said. "You'll get over Jenna. You'll find someone else. I bet in a year, you'll be talking about buying real estate somewhere with some pretty young woman you fell for while you were in some port."

I laughed. "Not likely, but whatever."

"He likes this woman he met last week," John said, a sly grin on his face.

"Oh?" Andy said and leaned forward. "Do tell."

I shook my head. "She's a great woman, but I'm a confirmed bachelor."

"He's falling already and doesn't know it," John insisted. "He's trying to deny it, but I know the truth."

Now Andy was all smiles. "Seriously? Who's the lucky woman?"

Then John relayed the story of how Alexa and I met.

"She actually pretended to be a call girl?"

When I nodded, he laughed.

"Oh, that is such a great story. You two can tell that one the rest of your life on the anniversary of your first date."

"You're full of it," I said, unable to stop smiling. "We're just a couple out of convenience. I'm faking it for her benefit, to keep the skinny Teaching Assistant out of her hair, and she's faking it for me so I can let my adoptive mother's best friend down easy that I'm not marrying her daughter."

"Faking it?" Andy said, a grin cracking his face. "Is he faking it? That's a real smile on his face."

John shook his head. "He really likes her."

"Keep deluding yourself," I replied and stood up, gathering up my files. "Well, enough girl talk. I have work to do finishing off the presentation. We can go over it next week before the meeting. I'll send it to you when I'm done."

We left the conference room and went our separate ways.

I was somewhat amused by Andy's and John's attempts to paint me as infatuated with Alexa. Sure, I'd love to fuck her brains out, but that was it.

They both had to get a life. I had plans for the next fifty years and they didn't involve becoming a lapdog to some woman just so I could get my rocks off.

I'd learned that lesson with Jenna and wouldn't make that mistake again.

The following Friday, I sat at my desk gazing out at the Manhattan skyline. I checked my cell to see if Alexa had pulled out at the last minute, like I suspected she might, but so far there was no text from her.

LUKE: *Hey, how are you today? Slay any international relations dragons? I hope you're still planning to come to Westhampton with me tonight. I need a sidekick to keep the wolves at bay...*

I sent the text and then waited, wondering what she'd say in reply.

When she didn't reply right away, I opened a file on my desk and tried to occupy myself. Finally, I heard a ding and checked my cell.

ALEXA: *I'm through with dragons for at least two weeks, I'm happy to say. If you seriously need me to come to Westhampton, I'm willing but I want a promise from you again that you're not going to try any funny stuff.*

LUKE: *I am a man of my word. I promise to only fake trying funny stuff. I will pretend to be so turned on by your mere presence that I can't wait to get you alone in my bed so I can ravish you the way you deserve. It will all be a total act, rest assured. ;)*

ALEXA: *Good because I don't do meaningless sex, no matter how wonderfully pleasurable it might be.*

LUKE: **sigh* Classic boy-girl divide. He wants meaningless sex, and she wants meaningful sex. Can I ask you something? Why can't plain old good sex be enough? Don't you like good sex? Maybe you haven't had enough of it to know what you're missing. I assure* *you, I would make it worth your while. It's been over a year after all...*

She didn't respond right away, and I felt that maybe I'd pushed a bit too hard.

LUKE: Of course, if you prefer to just fake it, I understand. Well, I don't understand, but I can accept it.

Another silence passed and I hoped I hadn't been really wrong to text what I had. I read over my text and tried to see what I might have written that would be taken in the wrong way.

LUKE: ??

Finally, after about ten minutes, she replied, and I felt a huge sense of relief that she wasn't going to tell me to fuck off and deal with my family and the Blakes on my own.

ALEXA: I have my reasons as I'm sure you have yours.

LUKE: Of course you do. Look, you can't blame a guy for trying. You're beautiful and sexy as hell. I can't not want to fuck you silly. You have to understand that. Right?

ALEXA: This is the source of all problems in the world between men and women. Men can't seem to see us without their dicks getting in the way. I'm more than just tits and ass...

Whoa. I really put my foot in it that time.

LUKE: Of course you are. You're much more and all of it is very attractive. I'm sorry if my bluntness insults you, but I'm only being truthful. I promise that I won't be too obnoxious when we're at the beach house for the weekend. Only as obnoxious as I have to convince everyone that we really are fucking our brains out, okay? Deal?

I waited for her response. From my way of thinking, I was complimenting her, noting how beautiful she was and how sexy. How pretty much every man I knew would feel the same way about her.

ALEXA: As long as you keep your end of the bargain, I'll keep mine.

LUKE: Deal. I'll pick you up at seven. By the time we arrive, there'll be a barbecue, bonfire and we can sit around, have a few drinks and enjoy the night. You deserve to relax and enjoy yourself and celebrate your successful exam. You can hold my hand a bit, we can gaze in a loving but entirely fake way into each other's eyes in front of the Blakes, put on a good show for my adoptive mother and then hit the sack. I promise to be a total gentleman when we're alone.

ALEXA: I'm holding you to it.

LUKE: Okay. See you in a while.

Damn, woman...

I thought she'd be flattered that I found her so attractive and desirable. I'd think she would like it, but apparently, it was a sore spot for her.

I'd be the perfect gentleman with her when we were alone, even though it would be hell to have her in my bedroom and not be able to actually use it the way I wanted.

With her on the bed, on the floor in front of the fireplace, on the sofa in front of the window, and in the bathtub. Wherever I could take her.

That was the normal red-blooded hetero male in me.

The other part of me, the part with a functioning pre-frontal cortex, knew I had to show her that I appreciated her as a person as well as a woman.

I'd make sure I asked her all about her thesis and what she was planning to do with her PhD when she finished it. I wasn't a total ignoramus when it came to women.

I'd been engaged to and ready to marry one.

Scratch that – I was a total ignoramus when it came to women, at least when it came to judging whether they were faithful. I thought Jenna was faithful, but I was wrong.

I wouldn't make that mistake again.

I went home and took a shower then packed my bag, throwing in a few pairs of swimming trunks and some clean boxer briefs, my golf hat, a Hawaiian shirt and some Bermuda shorts. I packed my shaving kit, and then added in a few condoms – on the off chance that Alexa changed her mind. I wanted to be prepared for all eventualities.

After I dressed in some jeans and a clean button down white shirt, I went to pick her up.

On the drive there, I was hopeful that we'd have a fun weekend, despite putting on a show. We enjoyed each other's company – I was sure of that much. I think if I could close my eyes and just listen to her talk, or if we kept it to texts, we could be great friends. I enjoyed her playful banter and of course, she was smart. Smarter than most guys I knew.

It was just that she was so damn sexy...

Buck up, soldier.

I'd have to be a perfect gentleman with her this weekend. No pushing myself on her. Let her come to me if she decided she wanted some...

I arrived at her apartment block and waited on the street, double parking while I texted her that I was outside. The sun was still high in the sky despite the hour, and the air was warm for September.

LUKE: Your knight in shining black armor awaits, m'lady.

ALEXA: Be right there.

About three minutes later, she appeared outside the door to her building, looking like a movie star in her white sundress with brightly colored flowers, a pair of sandals and a wide-brimmed hat and sunglasses. I hopped out of the car and helped her with her bag. She got in the passenger side when I opened the door and I threw her bag in the back beside mine.

I got back in the car and turned to look at her.

She was perfect. Everything – her hair, her dress, her sandals... she was the perfect date for a weekend at my family beach house.

"You look fantastic," I said and smiled.

"Thank you." She looked at me over her sunglasses, a grin on her lips. "You're not so bad yourself."

"We aim to please."

I drove off once she had her seatbelt fastened, surprised at how much I was looking forward to this weekend. Usually, I'd only tolerate things at my family's beach house, trying to wear headphones to keep from talking to people, even though they'd inevitably interrupt and try to make conversation. Sometimes, I'd bring work and sit at the table on the patio and hold my cell to my ear, shrugging to make it look like I was busy conducting business so I could dodge any conversations with people I would rather avoid.

This weekend, I was honestly looking forward to walking around the grounds with Alexa at my side, using her as a shield from having to do much socializing. I'd ensure that we pretended to be deeply involved in each other, and hope that if we kept to ourselves, they'd leave us alone. Surely, Mrs. Blake would finally get the idea finally that I was not interested in her daughter. With John there, I could relax and hope that she was pleased with the chance of matching her daughter up with him instead.

"What am I in for this weekend?" Alexa glanced at me as we took the freeway on the way to Westhampton.

"Fun, sun and lots of prying questions from my family. The usual."

"How much do I tell them about us?"

"Wing it," I said. "If they ask about Jenna, just say that I don't talk much about her, and that you feel it's better that way."

"Are you going to tell me about Jenna?"

I shook my head. "I don't talk much about her. It's better that way. Suffice to say she betrayed me. That's really all you need to know."

She watched me for a few moments. I felt her eyes on my face and tried not to say anything more. I didn't want to get into the whole business of my cheating fiancée, because it was a real downer and I wanted to put it all as far behind me as I could.

"Unlucky in love," she said and watched the passing scenery. "Join the group."

"You too?"

"I don't talk too much about it. I think it's better that way." Then, she glanced back at me, smiling softly. "The two of us are like the walking wounded."

"Not me," I said and took in a deep breath. "I'm completely over it. Never think of it unless someone brings it up. When they do, I try to put it out of my mind as soon as I can."

"That bad?"

"Worse."

We drove in silence for a moment, and I knew she was curious and fighting her desire to ask me more. Hell, I was curious about her sad story, too, and would have really liked her to tell me more.

Instead, I asked her about her family, and she told me more about them and her life traveling around the country with each posting her father got.

"It sounds like a great life," I said, thinking about how much I missed my own real parents, and how Dana and I used to imagine what it would have been like to have both of them still alive instead of two adoptive parents.

"It was a great life. I saw a lot of the country, met people from all over the world. My father taught me about responsibility and duty, and how important a strong family can be. He was a very lucky man to have been able to fly jet planes all his life. He stuck in the military rather than get out and go commercial like a lot of his fellow pilots did. He became a career military officer. He loved the life."

"I'd like to meet him. I bet he has some good stories to tell."

"Oh, yeah," she said and smiled. "Lots of them."

"Tell me one," I asked, wanting to pry more info out of her. "Tell me your favorite story of his."

She smiled and twirled a strand of hair, thoughtfully. "He and a couple of other pilots were on a cross country trip to Nashville, returning a visiting pilot to his home base. They went out that night and visited Hank Williams Jr.'s grave. It was past midnight and they were technically trespassing and very drunk, but they wanted to visit it while they were there. The police found them and were going to arrest them for trespassing and drunk and disorderly conduct. They asked for my father's ID and he saved the day. He was an honorable Colonel in the Confederate Army and had this joke ID card they gave out to people. The cop saw it and shrugged, followed them back to the hotel instead of arresting them."

I laughed, imagining the whole thing in my mind's eye.

"He was an honorary colonel in the Confederate Army?"

"It was a joke, of course. Something he got when he was in Louisiana or someplace on a cross country. He wasn't really a supporter of the Confederacy or anything but it did save their asses."

I smiled and wondered what kind of man her father was and

whether we'd get along. We came from very different backgrounds, but I thought I'd probably like the man regardless.

"What would your father think of me?"

She glanced at me quickly, and then looked away, chewing on a nail. She narrowed her eyes at me. "I don't know..." She smiled. "He'd probably tell you that he has a shotgun in the closet and knows how to use it."

I laughed at that. "He would?"

"Oh, yeah." She laughed. "You don't know how many times he pulled that one on my new boyfriends. Sometimes, he'd be cleaning his rifle when they came by, really slowly and methodically so they could watch him check the sight. It was so blatant. He was always so serious about it, but then he'd laugh his head off if he saw any fear in the guy's eyes and confess he was just kidding. One of my boyfriends actually bonded with him over his rifle, asking if he could help, that he was an expert marksman and wanted to join the Marines and become a Scout Sniper. My dad wanted me to marry him."

I could imagine it, smiling at the image in my mind's eye.

"But you didn't want to marry him?"

She glanced away. "I was almost going to. Things didn't work out."

"What happened?"

She looked back at me as if she was considering how much to tell me.

"You don't want to know, believe me," she said finally, her voice soft. She looked back out the side window, resting her hand on her chin. "He's the reason I'm here instead of Oregon or California. I also got accepted at Stanford and UCLA but I wanted to escape. Let's leave it at that, okay?"

Oh, so she left Oregon to escape a bad relationship? It was interesting to me, of course, but I knew enough not to pry. We both had bad experiences, but hers hadn't soured her completely against romance, while mine had. I put it out of my mind and turned my attention back to the road.

We drove the rest of the way, talking about everything under the sun except our bad relationships – high school, college, my business, the deal, my parent's deaths and how we ended up orphans. How neither of us could wait to get away from both our adoptive parents.

"I wish I could have stayed on the coast so I could be close to my parents," she said.

"You can still visit."

"No, I can't."

"The ex?"

She nodded. "Let's leave it at that."

So, it was more than just a bad breakup. "It must be some seriously bad stuff, if that's the case."

"It is," she replied and sighed heavily. "Like I said, you do not want to know and I don't want to talk about it. I'm not trying to be rude and I'm not trying to be mysterious or anything. There's a good reason I can't go back and there's a good reason I don't want to talk about it."

"Don't worry," I said, and smiled softly at her, wanting to ease the discomfort between us. "I'm just your fake boyfriend of convenience. You don't owe me anything except a pretend good time."

She smiled at that and I thought again how pretty she was, her lashes long over blue eyes. "Maybe a genuine good time? I could use one..."

"I'll do my level best to make it a genuine good time, okay?"

She nodded. "Okay. Sounds good."

She flashed me a quick smile and then turned to watch as we drove up the private road to the beach house.

Her eyes practically bugged out when she saw it. Even I had to admit it was pretty impressive for a beach house.

Let's face it – anyone would be happy to live there.

A huge colonial, it had nine bedrooms, twelve bathrooms, a pool and tennis court, and a strip of green that my father used as a putting course for golf. Plus a boardwalk along the private beach front where Dana and I held our beach parties while we were growing up.

"This is your *beach* house?"

Her mouth was open as we drove up the circular driveway in front of the entrance. Double doors led to the interior and a huge porch wrapped around the entire twelve-thousand square foot building with three wings. One wing was for entertaining, one wing was for family, and the final wing was for guests.

Yeah, it was worth in the neighborhood of thirty million.

There was a six-car garage and a small cabana on the beach where we often hired bartenders to serve our guests. Plus a huge stone wood-fired barbecue that could double as a pizza oven.

"I was expecting something more... modest. You know, like a cottage."

"We're wealthy," I said, trying to be as honest and up front as I could be. "This property is pretty old. My adoptive father renovated it about a decade ago, upgrading everything, but I basically grew up here in the summers."

"Wow."

I parked in the driveway in one of the slots for visitors, and noted there were three other cars parked, indicating we had guests. I opened her door quickly, wanting to be a perfect gentleman. I then grabbed our bags and took her hand, walking her up the stairs to the porch and then opening the door for her.

She stopped and stared in the front entryway.

Yes, it was ostentatious. A huge crystal chandelier hung from the second story ceiling over the entry. Across from the entrance was a wide stairway that curved up to the second floor, splitting off into two wings.

"You'll be staying with me in the family wing," I said. "There are enough rooms that you could have one for yourself and one for your bag, but I want there to be no doubt that we're a couple, so you'll have to sleep in my bedroom."

"No funny business, remember?" she said, frowning slightly.

"No funny business," I replied. "Unless you want some. If you do, hey, I'm a generous guy. I'll donate to the cause. Considering you've been out of commission for over a year..." I raised my eyebrows playfully, but she didn't seem to appreciate my sense of humor.

"Just kidding," I said, not wanting to hurt her. "I just want you to know that if you felt a need, I'll be here. Ready and willing. I won't push, I won't even try to seduce you, but I can't promise you won't eventually find me incredibly desirable and irresistible." I grinned and finally saw her smile as well, although she was trying hard not to.

"Don't get your hopes up."

"I never hope," I said. "I go after what I want and I usually get it. Usually."

"But not always," she said. "You've lost before."

"Oh, yeah," I said and peered around into the great room, expecting to see someone but the place was empty. "Everyone must be down at the beach."

Then, I walked her up to the bedroom on the second floor, down the long hallway of rooms for my parents, Dana, if she was going to be here, and then my room at the end. I opened the door and she walked in.

I could sense her amazement when she took it in.

A huge four poster king sized bed sat in one corner. Beside it stood a chest of drawers, a small plush sofa and chair. A set of double patio doors opened onto a personal balcony that overlooked the greens and ocean.

"This is fantastic," she said and opened the patio door. She stepped on the balcony and I heard her take in a deep breath of salt air. "It's heaven."

I went to her side and rested my hands on the rail. "Yeah, it's pretty great. At night, I like to hear the roar of the surf. We're close enough that you can hear it when the doors are open. You can see some pretty decent stars as well. There aren't too many houses around with any lighting."

She smiled and then turned to me. "So, Mr. Big Shot, what's first on the agenda?"

"Something to eat. If you look down at the beach, you can see my family is sitting around a table by the barbecue."

"Sounds good," she said and together we left the house and made our way down the path past the putting green and swimming pool, to the beach.

I wondered who was there. People usually arrived Friday night for one of our weekends, and stayed until Sunday afternoon, but people came and left all weekend for meals and meetings.

I took her hand and prepared to meet my family and their guests, wondering what kind of weekend it would be.

CHAPTER 13

ALEXA

If I was impressed with Luke's lifestyle and fortune before I saw the beach house, I was even more impressed – and a little overwhelmed – after. Sure, I saw it on Google earth, but a blurry tape was no match for the real thing.

I tried not to gape, but it wasn't easy.

"I feel like the country mouse coming to visit the city mouse," I said as we walked past a tennis court, an enclosed swimming pool, and a putting green to the beach where the barbecue was taking place.

"Don't worry," Luke said. "These are all flesh and blood people. Most of them inherited their wealth, and most of them have just as many flaws as anyone from your neighborhood back in Oregon. In fact," he said and leaned in closer. "Some of them are even more fucked up that your average middle class person. I bet your father is far more together than any of the men here, despite their wealth and privilege."

I smiled at him. "You think so?"

"I know so," he said, nodding. "These men have worked hard in their businesses, but several had it passed on to them and they merely took over the reins of power. They didn't build their businesses."

"They still run them," I replied, trying to dampen down my awe.

"Sure, but many of the wealthiest men I know only make decisions, and leave all the grunt work of running an organization to underlings. They spend a lot of time on the golf course, having business lunches, taking jaunts in their private jets to talk to other businessmen and have business lunches, play on different golf courses. It's an entirely different sort of thing from actually building a company from the ground up."

"Like you and John did with Chatter," I offered.

He squeezed my hand. "Exactly. I know what it's like to start from scratch. Yes, I had seed money, but I earned half that money myself, investing. Every business has to either bootstrap or use money they've begged, borrowed or stolen. I started with a hundred thousand dollar investment account that I accrued from years of selling comics and investing my inheritance. I used that to fund the startup. John chipped in his own savings, and we were off. The rest was hard work, a brilliant idea and a lot of legwork getting it started."

I smiled, impressed with his accomplishments. He was a bit cocky about it, but then again, he was waiting on a two billion dollar deal to come through. I figured he could afford to be a bit cocky...

"So, who all's here," I said when we approached the group of people sitting around a table under a huge gazebo.

He peered at the group and leaned closer. "My parents. The Blakes of course, just as I thought. Mr. and Mrs. B plus Felicia. I hope John shows up soon so Mrs. B doesn't give me the stink eye. And there's Jim Thorpe and his wife Marie. Plus my father's golfing buddy who's the CEO of a Wall Street investment firm you won't have heard of but which handles billions of dollars in investments of the rich and famous. Smile for the camera," he said and squeezed my hand.

He pulled me over to where his adoptive mother and adoptive father were sitting.

"Hello everyone," he said and bent down to kiss his adoptive mother's cheek. "Mother. Father," he said and smiled at the people sitting at the table. "Good to see everyone. For those of you who haven't met her already, this is Alexandria."

I smiled my best smile and tried to make eye contact with everyone as Luke introduced them.

"Luke," Mrs. Thorpe said, eyeing me up and down. "We didn't know you had a new girlfriend. How nice to meet you, Alexandria."

"Please, call me Alexa," I said and felt my cheeks heat.

"Alexa's doing her Master's Degree in International Relations at Columbia," Luke said, a note of fake pride in his voice. "We met there last year."

"How nice," Mrs. Thorpe said and I was surprised at how these adults looked on the children of their friends almost as possessions to be mated off to each other's children. On their part, the Blakes gave me acid smiles, Mr. Blake narrowing his eyes like he was assessing why I got Luke instead of his daughter. I thought the time of the aristocracy pairing off children to each other had gone, but I found it operating in full force in the wealthy business types in Manhattan. Who would have thought?

Luke and I went over to the barbecue where a chef wearing a

white chef's hat was moving pieces of meat around on the grill.

"Take a plate and tell Jean what you want. Looks like there's beef ribs, roast beef, steak and burgers."

I examined everything on the grill and opted for a small tenderloin steak. Luke took some ribs and then we served ourselves salad and bread, snagged a beer each and went back to the table. Luke pulled out a seat and I sat down, nervous about being with all these strangers, but at least Luke would be there to look after me. While I thought I could carry on a conversation about international affairs as well as the best of them, I had no idea what rich people talked about when they sat around a supper table.

I ate my meal and listened as they talked about the stock market, about the golf courses they were visiting during the season, about the election, and about mundane things like the weather and the price of oil. I kept my mouth shut and ate without contributing, and Luke was silent as well, seemingly hungry and focused on his food.

"Is your steak to your liking?" Mrs. Marshall asked, looking at me over top of her glass of wine.

"Yes, thanks," I replied, smiling. "Delicious."

"So, Luke, tell us about this deal we've all been hearing about," Mr. Thorpe said, focusing on Luke.

Luke recounted the upcoming meeting and how there were several buyers interested in acquiring Chatter, including Harrison, the Blake's son. I recounted how they were vetting each one to ensure they shared the company's vision for the business. Luke was smart and articulate and the others listened as he spoke. They were all rich as crap but they were also impressed with someone who could build a business worth two billion in such a short time.

"To what do you attribute your success, young man?" Mr. Thorpe asked. He'd pulled out a cigar and was smoking, blowing the smoke off to the side of the group. Beside him, Mrs. Thorpe waved the smoke away, making a face of disgust. She turned to Luke.

"Yes, Luke. Tell us what you think made your business so successful."

Luke put down his rib and wiped his hand, then took a drink of beer.

"It was timing and a lot of legwork plus the smarts of my co-founder. I'm the deal maker, John is the tech wizard. We work together really well, we're both equally ambitious and we had a product that people actually wanted to use. It filled a niche and there were enough people using it to make it very desirable to investment types."

People nodded and congratulated Luke on his success and I smiled as I watched him enjoy it, basking in being able to talk about his business.

"What will you do now?"

"I'm going to take a year off and sail around the world," Luke replied, then filled them all in on his plans, talking about building a custom-made catamaran from the ground up and then take it around the world with a crew.

"What about you, dear?" Mrs. Blake asked, her face a bit gloating. "Will you be going with Luke?"

"Oh, no," I said and felt incredibly nervous, coming up with a story on the fly. "I couldn't take the time off. I'll be starting my PhD and I don't want to delay it any longer than I have to."

"Alexa will fly and meet us at various locations while we're in port," Luke said and took my hand, squeezing it and then kissing my knuckles in a gallant gesture that was pure performance. "It'll be hard to be apart for that long, but we'll find ways to see each other during her vacations and on long weekends. I'll fly her anywhere she wants to go when we get into port."

I smiled, wishing that were the truth and not just a story he told to make sure Mrs. Blake gave up on her dreams of marrying Felicia off with him. I turned to see what Felicia was doing but she was looking down at her plate, pushing food around. I felt truly bad for her because it was obvious Mrs. B was a domineering type who tried to control her daughter's life.

I couldn't stand it if my mother was that much of a busybody, trying to marry me off to her best friend's son. Felicia herself was quiet and I hoped John showed up soon so she could enjoy the night. John seemed to be interested in her when we were at the family dinner at Cipriani's. Felicia was pretty and she was sweet in a quiet sort of way. I felt no ill will from her and when she met my eyes, she wasn't shooting daggers at me the way her mother was.

For the next hour, we sat with the group and ate our meals, and once we were done and the bottles of wine were empty, Luke's parents, Mrs. Thorpe, Felicia and the Blakes went up to the house. Mr. Thorpe stayed behind with us and Luke and Mr. Thorpe talked business.

"I'll stay here for a while if you two lovebirds don't mind," he said and pointed to his cigar. "I'm *persona non grata* nowadays due to my filthy habit."

I smiled at him. He seemed like a good-natured man who listened intently as Luke talked a bit more about the deal and what his plans were after he returned from his trip around the world.

"Well, I better leave you two alone for a while," Mr. Thorpe said and stood, throwing his cigar into the fire pit. "Mrs. Thorpe will want me there so we can socialize before we hit the sack. We're driving back to the city to do some shopping before the fundraiser tomorrow night but we wanted to come out here for a few days before the real work starts."

"Good talking with you," Luke said and I smiled at Mr. Thorpe. He stood up with difficulty, and then made his way up the boardwalk to the house, leaving Luke and me alone while the chef packed away his tools and an assistant cleaned up after the guests.

"Feel like taking a walk along the beach? Get your toes wet?"

I smiled. "Sounds great."

We left the table and made our way down to the beach, close to the surf. The sky was dark and the surf roared a few feet away as we walked along. A string of lights up and down in front of the property shone down on the sand but beyond on either side was dark. Luke took my hand and I was surprised, because we were alone and there was no need for a performance.

"Never know who might be watching from the house. My father has a telescope, but I've seen him turning it on the neighbors, so I want to be realistic just in case."

I laughed and let him take my hand, even though I didn't believe it.

"Does he have night vision as well?"

"We have to keep in character," Luke said and smiled. "Might as well play the parts as much as possible so it doesn't feel awkward."

We walked along the beach about a mile, talking the entire time about his family and mine, about everything except the main reason I was there – because he didn't want his family or their meddling friends to try to match him up with anyone, even though I could tell that they were all really attached to him and wanted to see him happy.

When we arrived back at the beach house, we went to the great room where the guests had assembled. The room was huge, filled with comfortable furniture, and had three separate seating areas, where people had gathered.

Luke pulled me over to one set of sofa and chairs and we sat together, side by side. He put his arm around me and pulled me closer and we sat quietly and listened as Mr. Thorpe and Luke's adoptive father talked about the stock market rally.

About nine o'clock, John texted and said he wouldn't be arriving until the next day.

Luke showed me the text.

"That's too bad," I whispered.

"I know. Mrs. B will be so upset."

Luke and I remained seated where we were, his arm around me, and we passed the rest of the evening that way. When the grandfather clock in the hallway chimed eleven thirty, I covered my yawn with my hand, surprised that I was so tired.

"Are you an early bird?" Mrs. Thorpe asked, peering at me with interest.

"I am," I said. "I'm used to getting up early and studying before class."

"Alexa just passed her comprehensive exam for her Master's Degree. She's been under a lot of stress preparing for it." Luke smiled at me, his expression proud.

"Oh, congratulations, dear," Mrs. Thorpe said. She smiled and I wondered what they'd think if they knew all of this was a big performance. That Luke and I had only ever really kissed once.

Of course, it was at that very moment that Luke leaned down and kissed me, catching me by surprise. I recovered quickly enough, and kissed him back, then he met my eyes when the kiss ended, a twinkle in his like he was enjoying it all a bit too much.

"I'm so proud of her," he said and squeezed my shoulder. He kissed me again, this time longer, lingering over it, so that I began to feel a bit embarrassed. We pulled apart and I glanced at Mrs. Thorpe, who was smiling like a Cheshire Cat, her face lit up like she couldn't get enough of our show of affection.

"It's so good to see you with someone again," she said to Luke.

"For a while, your mother and I wondered if you'd ever find someone else."

"No need to worry about me," Luke said and held his chin up, a grin on his face. "I've found someone so you can all just relax."

"It's too bad you're going away for so long," she said and looked at me, an expression of sympathy on her face. "How will you cope with him being away for all that time? A whole year? I don't think I could manage."

"We'll manage," Luke said, almost defensively. "We won't be separated the entire time. Like I said, I'll fly her to meet us and we'll see some of the sights together when she has a break from her PhD."

"That's good," she replied, and pressed her lips together. "Relationships and family are the most important thing in life. Everything else is just window dressing. Don't forget that in your quest to make a name for yourself."

"I've already made a name for myself, I think," Luke said. "Now I get to take a year just for myself, and then I'll think of the future."

She smiled, apparently pleased with his answer. "Don't let what happened to you in the past make you lose faith in life." She nodded meaningfully. I made a mental note to ask Luke more about his failed romance. It was something we had in common.

The evening went on, and Luke pulled me onto his lap, his arms around me, my legs thrown over his lap. Being so close to him in that way, the warmth of his body, the comfort of his arms, made me uncomfortably aroused. He squirmed a bit as well, and I wondered if he felt the same. A part of me wanted to just give in and have meaningless but fantastic sex with him. He was gorgeous, he was smart and funny, and very sexy.

The other part – the part into self-preservation – was leery of doing so. I knew what I was like. I couldn't just be a fuck buddy. I just couldn't.

171

I admired Candace's ability to be with a new man and enjoy him purely for the sex, but that wasn't me. I'd been with only a couple of men in my life and didn't find it easy to just fall into bed with a new one. I had to be warmed up.

I was definitely warmed up sitting that way with Luke.

One by one, the other guests got up and said goodnight, saying they'd see us in the morning on the patio for brunch. I felt strangely comfortable sitting there, performing for Luke's family and friends. If I let myself, I could imagine taking Luke's hand and going upstairs to bed, and fucking our brains out.

I couldn't let myself do that.

He was leaving, and that was all I needed to know.

I sighed when Luke's parents got up to leave and we said goodnight.

"Will you be staying the entire weekend?" Mrs. Marshall asked.

"She will be," Luke answered. He turned to me and smiled, squeezing me. "We plan on spending the entire weekend decompressing. Sun, surf and lots of beer is on the agenda."

Mrs. Marshall smiled, but it wasn't real. I knew she didn't approve of me. I wasn't likely up to her standards for her son. She wanted someone like Felicia Blake for Luke, not little old me from Oregon.

Well, let me tell you something about your son, Mrs. M. He doesn't want anyone. Not Felicia and not me.

He wants Mars.

When we were finally alone, Luke turned to me. The lights were low, with the glow from the gas fireplace making everything warm. It seemed entirely natural for him to lean in closer and kiss me, and it seemed entirely natural for me to kiss him back.

So I did.

The kiss went from warm and affectionate to hot and needy and Luke pushed me back on the sofa, lying on top of me while he continued to kiss me and inexplicably, I went on kissing him back without protest.

His hard length pressed into me in just the right places and I couldn't hold back a groan in response.

What the fuck was I doing? Apparently, not putting a stop to things...

When his hand slid down from my shoulder to one breast, he pulled back and looked into my eyes. He squeezed, his thumb finding my nipple and stroking it through the fabric of my sundress.

He didn't do or say anything, like he was waiting for me to protest.

I didn't.

I wanted it. For that moment at least, I shut off that part of my brain that would usually say *STOP! He won't love you.*

At that moment, I honestly didn't care if he didn't love me or wouldn't ever love me.

At that moment, all I wanted was for the moment to continue and for him to keep touching me, keep kissing me. I wanted to feel him inside of me. I wanted – I *needed* – that sweet sweet release that would only happen when I came while he was filling me up so completely.

It had been so long since I had been filled up completely.

"I want you," he said, his voice breathless as he continued to touch me, his hand moving lower, down over one hip. He squeezed my buttock and pulled my hips more tightly against him so that I could feel his erection press against me.

"I want you," I whispered, afraid to admit it, but unable to deny it.

He kissed me again, and this time, he pulled the other strap down and exposed my bra. He cupped my breast over the top of my bra, squeezing gently before he found the edge of the bra cup and curled his fingers inside it so that his bare hand touched my skin. I gasped into his mouth and arched into his hand when he squeezed my nipple between his finger and thumb.

"Fuck, I need you," he said and then slipped his hand down my dress to the hem, hiking it up, his fingers, beneath my panties, finding the lips of my sex and slipping between them.

"Oh, you're so nice and wet," he whispered, pulling his fingers out and licking them suggestively. "I want to eat you."

I inhaled at that, but glanced around the darkened room, not wanting to do anything there in case someone walked back in.

"We should go upstairs," I whispered, trying to wiggle out from under him.

"No," he said firmly. "Here."

"Someone might come in..."

"They won't," he replied, a gleam in his eye. "They've all gone to the bedroom wing. We're alone. I want to eat you right here in front of the fireplace. Then, I want to fuck you."

I closed my eyes, because he seemed determined to do so, despite the risk – or maybe because of it.

He slipped down both bra straps and pulled down the cups, exposing my breasts to the air.

"Your breasts are magnificent," he whispered and then squeezed one, nipping lightly at the hardening bud with soft teeth, making me squirm with lust. He closed his lips around it and sucked, sending a jolt of desire through me right to my clit.

"Oh, *God*..." My heart raced as he moved from one nipple to the other, my eyes shut, hoping no one came in and found us like that.

When he moved down and kissed a trail down my belly to my

174

mound, I gasped. Then he pulled my panties down with his teeth, a gleam in his eyes as I watched him. I helped him remove them, squirming around so that he could pull them down and off my feet.

He pushed my thighs apart and remained poised over my pussy, staring down at me like I was a delicacy that he couldn't wait to eat. Then, while I watched, he leaned closer and spread me before swiping his tongue up between the lips of my sex, finding my clit and pressing his tongue against me, swirling it expertly. I moaned in response to the sweetness of the sensations, closing my eyes because it was too much.

"Open your eyes," he said, his mouth over top of me. "Watch me eat you."

I did, and he very deliberately licked me again and again, unerringly finding my clit each time, his eyes never leaving mine.

"I'm going to make you come while I lick you and you watch."

I didn't reply, my gaze on him while he covered my pussy and sucked on my clit.

"Oh, God," I said with a gasp when he slipped his fingers inside of me. I could sense how wet I was, how swollen and ready.

"Oh, you are so wet for me, Alexa, so tight. I want to fuck you so badly..."

He stroked me with his fingers and tongue and soon, I could feel the buildup of pleasure that signaled my impending orgasm. Unable to stop myself, I cried out, thrusting my hips up to meet his tongue and fingers as I reached my climax, my body shuddering, my muscles spasming around him.

He didn't stop licking me, his tongue insistent and my orgasm went on and on so that it was all I could do to keep watching him, my eyes half-lidded as I stayed at that high for what seemed like an eternity.

Then it became too much and I slumped beneath his mouth,

reaching down to push him away.

"Stop," I moaned, the sensation too intense. "Stop..."

He did, pulling his mouth away, but keeping his fingers inside me. I could feel my muscles still contracting around him in the aftermath of my orgasm and lay back, my eyes closing, my heart rate slowly returning to normal.

"Oh, God that was good," I managed to say, my arm thrown over my eyes.

"You came fast," he said, and I could detect a note of approval in his voice. "You were ready."

"I was," I said with a sigh. "It's been a while..."

I heard him chuckle and glanced down, frowning.

"You needed it," he said. "You need even more. You need my cock inside of you."

"I don't know if I can come twice," I said, shaking my head. "I never have before."

"You've never been with me," he replied and I almost laughed at his boast, but I was also curious whether he'd succeed. "I'm going to make you come again."

I smiled in response when he rose and lay on top of me, kissing me deeply so that I could taste myself on his tongue. Then he knelt with his knees on either side of my body and put his hands on his hips.

"Suck me first," he commanded.

I squirmed up so that I could reach his belt buckle and very slowly and deliberately unzipped his jeans, before pulling them down around his thighs. Beneath them he wore a pair of black Joe Boxer briefs, his thick erection pressing against the fabric. I licked him through the material, tasting his saltiness. He groaned in response and so I teased him a bit before pulling down his boxer briefs, his long thick cock springing out, almost hitting me in the face.

I would have laughed, but didn't want to destroy the sexiness of the moment. Instead, I ran my tongue all along the shaft of his very hard and dripping cock, catching the thread of fluid on my tongue and then lapping the head.

"Oh, God," he said, his eyes meeting mine. "Suck me."

I did, taking the head in my mouth, my tongue licking the bottom of the crown.

"That's so good," he murmured in approval. Then he began a slow thrust, and I complied, taking his length in my mouth, between my lips, as far as I could without gagging. He was long and thick, stretching my mouth wide to accommodate him. I imagined him inside of me while he fucked me and I hoped I could come again. I was still slightly swollen and sucking him, seeing the desire in his eyes as he watched his cock moving in and out of my mouth, was turning me on again.

"That's enough," he said and pulled his cock out of my mouth, making a 'pop' sound when he pulled the head free of my suction. "I could fuck your mouth all night, but I want you to come on my cock first."

I didn't argue, letting him pull me up and then position me with my hands on the back of the sofa while he spread my thighs with a knee.

"Do you have a condom?" I asked, but he was ahead of me, pulling out a metallic wrapper from the pocket of his jeans. I craned my head and met his eyes as he ripped the package open with his teeth. "You were pretty sure of yourself."

He shook his head. "Only hopeful." Then he unrolled the condom over his erection. He leaned back over me and turned my head for a kiss. When it ended, he stroked his cock against me, one hand pressing it up so that he rubbed my clit again and again, working me back up again without entering me yet. I met his thrusts with my own, intensifying the ·sensations, my core throbbing with desire, aching to be filled up with him.

"I can't wait to fuck you," he whispered in my ear while he stroked me with his cock. "Tell me when you want it."

I closed my eyes and let the sensations wash over me as my desire built up once more. I thought I could come again with him continuing to rub against me, but I wanted to wait until he was inside of me.

"Now," I whispered.

"Now, what?"

I made a face. He was going to make me beg him to fuck me...

"I want you inside of me."

He kept stroking me. "What do you want me to do?"

I groaned in frustration, not used to being so vocal during sex. "I want you to fuck me."

Then, he pressed his cock against the entrance to my body and pushed, entering me slowly, just an inch, then two. He was so nice and thick, I could have come with him only partially inside.

He thrust a few times like that, just in and out, stroking my clit before pushing inside an inch or two.

"Tell me when you want more."

I closed my eyes and enjoyed the delicious sensations while he expertly built me back up, my body aching to feel him fill me up completely.

"Now," I said but he didn't comply. "I want you to fill me up."

He did, pushing inside me so that I was completely stretched and full.

He didn't move for a moment, and merely leaned over me, his cock filling me, his hand reaching around to press against my clit, he other squeezing a breast. He kissed the back of my neck and then bit my shoulder softly.

I ground against him, wanting more sensation.

"Impatient, are you?" he asked, his voice husky but amused. "Tell me what you want."

I exhaled in delicious frustration. "Fuck me," I replied.

"Fuck you, *what?*"

"Fuck me, *please,*" I said, thrusting back, enjoying this little game.

He did, beginning a slow thrust while he played with my clit. After a few delicious moments, he pulled out and turned me around, pushing me down on the sofa. He knelt before me this time and pressed open my thighs, pulling me forward and entering me once more. I leaned back and watched as he began to thrust, one hand over my pussy, a thumb stroking my clit in a lazy circle.

Our eyes met and he fucked me like this, leaning down to suck one nipple and then the other while he maintained his motions. Soon, I was surprised to find my body reaching once orgasm once more.

"Oh, God," I said, my eyes wide. "I'm there."

He smiled and began thrusting harder and faster, like he was trying to reach his own release when I did.

"That's it," he said when I closed my eyes, ready to come. "Come for me."

I groaned and felt the first waves of pleasure wash over me, my body clenching around his thickness, the intensity making me dizzy.

I barely heard his own grunts of release, but managed to open my eyes, watching him watch himself fucking me, his cock sliding in and out of me, then he drove in to the hilt and ejaculated, his face contorted in pleasure.

"Oh, *fuck...*"

Finally spent, he collapsed onto me and I slipped my arms around him.

On my part, while my body spasmed around him, I felt elated

to have been able to orgasm twice in one session. I had never before, even with Blaine, who I was with for several very long years. He'd never seen my pleasure as being his concern, focusing on his own like mine was incidental to the whole process. In my ignorance, I thought that's the way sex was supposed to be.

I could see that with Luke, it would be different. My pleasure was his focus and his own was only made all the better by mine.

He lay there against me, his breathing slowing, and began kissing my neck, then my cheek, and finally, my mouth. We kissed, his hand holding my face. When he pulled away, he met my eyes and we shared a moment. I don't know what it was, but I felt naked in a way I hadn't before with any man. Like he could see inside of me and I him.

Then it passed and he leaned down and kissed my shoulder before carefully pulling out.

"That was amazing," he said and leaned down to kiss each of my nipples quickly. "I feel like I barely got enough of your body. We're going to have to spend an entire day in bed tomorrow, only coming out for food." He glanced up at me, a grin cracking his full lips. "How does that sound to you?"

I smiled back, feeling like a kid being offered a day at Disney World. "Sounds fantastic. What about the sun and surf?"

He shrugged and laughed. "If you insist, I suppose I could take a few minutes out of worshipping your body..."

"I insist. The rest of the time, worshipping my body is fine."

He smiled again, and I was struck by his boyish charm with a touch of devilish charm mixed together.

"You're okay with this?" he said, his eyes meeting mine. "You're okay with really amazing but totally meaningless sex? I don't want you to feel pressured..."

"I'm more than okay with it," I said softly.

I watched as he slipped the condom off his now-deflating

erection and tied it off. He helped me up and we quickly dressed, then he took my hand and he led me out of the main great room and through the common entrance. The lights were out but there was enough of a moon shining through the large stained glass doors, that we could find our way around.

We climbed up the circular staircase to the other wing of the house where the bedrooms were located.

"I was worried someone would come back downstairs for a snack and find us."

"Don't worry," he said and laughed lightly. "I know what they do. Once they go down for the night, they don't come back up for air until the morning. We were fine. No one would come down, and if they did, they'd quickly leave unless they're voyeurs."

I laughed at that, my nerves overcome by how sure he was.

"So, your parents are okay with us sleeping together?"

"I'm a big boy," Luke said as we walked down the hall to his bedroom. "If you stayed in another room in the guest wing, they'd wonder if I'd turned gay or something."

I laughed at that. "They know you can't turn gay," I replied.

"Of course," Luke said. "I was just joking. They're happy to see me with someone new. You have to remember, they're both from the hippie generation even if they look like rich old coots."

"Rich old coots..." I smiled at him. "They don't look anything like rich old coots. Maybe comfortable middle aged people."

"They're that," he said and opened the door to our room for the weekend. "I'm going to take a quick shower. There's a bathroom across the hall if you want to change, brush your teeth – whatever."

I nodded and grabbed my duffle bag and went to the bathroom, wondering what the rest of the weekend would bring. On Luke's part, he undressed and threw his clothes on a chair by the large walk-in closet while I did the same, hanging my nightgown on the doorknob.

When he saw it, he shook his head. "No, no, no," he said and took it off the knob, putting it firmly back in the duffle bag. "I want you sleeping naked beside me. No pajamas for you."

"Will I get any sleep if I do?" I watched him as he took a toothbrush and began brushing his teeth.

"Guaranteed eight hours. I can't promise anything after that. I'm a morning person. But I do plan on getting as much out of your body as I can tomorrow. In the daylight." He leaned over and kissed my shoulder. "Again and again."

"It's yours to get as much out of as you can," I replied.

I took out my own toothbrush and brushed my teeth while he stripped off his boxers. While I watched in the mirror, I saw him cross to the bed, his delicious buttocks so nice and muscular, then he threw back the coverlet and crawled in.

I finished up and then stripped off, only a bit shy of walking naked to the bed while he watched me, his hands behind his head. I could see an expression of appreciation on his face and tried not to show any modesty. He was perhaps the most desirable man I had ever met. Not only was he gorgeous, he was smart. He was funny. He was ambitious.

The wealth was impressive, but it was the fact he'd made so much money so young, and from his own ideas and concepts, that was impressive. If it was only a million, instead of a billion, I wouldn't care.

He enjoyed my body – that much was clear.

He could enjoy it as often as he wanted over the weekend. I hadn't had sex for almost a year. I needed it.

I *wanted* it.

Most of all, I wanted it from him.

The look in his eye when he watched me climb into the bed suggested I'd get it.

CHAPTER 14

LUKE

Despite the novelty of having a woman sleep in the bed beside me, I fell asleep almost immediately, with Alexa spooned beside me, my arm thrown around her body.

In the morning, after a solid night's sleep, I woke to find the bed empty beside me. Alexa must have gotten up and gone to the bathroom. I rolled over and waited, watching the door to the bedroom for her return.

When she emerged from the ensuite, she covered herself up demurely when she saw me watching.

"Don't hide yourself," I said, already aroused at the sight of her curves. "You're beautiful."

She smiled and I could tell she forced herself to drop her arms from across her breasts. The sight of them made me instantly hard, my dick throbbing. Still, I didn't want to greet her with morning breath, so I jumped up and passed her, not hiding the evidence of my own arousal. Let her see it and think about it. I wanted her ready for another round or two when I returned as well.

I quickly took a piss and then brushed my teeth as I saw she had done and then went back to the bed to find her under the covers, a smile on her face when she saw me standing at the side of the bed, my cock now at half-staff.

I knew she was interested in another round when she pulled back the covers for me. I hopped in beside her, always the gentleman, pleased to give her exactly what she wanted.

Once I was lying down, she rolled over and lay on top of me, still smiling.

I honestly couldn't have asked for a better way to wake up.

Later, much later, when both of us were satiated and now were only hungry for food rather than each other, we showered and dressed, then went down to the main wing and the kitchen.

The double patio doors were open, and the breeze off the ocean was cool and salty. Outside on the patio, a long table was set with linen and dishes, and several of the guests for the weekend were there, eating the brunch laid out on the table in the kitchen.

"Wow," Alexa said. "Is this breakfast?"

"Brunch," I replied. "On the weekend, it's here for guests to serve themselves whenever they get up."

I watched Alexa's eyes bug out at the spread, which was normal for my family but I was sure was reserved for special occasions for hers. I had to remind myself that not everyone grew up the way I did – with privileges. What seemed like a treat to Alexa, I knew was business as usual for my family.

There were scrambled eggs and Eggs Benedict, biscuits, home fries, bacon, sausage, sliced ham, toast, waffles and fruit. Fresh coffee, juice and milk were in thermal flasks next to a collection of cups and mugs, glasses and plates.

We fixed our plates and then went to the table, taking a pair of chairs at one end, saying good morning to everyone as we sat down and dug in.

"Sleep well, dear?" Mrs. Marshall asked, taking a sip of her coffee.

"Never better," I replied, glancing sideways at Alexa, who was holding back a grin. "We slept very well, didn't we?"

"Yes," Alexa said and took a sip of her juice, a twinkle in her eyes.

"I hope that old bed is good enough for you. We brought it out from the city to use as a spare instead of getting a new one."

"It was fine," I said and took a sip of coffee. "We both slept very well, didn't we, sweetheart?"

"We did," Alexa replied, narrowing her eyes at my use of a term of affection. Might as well go all out.

I was glad I could truthfully say that we had a great night, even if we were just performing the boyfriend-girlfriend part. I slept amazingly well, despite the fact I wasn't used to a woman in my bed. I usually kicked them out, sending them home with my driver at as early an hour as I could so I could sleep alone and get up early, refreshed. On the weekends, I could be forgiven for letting Alexa stay overnight. Besides, I was pretending she was a real girlfriend.

After last night, I felt we could give an even better performance than we had already. At least we got the sex part of the relationship right, even if everything else was an act. I could tell by the way her pussy clenched down on my fingers and cock that she wasn't faking that part of the relationship...

We ate our meals, listening to the sound of the surf, and the talk of the people at the table about their plans for the rest of the weekend. When we were finished, we left the table and went for a walk down to the beach, hand in hand.

It felt strangely real to me, walking along the beach with Alexa. I could keep up this façade without any effort. Alexa was smart, beautiful, and great in bed. There was nothing about her that I didn't like and I felt no inclination to take her home so I could be alone and work, as I usually would with a sex partner. In fact, I looked forward to spending the weekend showing her around the Hamptons, and maybe taking her out for a sail if the weather held up.

"Hey, would you like to go to see my boat?" I said as we turned around and made our way back to the house. "The builder's just down the coast at Patchogue."

"Sure," she said and smiled. "I don't know anything about boats but I'd like to see it."

"Deal. I'll call over and we can meet Dave, who's in charge of building it."

We arrived back at the house and then collected our things. Before we left, we passed by the library, just off the great room. Inside, Mr. Thorpe sat reading the Saturday times and drinking coffee.

"What are you two up to?" Mr. Thorpe asked when we walked by.

I grabbed Alexa's hand and pulled her to my side. "Going to take Alexa to see my catamaran at Alpha Yachts in Patchogue."

"Lucky Alexa. I'd love to see it someday," he said, turning a page in his copy of the paper and looking at us over the edge. "What an adventure, sailing around the world."

"When the cat's finished, I'll take you sailing before we leave on the trip if you want to go."

"I'd like that," he said and nodded. He returned to his paper, his half-eye reading glasses perched on the end of his nose.

I led Alexa outside and we hopped in the SUV to drive down the coast to the ship dealer in Patchogue.

As strange as it felt to be taking a woman to see my catamaran, I wanted the weekend to be enjoyable for Alexa and so I thought it would be a great idea to take her along with me. If she was going to pretend to be my girlfriend, I wanted her to feel the effort was worth her while, treating her to a deluxe weekend at the beach house with all the trimmings. Sun, surf, maybe a late afternoon sail, great food and even better sex than I hoped she'd had in a long time.

From her reaction to me the previous night and that morning, I felt pretty sure she had been in real need of a great fuck.

It was the least I could do, given how much she had done for me...

We spent about an hour at Alpha Yachts while my dealer, Dave, showed us the catamaran and how the build was going. They were still outfitting the interior, which had two main compartments for sleeping, including a set of bunks, a double bed and a pull-out bed that could double as a sofa slash eating nook. The finishes were all of the highest quality. I told Dave to spare no expense. The galley had a full kitchen, if in miniature, with a small stove, refrigerator, sink, and even a tiny dishwasher. Although I'd been used to a much less fancy ship before, where we had to actually wash our own dishes, I decided that the boys and I were not interested in spending our time cleaning dishes.

I'd even install a gas line for a barbecue so the four of us would be able to grill fish and whatever fresh meats we came across on our trip.

"What do you think?" I asked Alexa, who was standing on the front bow of the catamaran, watching as the workers installed some storage compartments. "Do you think you could manage a trip on this?"

"It's amazing," she said and glanced around at the ship, which was almost finished. "I've never been on a ship before. Do you get seasick?"

I shook my head. "Some people do, but I never have. When the seas are calm, it's like being on a boat on a lake."

"When the seas are rough?"

I shrugged. "Then it can be a bit tough, but we pay close attention to weather reports and stay in port if there are going to be rough seas. We won't have any deadlines, so it won't matter if we stay several days extra in any given port."

"It's a once-in-a-lifetime trip," Alexa said, her voice wistful. She ran a hand along the smooth fiberglass surfaces of one of the bulkheads. "I don't know if I'd be able to sleep on a ship."

"You would after the first or second night, believe me. I've done it. After a while, you don't even notice the motion."

After we finished the tour and Dave updated me on the progress to date, we drove back to the house, the windows open, the breeze blowing through the vehicle. I loved being out at the beach house, the salt air a reminder of all the happy summers I'd spent there as a kid with Dana and whatever friends we had at the time. For a number of years, we were each the other's only friend, but once my parents died, we began to have other friends.

I looked forward to seeing Dana. She and dickface were due out after lunch, and it would be nice to spend time with her. I could tell Dana approved of Alexa for my girlfriend. Even if she wasn't my real girlfriend, I wanted Dana to think I was happy now. She'd been worrying about me for the entire year since Jenna and I broke up, ending our engagement and cancelling our plans for marriage.

As we drove up to the beach house, around the circular

driveway, I saw that, as I expected, Dana and Eric's Mercedes SUV was parked in one of the slots. There was also a vehicle I didn't recognize – a red Audi with a license plate I didn't know.

Who else was coming this weekend?

I took Alexa's hand as we walked up the stairs to the porch.

"Ready for another performance?"

"As ready as I'll ever be. I'm looking forward to some time on the beach."

I nodded. "That was my plan as well. Dana's here so we'll say hello and then go down.

"Maybe I'll go up and use the washroom first, if you don't mind. All that coffee's hit me."

"Sure," I said and squeezed her hand. "Come on down when you're finished. People are probably out on the porch out back. We can say hi and then go down to the beach later."

She smiled and climbed the staircase to the second floor family wing and I went through the entry to the back of the house, past the great room and kitchen. Sure enough, the double patio doors were still open and a number of people were sitting around the table.

I saw Eric first, his annoying voice rising above the rest of the group.

"It's been so long," I heard him say. "So good to see you again. Terrible, terrible what happened..."

I frowned and poured myself a cup of coffee before I went outside, and when I did, I went right over to Dana, bending down and giving her a kiss on the cheek.

"Good to see you, sis," I said and squeezed her shoulder. "How's my little mommy doing?"

She gripped my hand on her shoulder and smiled, but she bit her lip and then tilted her head to the side, like she was trying to signal something.

"What?" I asked and glanced to see what she meant, eyeing Eric, the bastard. He had this grin on his face that seemed really gloating. I frowned and glanced down the long table to see the usual suspects – Mr. and Mrs. Blake, Felicia, Mr. and Mrs. Thorpe, my adoptive mother and adoptive father...

And then I saw her.

Jenna.

She was sitting at the far end of the table, her mother sitting beside her.

I felt the blood drain from my face. Adrenaline surged through my body.

What the fuck?

What the *hell* was she doing here?

How did she gather the nerve to come to the beach house when she knew I would most likely be there – and with a girlfriend?

"Luke, darling, look who showed up unexpectedly? Jenna and Mrs. C. What a surprise, isn't it?"

"*Jenna,*" I said, trying to keep my voice level. "Mrs. Cornwall. If you'll excuse me, I just wanted to say goodbye to everyone. Alexa and I will be going back to the city."

"Don't leave because of us," Jenna said and frowned at her mother. "We had no idea you'd be here this weekend, did we, *mother...*"

"Not at all," Mrs. Cornwall said, but I didn't believe her for one single moment. "When we were invited, we didn't expect you'd be here. We thought you'd be holed up in Manhattan negotiating the sale of your company."

I turned to my mother, who shrugged, her eyebrows raised. "I must have forgotten to mention you were coming."

I turned to my father, who quickly hid his face behind the Saturday *Times*, shaking the paper and clearing his throat. I knew he had nothing to do with this, but there was no way I believed my adoptive mother failed to tell Mrs. Cornwall that I was going to be here. That was probably the only reason she and Jenna were there.

From the time Jenna and I had split, my mother had been trying to either make amends between us, or match me with Felicia. When I had repeatedly told her Jenna and I could never reconcile, she gave up and pushed poor Felicia at me.

In that moment, I had no doubt that when I had made it clear I wouldn't be hooking up with Felicia, my mother turned back to her original plan to push Jenna and me together once more. She begged me to forgive Jenna. Said that it was a mistake and that if I couldn't forgive someone I loved so much for a mistake, I could never be married.

"That's right," I remembered saying. *"I can never be married if it means forgiving a cheating bitch."*

"I have to go," I said and turned on my heel, leaving the group to return to the house.

I got a few steps inside and heard footsteps behind me. When I turned, I expected it would be Dana following me to console me, but instead, it was Jenna.

She came over to me where I stood at the kitchen island, dumping my cup of coffee into the sink.

"I'm so sorry," she said and laid her hand on my arm, an expression of sadness on her face. "I had no idea you'd be here. Honestly. I asked and my mother said that you were staying in Manhattan this weekend because of the negotiation. I never would have come out here if I knew you'd be here."

"I'll believe that when pigs fly," I said, barely able to control my anger. "I have a friend with me and there's no way I want her to see you, of all people."

"Don't leave because of me. We'll go. I'll tell my mother that we're leaving. If she wants to stay, I'll go back. I'll take the car and leave. She can stay. I know she was looking forward to spending time with your mother."

"Don't bother," I said and rinsed off my hands in the sink. "I have a bad taste in my mouth now and think it's best if I leave. I know my mother and your mother arranged all this."

"Do you think so?" she asked, frowning. "I don't think—"

"Of course they arranged this accidental meeting. Of course they planned it and then hoped that seeing each other would push us back together again. If you can't see that, you're not as smart as I thought you were."

She sighed and stepped closer. "Seriously, Luke, I never thought you'd be here."

She put her hand on my arm once more, moving even closer like she wanted to hug me. She reached up and touched my cheek, then brushed hair out of my eyes.

I stared at her, unable to believe that she was acting all sad and sorry about what happened. How could she be so deceitful?

Finally, I pulled back, sick to my stomach about the nerve she had to try to cozy up to me after everything that happened between us.

"Where's Dylan, anyway?" I asked, acid in my tone.

"Dylan and I broke up a while ago. He took a new job and moved to Riyadh. He's flying planes for one of the princes, if you can believe it."

I shrugged, not caring what her bastard of an ex-boyfriend was doing with his time. I didn't care that the reason she agreed to marry me – the reason she pretended to want to marry me – was because he didn't want to get married. He wasn't rich enough for her mother either. A pilot for a small regional airline after he got out of the service, he was a playboy. She'd apparently been in love with him forever but he was never the right kind of man for her family.

I had been the right kind of man for them, but apparently not her.

Yeah, I was still hurt by her betrayal. I didn't love her anymore – I knew that the moment I saw her. I only felt contempt. But I still had the wound from when my trust and love had been thrown away for a night of sex with her true love before she committed to me.

That was her excuse, anyway. One night of hot sex to say goodbye forever to the man she had loved for years so she could commit fully to being my wife and the mother of my children.

Thing was, I could never trust her again when I knew she'd slept with him. She claimed it was a one-time only thing, to say goodbye forever, and that she hadn't slept with him the entire time we were engaged, but I didn't – I couldn't believe it.

I could never imagine sleeping with her again, as much as I thought she was very beautiful and smart.

She was a cheat.

That was enough to break it off completely.

A clean break with a promise I never wanted to see her in public again. I never wanted to go to any function she was at or want her at any family gathering. Her family was very close to my parents, but I had told them in no uncertain terms that if she or her mother were going to be at a function or at the house or at the beach house, I wouldn't be there and not to invite me or expect me to attend.

I'd spent several months in a funk, drinking myself crazy, smoking too much pot with my old buddies from college. It was only six months after we split, when Dana announced she was pregnant, that I came out of my funk and started to think about re-entering life.

That's when serious work on taking Chatter to the next level happened. That's when I focused all my energy on making it the best app possible. That's when it took off and we saw an exponential growth in its user base.

So, while my heart and pride took a beating when Jenna betrayed me, the rest of my life took off and I would finally have total and complete independence from my adoptive parents and the family money.

I now counted my blessings that I found out about Jenna's cheating ways before the wedding instead of after. It made me think even harder about how I was handling Eric's cheating on Dana.

"Whatever," I said and pulled my arm away from her. "I'm taking Alexa and going back to the city. You stay here. Enjoy your time with your mother. My weekend's been ruined."

I turned and left her, walking out of the great room, and taking the staircase to the second floor family wing. I went to my bedroom and found that it was empty. Alexa wasn't there. I checked for her bag, but it was gone as well, and her things were gone from the ensuite bathroom.

I hadn't seen her walk out to the patio where the family was so I went back down the stairs and checked the great room once more. There was no sign of her. I went out to the patio and checked but she wasn't sitting at the table with everyone. I could see Jenna sitting with her mother. She glanced away when she saw me.

"Has anyone seen Alexa? She's not in our room."

People shook their heads.

"No, dear," my adoptive mother said. "She hasn't been out here since you got back from seeing the boat. Did she go for a walk on the beach?"

I walked down to the surf and looked in both directions, but didn't see her. I sighed, and went back to the patio and through the house to the front entrance. I opened the door and checked out the driveway, but there was no sign of her so I took out my cell.

LUKE: *Where are you? Did you leave?*

There was no answer.

LUKE: *Please answer me so I know you haven't been kidnapped or drowned when you snuck out to take a swim without me...*

No answer.

FUCK.

CHAPTER 15

ALEXA

I took a quick pee and brushed my hair, which had blown in the wind as we drove along the coastal highway with the windows open. I had enjoyed the trip to see Luke's catamaran. It was really exciting to imagine what it would be like when it was complete and he went sailing, visiting any number of exotic tropical spots in the Pacific.

What an amazing future Luke had planned.

It struck me how much freedom he'd have to do whatever he wanted from now on. He was so lucky...

I went back down the stairs to the great room and saw Luke standing close with a woman, her hand on his arm. It took me a second but I recognized her from the google search Candace and I had done before I agreed to meet him. It was Jenna — his ex-fiancée.

She was beautiful. Dark hair, dark eyes, fit lean body.

She was everything I wasn't, in other words.

She reached up and touched his cheek, then brushed hair out of his eyes in a gesture that was so tender and intimate, it made my heart skip a beat.

At that moment, I had an epiphany.

I was getting too close to Luke. I was enjoying him far too much. I was imagining being with him on his boat, sailing to exotic locations and waking up with him beside me. I had this ridiculous fantasy in the back of my mind that he'd fall in love with me and realize he wanted to be married and have a family after all. That his broken heart had healed and he now wanted a real life with a real family.

That staying on Earth – with me – was what he really wanted after all.

What a *fool*.

Seeing Luke with Jenna made my throat choke up and a surge of regret flow through me.

What the heck was I doing at his beach house with him? What was I doing actually having sex with him when there was no way that he and I would get together?

First, he didn't want to get married.

Second, he was from a wealthy family and was going to be one of the richest men under thirty in the world.

Third, I could tell by the way he was looking at Jenna that he was probably still in love with her. His expression was intense, and he was looking in her eyes the way I wanted him to look in mine.

I went back up to the bedroom and quickly packed my bag, deciding then and there I had to leave.

On my way out, I ran into Mrs. Marshall, who was just coming up the stairs.

"Oh, Alana, there you are," she said and stopped when she saw me with my bag in my hand. "You're leaving?"

"I am," I said and tried to go past her, not wanting to talk. "And my name's not Alana."

"You know he's still in love with her," she said as I passed her and took the stairs. "He doesn't want to admit it, but he is. A mother knows these things."

"Whatever," I said and ran down the stairs.

"It's better for everyone," she said, following me down. "He's on his way to big things. You're not quite in our," she said and hesitated like she was searching for the right word. "Circle of friends and acquaintances."

"What?" I said and turned back, frowning.

"You know what I mean. It's best that you two stop seeing each other."

I didn't know what to say so I just left, taking the front door and practically running down the driveway in hopes that Luke didn't see me and try to stop me.

I grabbed my cell and called a local taxi service, requesting a car to take me back to Manhattan. I'd walk a few blocks down the road and meet the taxi there rather than in front of the house in case Luke came to look for me.

I'd text Luke afterwards, when I'd calmed down, and tell him it was a great night but that I had to look after myself. I couldn't be pretending to be his girlfriend anymore. He'd have to tell everyone the truth – that he didn't want a girlfriend or wife. That he was planning on leaving Earth one day and there would be no family for him.

No heirs. No dynasty to carry on.

It choked me up, but I kicked myself mentally in the head for being such a romantic fool about Luke. Like Mrs. Marshall said, I wasn't part of his world and he wasn't part of mine. It was better that we ended it now. I couldn't imagine a life with Mrs. Marshall as my mother-in-law.

Having sex with Luke and doing the few things we did together had fooled my stupid mind into believing that he really felt those things and was right for me. I started to have real feelings for Luke, imagining us together. Happy.

I walked down the street, slipping my sunglasses on to hide my tears, and waited for the taxi to come and pick me up.

Later, on the way to the city, I got a text from Luke.

LUKE: Where are you? Did you leave?

That choked me up even more. Yeah, I left. When I saw the way he looked at Jenna, I realized that he hadn't gotten over her, despite all his protests. Then, Mrs. Marshall drove home just how different we were...

LUKE: Please answer me so I know you haven't been kidnapped or drowned when you snuck out to take a swim without me...

I wasn't going to answer. I didn't want him to apologize. I didn't want to read his lies about how he didn't feel anything for Jenna and that what I'd seen was a mistake.

There was no mistaking the way he looked at her and the way she looked at him.

I wasn't sure if he could forgive her, but I realized that me spending even more time with him, having sex with him again, might be fine for him, but it wasn't fine for me. I knew it would only end up hurting me.

We were from two different worlds.

I had to quit him and fast. Put him out of my mind.

I put my cell away and turned off the ringer, not wanting to hear in case he called.

Then I changed my mind.

I pulled out my cell and sent Luke a message that I hoped would end things between us for good.

ALEXA: I'm fine and no I didn't drown. Sorry about leaving without telling you, but I realized I can't keep up this façade of being your girlfriend. The sex was great, but I'm just not built to deal with casual hookups. It's not who I am. You're going to have to talk to people and tell them the way you really feel. You can't keep pretending, Luke. Be real with them and they'll finally realize you are your own man and have your own plans. Honesty is the best policy, or so they say...

Then I turned off my cell and turned off the ringer, not wanting to read his response.

I arrived back at the apartment and went upstairs, feeling like I had a huge weight on my shoulders. I had to buck up and be strong. It wasn't like Luke and I had any future, as Mrs. Marshall said. I knew that when I agreed to go with him to the beach house, but my silly romantic mind had let myself believe otherwise even if I was denying it.

Candace was sitting at her desk, one foot tucked under her, reading emails, when I walked into the room we used as an office.

"There you are – why are you home so soon? I thought you were going to stay for the entire weekend?"

I plopped my duffel bag down on the floor and slumped on my chair.

"The ex-fiancée showed up and I realized I was fooling myself if I thought he'd ever be interested in me for more than a stand-in fake girlfriend. Plus the mother pointed out that Luke and I are from two different classes and are not right for each other."

"What," she said and made an angry face. "That's bullshit. I'm sorry, kiddo. He's a real hunk of man, and this class shit is just that – crap. I saw him with you. He really likes you."

"He may, but you should have seen the way he looked at her."

"Aww, I'm sorry." She smiled and squeezed my arm. "But if he's really not into it, you should just put him out of your mind. Someone new and better will come along."

"I know, I know, but my stupid girl mind – the one who believed in princesses meeting handsome princes surfaced despite all my efforts to choke the living daylights out of her."

Candace laughed softly at that. "Yeah, I know. Too much Ariel and Anastasia in my past as well. We have to be realistic about guys. They're not Prince Charmings. They're guys from Seinfeld, like Georges and Newmans. Some look better than others, but they're all little boys underneath."

I nodded and took in a deep breath. "But man, he's as close as you can get to a Prince Charming, without the wanting to be married and have a real family part."

"He's a hunk of a billionaire man, that's for sure."

"That he is..."

I took out my cell and checked to see if he'd responded to my last text.

LUKE: *I'm sorry you felt you needed to leave. If you saw me with Jenna, you should know I feel nothing for her anymore but contempt. I would have enjoyed spending the weekend with you, and now I feel bad that you didn't get any sun and surf in like I promised. But you're right. I have to start telling the truth to my meddling family. Thanks for everything you did to help me fake them out. I truly enjoyed being with you, and the sex was great. There – some honesty from me.*

I read it over several times, feeling a bit sick to my stomach. I believed him that he enjoyed the sex. That much was clear. I believed him that he felt bad that I missed out on the sun and surf. I even believed that he enjoyed being with me.

What I also believed was that there was no future for us, no matter how much we enjoyed each other's company.

From his message, I gathered he realized it as well.

It was best we break things off and make a clean start of it, no longer pretending to be together as a couple. I could feel myself being drawn into Luke's world. It would be so easy to just let things continue between us, with me acting as his pretend girlfriend and us having great sex whenever it was possible.

But I knew it would be me with a broken heart. It would be me waving goodbye to Luke as he sailed away on his catamaran to the South Pacific and then off to Mars or wherever it was he wanted to live.

So I had to protect myself.

Luke was gorgeous. Smart. Rich. Ambitious. A great lover.

He wasn't and would never be mine...

"He sent me a text, apologizing and claiming I misread things between him and his ex."

"I'm sure he hates her," Candace said. "Who wouldn't hate your fiancé for cheating on you a week before your wedding? I sure would."

"Me, too," I said and re-read his message. "I was looking forward to some sun and surf, but it would have become really uncomfortable with the ex there. Plus, we actually had sex and you know me. I'm not into meaningless sex, no matter how fun it might be."

She leaned forward, her eyes wide. "You did the deed? Oh, my God, tell me. Deets, please!" She reached out and touched my arm. "I mean, I'm really sorry things didn't work out, but you have to be pleased to get some..."

I told her about my night with Luke and how good it had been.

"It just kind of happened naturally," I said, remembering how easy it had been to kiss him and to just have sex right then and there. How exciting it had been to do so in the great room despite the fact we might have been caught.

"Naughty girl," she said, her mouth wide. "I can't believe you did that! He's a bit kinky, huh?"

"Not really," I said. "At least, I didn't see anything other than he enjoyed talking dirty and risked getting caught."

"Was he good at it?" she asked, moving her chair closer to mine, eager for more details. "Some guys are good at it, and others are bad and say the most ridiculous things."

"I don't have much experience..." I said, remembering back to the few guys I'd slept with. None had been dirty talkers. Blaine was pretty quiet when we had sex. "It was a turn-on though."

"Oh, God, he's so good looking," Candace said. "I can imagine it must have been hot to have him talking dirty. What did he say? Give me some examples..."

"I couldn't," I said and shook my head. "You had to be there."

She laughed. "You are a party-pooper. Okay, keep your secrets. At least you got some, which is more than I can say for me, stuck here in a man-drought..."

"Man-drought," I said, laughing with her. "You are terrible."

She gave me a fake bow. "I'm here every Saturday."

The rest of the night, I tried to distract myself from thinking of what was happening back at the beach house in Westhampton. Did Jenna stay the night? Did she and Luke have a deep serious talk and make up? He'd said he felt nothing but contempt for her, but I had heard that the line between love and hate was pretty thin.

I couldn't help but imagine the two of them fighting and

arguing and then falling into each other's arms for a bout of mad passionate make-up sex. It was supposedly the best sex you could have because of the intense emotions. He had been in love with her. He could probably forgive her. Or at least, have sex with her.

I tried to push thoughts of him and Jenna out of my mind, but it was nearly impossible. I kept going over what I saw in the kitchen at the beach house and how he stood and looked in her eyes, and she reached up to touch his cheek, run her fingers through his hair. How they looked perfect together...

Then Mrs. Marshall's painful words.

I finally gave up.

"I gotta stop thinking of him," I said and chose an action adventure movie on my Apple TV so I could distract myself from thoughts of Luke and Jenna. "Bring me a beer. I need a distraction."

Candy complied and brought back two cold beers from the refrigerator. She handed me one and sat down on the sofa beside me. We clinked the necks of the two bottles and spent the rest of the night studiously not talking about Luke or my weekend at the Hamptons.

CHAPTER 16

LUKE

She finally responded.

ALEXA: I'm fine and no I didn't drown. Sorry about leaving without telling you, but I realized I can't keep up this façade of being your girlfriend. The sex was great, but I'm just not built to deal with casual hookups. It's not who I am. You're going to have to talk to people and tell them the way you really feel. You can't keep pretending, Luke. Be real with them and they'll finally realize you are your own man and have your own plans. Honesty is the best policy, or so they say...

She was right, of course.

She did want more and deserved more, but I wasn't the one to give it to her, no matter how much I enjoyed her.

When I sent her a text, I hoped to be able to convince her that Jenna was the last person I wanted to see, even if I had to admit that she was right and there was no future for us. As much as I wanted to go after her, and as much as I was all ready to go and bring her back, explain to her that Jenna was nothing to me, she was right. I had to man up and start telling the truth.

LUKE: I'm sorry you felt you needed to leave. If you saw me with Jenna, you should know I feel nothing for her anymore but contempt. I would have enjoyed spending the weekend with you, and now I feel bad that you didn't get any sun and surf in like I promised. But you're right. I have to start telling the truth to my meddling family. Thanks for everything you did to help me fake out my family. I truly enjoyed being with you, and the sex was great. There – some honesty from me.

I had to start telling my family the truth. I had to start telling myself the truth.

I went to the kitchen to grab a bottle of ice tea for the trip back into the city. My mother came inside when she saw me.

"There you are," she said and came over to me, standing on her tip toes to give me a kiss on my cheek. "I was looking for you—"

Before she could coax me to stay, I cut her off.

"I'm not staying for dinner," I said, closing the door to the fridge a little too hard. She leaned against the table in the kitchen while I stuffed the bottle into my duffle bag. Outside, guests were assembling at the table by the barbecue, getting ready for cocktails before dinner. "I'm going back to the city."

"Oh, don't go. Stay," she said and grabbed my arm. "Be sociable. Everyone wants to talk to you about your business."

I looked down at her, exasperated that she just couldn't understand.

"I don't know why you invited Jenna and her mother. I don't want to spend any time with her. Not after what happened."

"I might have mentioned the weekend at the beach house to her when we were talking, but this was before you invited Alana."

"It's *Alexa*, and you also invited Felicia."

"But dear—"

"Mother," I said, exasperated. "I wish you could stop trying to match me with the daughters of your friends. I never wanted to see Jenna again. You knew that already. I told you that I never wanted to see her in public and I certainty didn't want to have her at any private family function. I didn't think you'd actually invite her to our house on a weekend when I'd have my girlfriend with me."

"Don't start on that now," she said and shook her pointed and well-manicured nail at me. "Jenna's mother is a dear friend of mine. You know that. You and Jenna should mend fences. There will be times when you'll be in the same crowd. You have to move on with your lives and can't always ignore each other."

"We *moved* on. She chose him over me. I started Chatter. I have Alexa. I'm not going to be moving in the same circles as Jenna and her family. I'm going to sail and then I'm relocating to California so there's no need for me to mend any fences with her and her family. That's really all there is to it."

"Who is this Alexa girl, anyway? She's not one of *our* people. Why are you with her? She's a pretty little thing, but she's practically white trash."

"*Mother*," I said, my fists clenched. "She is *not* white trash. Her father was a career fighter pilot in the Air Force. She's doing her Master's degree in International Relations. She's beautiful, she's smart and she's got a good heart. She is the farthest thing from white trash *ever*. And anyway, even if she was white trash, if I love her, you should be supporting me and welcoming her into your arms." I turned to leave, unable to hold back my anger and needing to get away. "I'm going back into the city."

"But Felicia—"

"I'm not interested in Felicia Blake," I said and turned back to her. "Get it through your head. I'm not going to *ever* be interested in Felicia Blake. I'm not going to get back with Jenna. That's it, mother. That's all you have to know."

She came over to me. "Don't go. Stay and visit with the Thorpes, at least. You know how he always enjoys talking to you. He was so looking forward to talking more about the negotiations..."

"Sorry. Not going to happen." I shook my head. "Give my regrets to everyone."

"But the Thorpes—"

"*Goodbye*, Mother."

Then, I left, duffle bag in hand.

I hopped in my car and drove off, leaving the whole bunch of them behind. I felt incredibly disappointed that the weekend didn't turn out the way I wanted. I had hoped to spend it with Alexa, lying in the sun and relaxing. Even if we were only pretending to be a couple, I was enjoying myself. She was so easy to be with...

The sex was great.

Instead, we had one great night and morning and then BAM. It was all over and I was alone again.

I wanted to spend time with Alexa, so I could watch her enjoy herself. I wanted to take her to my bed again that night and enjoy her body the way I had the night before. Being with her felt totally natural. We laughed easily, and we talked easily. The sex was better than great.

But she was just acting. She didn't really feel anything for me as a man although she definitely enjoyed the sex.

Strangely enough, that didn't feel like enough for me anymore. I wanted more.

That surprised me. I hadn't felt so comfortable with a woman for a long time. Not since with Jenna.

I had to push that thought out of my mind, because we all

knew how that turned out – a disaster that took me a good six months to recover from. No, I wasn't going to let myself get hooked back into the whole relationship thing only a month before I was scheduled to take the catamaran and sail down to the Caribbean and then through the Panama Canal to the South Pacific.

I had to keep that in the front of my mind. Once the deal went through, and I was sure it would, the ship would be finished and the guys and I would sail away for what I hoped would be the greatest year of my life – so far.

I arrived back at my building just as the sun had set and walked into an empty apartment, throwing my duffle bag and keys onto the table in the entrance. Then I went to my living room and stood at the sliding door to the balcony. I opened it and went to the railing, looking out over the city at the lights from the Hudson. A light breeze blew in from the water.

I thought once more about Alexa and how Jenna's presence had ruined everything. My adoptive mother just couldn't resist trying to control my life. I really had to make a clean break with her and my adoptive father once the deal went through.

Then, I could finally live my own life the way I wanted.

I sat on my sofa and watched the late local news, my mind only half-focused on the report on some crime committed down some dark back alley. I took out my cell and checked my messages once more, in the vague hope that Alexa might have a change of heart and text me, asking me to come to her place so we could spend the evening together, but no luck.

I was tempted to send her a message and suggest it. The hour was late but I hadn't eaten dinner and could have used a late supper.

LUKE: Look, I know that there's no future for us, because I'm leaving in a month for the Panama Canal, and you're starting your PhD and want to live in Europe, but I'm craving some pizza and was hoping you might feel like joining me. I feel like I owe you a fun night after what you did for me at Cipriani's and after coming out to the beach for the weekend. I can't talk you into a slice at Familigia's? It's close to your place... Afterwards, I could bring you back to my place for a wild night of really great sex... ;) But if you're not into really great sex, I could use company for a slice or two.

I should have just let things be, but I couldn't. I wanted to talk to Alexa. I wanted to see her smile and hear her laughter as I told her tales of my adoptive mother's meddling. I wanted to fuck her again and again, watching her face in pleasure.

I read my text over and then sent it, throwing caution to the wind.

Then, I waited. I checked my watch. It was now close to nine and I knew the streets would be busy along the Hudson as Saturday night revelers would be out, and Familigia's would be busy with customers. I wanted to walk down Broadway with Alexa and sit on a bench, watch people for a while.

Sure, maybe she'd go back to her place afterwards, but I felt incredibly lonely at that moment and wanted to be with her.

Finally, after about ten minutes, I heard my cell ding and knew she'd replied.

ALEXA: Familigia's? What are you, an agent provocateur? I can't resist a slice from Familigia's...

I smiled, and replied right away, before she could change her mind.

LUKE: I'll pick you up in 15.

ALEXA: No, that's fine. I'll meet you there.

LUKE: *Seriously, let me pick you up. The streets will be busy this time of night. Besides, it's dark out.*

ALEXA: *I'm a big girl and I've been around Manhattan for three years, now. I'll see you there in fifteen. You'll know me by the jade Mala bracelet with the tree of life charm. ;)*

LUKE: *If my lady insists... See you in 15.*

I grabbed my jacket and was just about to leave when my cell dinged. I took it out, thinking it might be Alexa texting to cancel after having second thoughts, but it was John.

JOHN: *Hey, Luke. Looks like trouble brewing on the Chatter front. We better meet and talk. Andy and I are going to Bonaventure on Fifth. Meet us there.*

Crap. I didn't want to cancel my plans with Alexa.

LUKE: *I'm busy for the next hour, but I can meet you there for a late drink at 10:30. What's the problem?*

JOHN: *One of the investors is thinking of pulling out, which means the deal would drop until they can find someone else to make up the difference.*

LUKE: *Crap. Let me guess... It's Harrison Blake.*

JOHN: *How did you know? Seems like your rejection of his little sister made him have second thoughts.*

LUKE: *What a bastard. OK, I gotta go. I'll see you at Bonaventure at 10:30.*

I put my cell away and stood for a moment, my hand on the door knob. I hated the fact that Harrison had that much power over me, punishing me for not wanting to play family with his sister. He was a bastard, and I should have known at the outset that we shouldn't do business with him, but I was as eager as John to see the deal come through.

Whatever happened, I wanted to see Alexa and have a slice of pizza with her, talk over the deal with her and maybe, convince her to come back to my place after my meeting with John.

I left my apartment, a blanket of gloom over me that just a few minutes earlier, had not been there.

I found a parking spot about four blocks away from Familigias, and walked the rest of the way to the restaurant. There was a line of customers outside, waiting for a slice and a can of soda. I glanced around, searching for Alexa, and was dismayed that she wasn't there. I didn't want to see her pull out as well and checked my cell in case she'd sent a text and I'd missed the alert.

There was nothing so I went closer to the store front where they dished out slices and leaned against the light pole, my arms crossed as I waited for her to arrive.

After about ten minutes, I texted her.

LUKE: Hey, Alexa. I'm here and you're not.

I waited, and then her text came.

ALEXA: Sorry. I was late getting out of the apartment. I'm five minutes out. See you soon.

*LUKE: Phew! *wipes sweat* I was worried that you'd changed your mind at the last minute.*

*ALEXA: What? And miss a free slice of Familigia's pizza? Do you think I'm crazy??? *evil grin**

LUKE: Hmm. I hoped you wouldn't want to miss spending time with me and my witty and deeply engrossing conversation.

ALEXA: That, too. :)

I smiled and put my cell away, then returned to watching the street life as crowds on Broadway moved down the street around me, happy to be lost in their midst.

"What are you smiling about?"

I turned and there was Alexa, a grin on her face.

"You're here," I said, surprised to see her so soon. "I thought you were five minutes out."

She sighed audibly. "I was giving myself time to change my mind if I needed it."

I shook my head, my smile fading. "What are you so worried about? It's just an innocent slice of pizza..."

"Because it would be easy to just let things happen," she said and took in a deep breath. "And that would be a mistake. But then, I decided, what the hell. You only live once, right? Besides, Familigia's pizza is to die for, so..."

I put my arm around her shoulder. "Do you want to go inside or do you want to get a slice and walk along the street?"

"Let's sit," she said. "I went for a run and need a rest."

We went inside and waited in line for a table. The hostess told us it would be about ten minutes, and so the two of us stood in the entry way behind a line of hopeful customers.

"The line is small, considering what time it is. Usually, there's no way we'd get in."

"I know," she said, leaning against the wall across from me. "It must be a sign."

"It must be." I smiled at her, my gaze moving over her from head to foot and back again.

God, she really was a pretty little thing. She was wearing a sweater that hugged her curves very nicely, with a deep cut v-neck that showed a bit of delicious cleavage. Beneath was a jean skirt and then some sandals. I felt very much like we were boyfriend and girlfriend going out for a meal together, and not a couple of frauds who met through a misspelled email and had pretended to be something they weren't.

If I wasn't going away on the catamaran for a year, I'd definitely want to keep seeing Alexa. She was so easy to be with, so funny and smart. I felt both excited to be with her and relaxed, like she was comfortable.

"I just got a text from John that didn't make me happy," I said, wanting to talk about the problems with the business deal.

"What?" Her eyes widened, concern for me clear on her face.

"Seems like Harrison Blake is considering pulling out of the deal. With him goes about one quarter of the money so they might have to wait until they find another backer."

"Harrison Blake of the famous Blake family, with the daughter who was in want of a wealthy husband?" She smiled at me, a playful expression in her eyes.

"The very one," I said and shook my head, still in shock that Harrison would consider pulling out merely because I wasn't into his sister. "I knew he liked me as her husband but I really didn't think the deal rested on it."

"I'm so surprised at you super-rich people and the old-fashioned ideas you still have about marriage."

"You middle class people never consider money when you become engaged?" I said playfully, matching her joking tone. "You don't consider your would-be husband as a provider?"

She laughed. "We consider *ourselves* as providers. We have to think that if the marriage failed, we'd be expected to hold up half the sky, at least financially."

"Well, I guess my class wants to consolidate fortunes and carry on dynasties. That's the old money but I don't know what the *nouveau riche* think. Probably aren't as concerned with passing on fortunes, since they're so new."

"So your family must have been really upset when they saw me with you. Me, from Oregon. I mean, I'm not even *nouveau riche* and besides, who's from Oregon anyway? Your mother said as much..."

"When?"

She shrugged. "After I saw you with Jenna. She came up and

told me that you and I were from different social classes and would never work."

"What?" I said, fuming. "That old witch. You have to know I don't believe any of that crap."

"It made me feel even worse, but then I got my back up. You texted me at the right time. An hour earlier and I would have said no."

"Thank God for good timing," I said. We both grinned and I leaned in closer to her, feeling an urge to kiss her then and there.

So I did.

I kissed her, a smile still on my lips, and she kissed me back, a smile on her lips as well. The kiss lingered for a moment, and then it broke on its own time and we pulled back. She glanced away, a smile still on her face.

Yeah, she felt it, too. That connection we had that went beyond pure lust. It was more than that, although it was that as well. It was affection, despite the fact I knew her for only a few weeks. It was attraction to her as a person. Someone I could talk to about things that were beyond popular media or music or films – the usual things I talked about with the other women I fucked on a regular basis.

With Alexa, I felt I could talk to her about the most familiar and most unfamiliar things – my family and the business world. My ex-fiancée and my trip around the world. My business deal and my family dynamics.

I realized I had barely asked her about her family, since mine had been so dominant over the past week.

"Tell me about your father and mother. I know they have a great marriage, but what do they do now that he's retired?"

She went on to tell me about her parents and her brother, and how she missed them, but was unable to go back. She opened up and told me more about Blaine. We talked about his obsession with her after they broke up, and how she was afraid to go home. News got around too quickly for her to feel safe in her home town. She had to meet her family at vacation spots and the location would be kept quiet until the actual date they left.

"It must have been scary having a stalker."

She sighed, and glanced away. "The police arrested him after he pretty much abducted me. He was in jail for a while, but got out. After that, I never feel safe in town, like he was always watching. Like he was waiting for the chance to abduct me and kill me."

I frowned, shocked that she was really that afraid. "Do you really think he would?"

"Who can say?" She met my eyes. "He crossed the line into deviancy. He's dangerous. The police told me to be extremely careful and to never be alone in case he tried to abduct me and I thought, to hell with that. I decided to move away and not tell anyone where I was going. You can imagine I don't really want to go back home as long as he's there."

"I'm sorry you had that happen to you," I said and reached out, pushing a strand of hair from her cheek. "He's obviously a nut case. I was upset after Jenna and I broke off the engagement, but I wasn't going to stalk her. I didn't want anything to do with her ever again. It was my family and her family that kept trying to get us to kiss and make up."

"You don't think you could?"

I shook my head firmly. "Never. How could I?"

"I couldn't," she said and shook her head. "Cheating is beyond anything I could accept. If – when — I get married, I want my husband to know that he can come to me anytime and tell me if things are a problem. If he needs more than I'm giving him. When I get married," she said and glanced away. "I'll do everything I can to make sure my husband is happy."

"That sounds easy in theory, but I think it's harder in practice. Sometimes, people don't know what they want or need."

"Then, people have to grow together and learn to tell each other what they need."

"You make it sound so easy. Marriage is hard."

"Everything worthwhile is hard."

I nodded, but I wasn't as sure of it as she was.

Marriage seemed like a hard mountain to climb and a happy marriage like the pinnacle. Only a few ever reached it. Everyone else fell short and many people died along the way...

We finally got a table and ordered, then spent the next half hour talking about everything and anything, laughing and enjoying each other's company.

It felt so comfortable and exciting at the same time. I didn't want it to end, wishing we could take it back to my place for the night, but I had my meeting with John and Chris and that could not be put off. We were meeting on Monday to finalize things and needed to discuss our strategy.

"Well, I hate to say goodnight," I said and glanced at my watch, "but I have to meet John and Chris in about ten minutes. I gotta go."

I paid the bill and then we walked out of the restaurant past the throng of people waiting at the front for a slice and those waiting in line to get a table.

We stood on the brightly-lit street outside the restaurant and I regretted that John had called and the deal was now uncertain. It felt like Alexa would come home with me if I asked. I would have liked to invite her to my place after my meeting with John and Chris, but that seemed so calculated, like I was hoping to fuck her but had other more important matters to attend first. I wanted things to feel unforced and natural.

I couldn't ask, not this way.

"I better go," I said and leaned in, kissing her gently on the lips. She kissed me back and then I pulled her against me, her body pressing into mine, her curves so delicious that I could get a hard-on just standing there with her.

"Damn," I said, looking into her eyes when our kiss broke. "I wish you could come back to my place. I wish I wasn't going to meet John..."

She smiled, and pulled back.

"Maybe some other time," she said and squeezed my hand. "Before you go. I'd like to see your boat when it's finished."

"It's a date. I'll take you on a sail before we leave. How does that sound?"

She nodded, but her expression was serious, like she didn't really want to think of me leaving.

I felt so conflicted at that moment. Part of me couldn't wait to get in the boat and leave all my worries behind me, sailing down the coast to the gulf and then through the Panama Canal on my way to the Marqueses Islands in the South Pacific. After such a tumultuous year, after the breakup with Jenna and the business going stratospheric, I felt a strong need to get away, to think and just breathe for a few months.

For a year.

At the same time, I hadn't felt this way about a woman for a long time. Maybe not since I met Jenna and we were first together. I hated the thought that I'd be leaving and nothing more would come of this thing between us – whatever it was.

If I wasn't leaving, I would have kept trying to see her.

If I wasn't leaving...

Then I thought about the deal and wondered if Harrison Blake pulling out would stop the deal in its tracks. If so, it could take us months to find another partner and negotiate a new deal. I hoped not. I wanted to leave Manhattan so badly. I had dreamed of sailing away on my catamaran for years, and now, it was so close, I could almost smell the salt water and feel it on my skin as I sailed to the South Pacific.

I glanced at Alexa and wished...

Fucking hell...

"Dammit, I have to *go,*" I said reluctantly. "I don't want to go..."

I leaned in to kiss her once more, only intending it to be a quick kiss goodbye, but it ended up being much more passionate. All at once, I didn't care anymore and so I grabbed her and picked her up, kissing her even more deeply. In response, she wrapped her arms around my neck and kissed me back. I was certain at that moment that she felt the same – wanting to be with me, not wanting me to go...

Then I put her down and turned, walking away, regret filling me, but resolve pushing me forward.

CHAPTER 17

ALEXA

I watched Luke walk away, his dark hair shining in the overhead streetlights as he dodged pedestrians and then crossed the street to his SUV. I sighed to myself, feeling a tug in my chest that he was leaving and I would probably never see him again except in the Cultural or Business pages of the *Times*. Although he'd said he'd take me for a sail on the catamaran before he left, I didn't believe it.

It would be best for both of us not to see each other again.

I took out my cell and was just about ready to delete his contact information when I got a text from him.

LUKE: *I really hate leaving you now, but I have to go to this meeting. I hope you understand. I know you probably think we should stop this now, before I go on my trip, but I want to see you again. Like, tomorrow night. Will you do dinner at my place? I want to cook for you. And other things...*

And other things...

I didn't have to wonder what that meant.

I chewed on my bottom lip for a moment, debating whether to answer or just delete him from my contacts and from my life entirely. I knew it would be the far better thing to do for my heart and for my sanity. I don't think I could stand to be apart from him for a year if we did decide to keep seeing each other and start a relationship. Even if he did fly me to whatever port he was in for a weekend or week when I had a holiday from college. Long distance relationships were not my cup of tea. I'd always be wondering if he was cheating on me in some port with some exotic woman and wouldn't feel sure of his commitment to me.

So, instead of answering right away, I tucked my cell into my bag and walked back to my apartment, determined to just let things die a natural death.

I got back into the apartment and found Candace sitting in her chair watching Netflix on her iMac. She had a bag of microwave popcorn and was munching away.

"You back so early?" she asked, stuffing a handful of popcorn into her mouth.

"Yeah," I replied and threw my bag onto my desk. "He had a business meeting. Seems there's an issue with the deal and he's meeting with the other guys to talk over last minute strategy or something."

"That's too bad. I hope it goes through..."

"He said it might delay the deal if they had to look for another investor to make up the difference."

"What happened? Why did an investor pull out?"

I shrugged. "It's the brother of that woman his mother was trying to match him with. I guess he thought he'd be investing in his future brother-in-law and now that Luke made it clear he wasn't going to marry Felicia, Harrison decided to pull out. At least, that's what I think happened."

"That sucks. Why do these rich people think they can control their kids that way? Like my parents would never think of saying no to a person I chose to marry, or force me to marry someone they chose for me because of wealth."

"They're old blue bloods and want to preserve their fortunes or something like that."

"I got news for them. It's the twenty-first century, yanno..."

I laughed and peered over her shoulder at the screen and saw it was Love, Actually. I'd never watched it, and was curious.

"You're watching that again? Don't you get sick of it?"

"Never. Speaking of love, what's going on with you and Mr. Big Shot?"

I sighed and flopped down on my chair. "He wants to cook me supper tomorrow night at his place. And other things..."

"Ohh, I like the other things. Lucky girl." She grinned at me lasciviously. "Supper sounds good, too. Why do you look so glum?"

"Because he's leaving on a boat in a month and will be gone for a full year, that's why."

"So?" Candy leaned forward. "Go and enjoy him while you can. Live a little. Get some, for God's sake. You need it."

"You're not the one whose heart will be broken when he leaves..."

"Don't let it get too attached. Use him for some great sex and good food and then wave goodbye happily when it's time for him to go. Be more like a man for a change."

"You think I should?"

She leaned forward and squeezed my shoulder. "Of course I do. You're not going to find a man as good looking, successful or smart as him for a long time, sister. Enjoy him while you can."

I nodded, realizing that she was right. "I guess. What's the worst that could happen? I fall in love with him and he leaves. I'll be alone. There's nothing different from how I am now – alone."

"Exactly. Plus, maybe he'll fall in love with you and decide he can't live without you. He'll invite you to come on the ship with him and the two of you will sail off into the sunset."

"Dream on," I said and laughed, a small part of me wishing that could be my future, and the big part of me kicking her in the ass for being so stupid.

"Grab your chair and sit down with me. We can watch Love, Actually and stuff ourselves full of popcorn."

"Sounds like a plan," I said and did just that.

Later, after the movie was over and we were done deconstructing it and raving over everything, I went to the bathroom to get ready for bed and remembered that I hadn't answered Luke's text.

ALEXA: *Supper sounds wonderful. As do other things...*

I put my cell down and began to brush my teeth and within a minute, his reply came and my cell dinged.

LUKE: *I promise that you won't regret it. I'll be the consummate gentleman, cooking you a delicious meal and providing you with very enjoyable entertainment. I have a meeting all afternoon and the meeting will probably go on until seven. Then, I'll go home and shower, and pick you up at eight. How does that sound?*

ALEXA: *Sounds fine. See you then.*

LUKE: *I'm glad you didn't decide to throw me over.*

ALEXA: *I almost did.*

LUKE: *I know. You shouldn't. We should enjoy what we have while we can. Life is short. People die.*

ALEXA: *They do. Goodnight.*

LUKE: *Goodnight.*

I put my cell away and finished brushing my teeth, a smile on my face. I glanced at myself in the mirror and focused on the little thrill that went through my body at the thought of the other things, very enjoyable things, that I knew we would get to tomorrow night. It had been so long since I'd had a boyfriend and had real sex. Well, Luke wasn't technically a boyfriend, but he was a lover.

I had a lover.

I smiled to myself and finished getting ready for bed. When I went to the kitchen to grab a bottle of water out of the refrigerator, I saw that Candace was still up, dressed in her nightgown and reading her emails, her knee bent up under her chin.

I sat on my chair beside hers.

"I have a lover," I said to her as I unscrewed the bottle and took a long drink.

She turned and glanced at me, grinning crazily.

"You do," she said and pushed me playfully. "You have a lover. It's so exciting! Finally, my girl is getting some. You deserve it."

"I do deserve it."

"After all you went through with Blaine, you deserve someone like Luke."

I nodded and of course, thoughts of Blaine ruined my good feeling about Luke. The two could not be further apart in temperament, which was probably why I was attracted to Luke.

Luke was so easy-going and laid back, despite being a very successful businessman. He could have fun and laugh, while Blaine seemed to be in a perpetual somber mood. I always thought it was because he was deep, but I realized instead that he was always on guard, looking for every slight to his ego.

He was a control freak. He had to control everything. Me, especially.

I'd been easy to control at first, because I was so in love with him and his handsome face and great body, plus what I perceived to be his deep thoughts and intelligence. When things started to sour between us, when I realized he wasn't all that deep after all, but was just quietly observing everything so he could measure how people treated him against his high standard, I started to assert my independence.

He never once hit me, although he did grab me a couple of times, held me still while he lectured me on this or that infraction I'd done against his rules. When I broke it off with him, he wouldn't take no for an answer and it wasn't just him pleading with me, telling me he loved me. He started to stalk me and then he attacked me.

"You're mine, no matter what you do, Alexa," he said. *"You can have your freedom for a while, if you want, but remember that I own you. I own a part of you that can never be owned by someone else. You can't ever really leave me completely, no matter what you do and where you go. I'll always be here,"* he said and pointed to my head. *"And here,"* he said, his hand grabbing my crotch.

I thought he meant he was my first lover and that meant he owned my virginity. He saw that as ownership of a part of me. I figured he was just being weird and thought nothing of it. But I was wrong.

For the first couple of weeks after we broke up, he let me be, and I thought I was a free woman once again and glad to be free of him and his suspicious and controlling ways. But soon, I noticed he was following me. I'd catch sight of his car following mine down the main street. I'd see him enter the little café where we used to eat our lunch. He'd catch my eye and then pick up food to take out. I'd go to a party and he'd show up later, walk through the party, talk to a few people and then leave.

I couldn't fault him because it was such a small town and there were only so many places either of us could go. Besides, my places were all his places as well.

So at first, I thought it was just coincidence that we ran into each other or I saw him at places where I went.

But later, I realized he was deliberately stalking me.

One night, I took the dog for a walk and saw his car parked at the end of our street. I turned the other way and went back home.

"Why are you back so early?" my mother asked, frowning when she saw me.

"Blaine's car is parked at the end of the street," I said softly, not wanting to alarm her, but feeling nervous myself. "I'm going to take Molly out the back."

I took my dog out the back way to the alley behind our house and walked her there instead, but the alley was dark and I felt immediately creepy. Molly was used to going out before bed and I didn't want to deny her a walk just because I was spooked by Blaine. He might have been visiting someone, after all...

As soon as Molly was done, I went back to the house and found my mother was on the phone.

"Here she is now," my mom said and handed me the phone. "It's Sheriff Dawson. Tell him about Blaine."

"*Mom*," I said and frowned, taking the phone and covering the receiver. "What did you do? You called the police?"

"Yes, I did. Blaine's stalking you and they need to know. Tell Sheriff Dawson what's going on."

I spent the next half hour on the phone talking to the Sheriff, who was a friend of my dad. I told him about Blaine and how I'd noticed him following me since we broke up.

"Has he said anything threatening to you? Has he actually touched you at any time?"

"No," I said, for he hadn't come within fifteen feet of me in the past month since we broke up.

"Has he contacted you on social media? Has he sent you any threatening emails or texts? Made any threatening posts on your Facebook?"

"No, he hasn't. He's just following me around. He stays far enough away, but it's scaring me."

"It's a small town, Alexa. You two are going to run into each other now and then. Are you sure it's stalking and not just accidental?"

"I'm pretty sure," I said, chewing a fingernail and feeling stupid all of a sudden.

"Pretty sure isn't good enough. I can't arrest him unless he's threatened you or touched you. There's nothing we can do except get a temporary restraining order against him, force him to stay a certain distance away. Do you want to do that?"

"I don't know," I said and turned to my mother. "He wants to know if we want to get a restraining order against Blaine."

"Yes," she said and took the phone from me, putting it on the speakerphone. "He's got to get over this and leave her alone. He's got to move on with his life. Maybe if he has a restraining order on him, he'll think twice."

We talked about the process for getting a restraining order and I promised to follow through the next day. When I hung up, I felt more unnerved because that might make him even more angry at me.

Things had gone way too far if I had to get a restraining order against Blaine.

"I'm scared," I said to my mom. "He's going to get really mad now."

She put her arms around me and squeezed me.

"I know you're scared," she said, kissing my forehead. "So am I. This is necessary to protect you. When your dad gets back from Phoenix, we'll talk about getting a better security system. You'll be going back to school soon, and he'll be as well. Maybe he'll get over this obsession with you."

I sighed and held onto my mom, hoping that would be the

case, but there was a part of me that felt an increasing sense of threat from Blaine.

I hoped I was just imagining things...

I hadn't been.

Blaine found out that I talked to the Sheriff about getting a restraining order. Someone close to his family who worked at the Sheriff's office squealed and told them what we were doing.

The next day, he found me. I was afraid he'd kill me if someone hadn't come along and found us.

I'd been in the back yard, sun tanning, trying to catch a few rays before school started and I'd be back inside all day.

He showed up, coming in through the rear gate off the alley. I had my eyes closed and my earphones in when I felt the sun blocked. I opened my eyes and before I could say anything, he had his hands around my neck, his face an inch from mine.

"What the *fuck* were you thinking, Alexa? Getting a restraining order against me?" he hissed.

I tried to fight back, grabbing his hands, which were definitely too tight around my throat.

"Stop!" I cried out, trying to wrestle away from him. "You're hurting me!"

"You're lucky I don't really hurt you," he said and finally let go. He grabbed my hand and pulled me with him towards the back gate. "I can't believe you even considered getting a restraining order."

"Let go," I said, fighting with him, hitting his arm, trying to wrest my hand out of his. He fought me, pulling me into the back alley. I saw his car was parked at the end of the alley. I knew enough that I couldn't let him take me. Once you got in a car with an abductor, it was usually game over.

Luckily, my neighbour Mr. Scott shouted over the fence. "Hey! What are you doing?"

Blaine startled, like he was waking up from a dream. Then he looked at me, stepping closer. "You're *mine*," he said and held his finger in front of my face. "You can't hide from me."

Then, he let go and I ran back to the yard, trying to catch my breath and recover.

Mr. Scott came over, his face white as a ghost.

"Are you okay?"

I nodded, my legs like rubber. "I'm okay. Thanks for yelling at him."

"He was going to abduct you. Do you want me to call the police?"

"No, I will. But thanks."

"If you're sure..."

"I'm sure."

When Mr. Scott left, I went into the house to the bathroom and checked in the mirror. There were red marks around my throat where Blaine had grabbed me and my wrist was red as well. The skin was sore and I was sure there'd be a bruise the next day.

He *could* have abducted me and if he had, he might have killed me.

It was then I realized I wasn't safe anymore. I'd been alone at the house. My mom was at work and my dad was still in Phoenix. Only Molly was there and she was in the house, deaf and almost blind with cataracts.

Blaine could have choked me to death and there was nothing I could have done about it. He could have hauled me into his car and there was nothing I could do about it.

He was too strong.

Thank God for Mr. Scott.

I went to the phone, my hands shaking, and called Sheriff Dawson.

"What happened?" he asked when I told him Blaine had attacked me.

I relayed everything from start to finish and he sighed audibly on the other end of the line.

"I was afraid of that," he said. "Sometimes, when women do something to fight back against an abuser, the man becomes more unreasonable, unhinged and lashes out. You're at your most vulnerable right after you break up with someone like that, and most at risk. You really shouldn't be alone if you're going to go through with this."

"I can't even be alone?" I said, feeling like I'd just made everything worse by even considering a restraining order. "What kind of life is that?"

"I'm real sorry, Alexa, but it's a fact. You and your mom better come down to the office and talk with us about what you can do. When is your dad back from Phoenix?"

"Later in the week," I replied, going around the house and locking the windows and doors.

"I'll make sure to have the boys drive by your place when they can, keep an eye out. You don't hesitate to call me if he comes back or if you see him following you."

I agreed and then we said goodbye. I sat at the island in the kitchen, the phone in my hand, and waited for my mother to come home from work, jumping at every noise and every time Molly barked.

It was a very long and nerve-wracked afternoon...

Now, here I was in Manhattan, far far away from all that, and I finally met someone I could imagine being with for a longer term but he was leaving. He would never be a long-term boyfriend.

I felt sad that the next couple of weeks would be all we had, and was still torn between wanting to protect myself from being hurt when he said goodbye, and not wanting to miss out on any time with him.

It was a hard choice, but I'd enjoyed him so much, that I decided that I only had one life. I didn't want to waste it always trying to protect myself from being hurt.

A broken heart meant that you loved someone once. That was better than always being alone...

The next day, I spent my time lounging around the apartment, watching news coverage, and reading the papers. My stomach was all butterflies as I thought about having dinner with Luke and what would happen afterward. As a result, I went around a little aroused, my body responding to memories of our time together, and looking forward to more of it later that night.

"Quit pacing like a caged lion," Candace said when I walked past her for the third time, moving from the kitchen to my desk and back because I couldn't focus and kept forgetting things. "Go out for a run or something. Do some yoga for God's sake, girl. You need to chill."

"I'm excited about tonight," I said and plopped down on my chair across from her. "Now that I've decided to live dangerously, I can't stand the wait."

"Go for a run, like I said."

"Don't want to exhaust myself, just in case we get busy," I said and wagged my eyebrows.

"In case?" she said in mock horror. "You damn well better get busy tonight or I'll kick your butt. You don't have access to a man as fine looking as Luke and not get as busy as you possibly can. Do you hear me?"

I laughed and nodded. "Loud and clear."

At seven, I took a shower and got ready for my date, shaving and waxing and brushing and doing everything to make myself as desirable as possible in case – for when – we got busy later that night. When I was done, I looked in the mirror and even I had to admit I looked good, dressed in a strappy little black number that hugged my curves. I figured I had to play up my best features and make Luke glad that he invited me to his place for supper.

"How do I look?" I asked Candace, who stood beside me at the mirror in the bathroom, her critical eye giving me the once over.

"You look fabulous. He'll drool when he sees you and he'll probably want to strip off that dress and make you the main course instead of supper."

"Oh, you," I said and hip-checked her one. "That's all you can think of. You should get yourself some."

"I know, I know," she said with a laugh. "I'm working on it."

"Oh, yeah?" I said and turned to face her, wondering what she meant.

"Yeah," she said and looked all coy. "I may have met someone when I was out today at the bagel shop. He may have been smiling at me for the past few weeks when I've gone there. We may have agreed to meet for coffee there tomorrow after he's done work."

"Oh, my God, Candace! That's great. What does he look like?"

"He looks like Thor, with shorter hair." She wagged her eyebrows and I knew what she meant. She'd been in love with the actor who played Thor for several years and was always looking to meet a guy who looked as much like him as possible.

"You go, girl," I said and playfully punched her shoulder.

"I know, right? Who would have thought the two of us nerd girls would find two hunks and both be getting some at the same time? The stars must all be aligned just right or something."

Right on cue, my cell dinged and I checked it to see if it was Luke.

LUKE: *Your ride awaits, m'Lady.*

"He's here," I said with a grin. "I'm off. I don't know if I'll be back or whether I'll be staying at his place tonight."

Candace gave me a little hug and smiled. "I'm a big girl. I can stay by myself."

"You won't be lonely?" I asked, feeling slightly guilty that I was leaving her alone.

"I have popcorn and the latest Thor movie on Netflix. I'm fine," she said and waved at me dismissively. "Go. Have a wonderful time."

"Okay, this is me going." I took in a deep breath and then I left the apartment, taking the stairs to the main floor.

Outside, double parked, was Luke standing beside his very expensive SUV. I smiled when our eyes met and then he opened the passenger door and I got in, excited for what the night would bring.

CHAPTER 18

LUKE

Alexa looked ... *amazing.*

I had to pinch myself that she was mine for the night when I saw her in that dress that hugged her very delicious curves. She was built, and she was beautiful. I wondered why she was single and had been for so long. I knew she had recently escaped a bad relationship and didn't feel able to go back to her small-town home, but could that bad relationship have turned her sour on men?

I hoped not. She seemed to enjoy being with me, but to go for a whole year without sex?

I couldn't imagine it...

"Hello," I said and leaned over, kissing her softly on the lips. "I'm so glad you decided not to throw me over."

She smiled, her expression softening. "I'm glad you asked. I was feeling bad that I'd probably never see you again. In fact," she said when we drove off. "I decided to ignore your text and delete your contact info from my cell so I wouldn't."

"You were really going to delete me?" I said, and made a face of mock horror, although I really did feel badly that she considered it. "I'm crushed."

She glanced away, a smile on her face. "Self-defense. Who needs a broken heart?"

"No one," I said, pulling out into traffic. "We won't break our hearts. We'll just enjoy each other while we can. How does that sound?"

She shrugged. "I'm going to try."

I took her hand. "Look," I said, trying to find the right words. "We've both got plans. You're starting your PhD. I'm planning to sail around the world. We should consider ourselves lucky that we met at all, considering everything. It was fate, I tell you."

"Fate?" she said with a laugh. "It was an accident. A slip of the fingers on your keyboard."

I maneuvered through traffic and drove down Broadway to 8th Avenue and my apartment in Hell's Kitchen.

"Thank God for that slip of my fingers." I turned to her and squeezed her hand. "I'm glad I met you instead of the real Lexxi911."

"But your plans to teach Eric a lesson fell through."

"No, I don't think so. I think we gave enough hints that I knew about his use of Lexxi911 that he got the message, even if it wasn't you. Besides, she's not nearly as pretty as you. Or as smart."

"You flatter me, sir," she said, a hint of protest in her voice but she smiled, hiding it behind her hand.

"I speak the truth," I replied. "After that first night, when I discovered you weren't Lexxi911, John spent some time searching through his recycling for the piece of paper with Lexxi911's contact info. When he found it, John sent her a PM asking for a pic. She sent him one so I actually saw her. There's no competition. Not in looks and I'm sure not in brains either."

"Plus, I don't sell it." She grinned at me and I felt a surge of affection for her. I *liked* her. Really *liked* her...

We arrived at my building and drove into the parking garage. I slipped into my parking spot and hopped out, helping her out of her door. I took her hand and led her up into my building, which was an entire brownstone owned by my family. It had been renovated with top of the line fixtures and had been featured once in the *Times* real estate section.

"This is amazing..."

I could see the awe in her eyes as we took in the entry, which retained the original dark wood paneling, crown molding and plaster, but which now included all new hardwood flooring, new electrical and pretty much new everything else.

"When I'm with you, I forget how rich your family is. How even more rich you're going to be."

I smiled and closed the door behind me. "It means nothing to me except a way to do what I want. I'm not into possessions as much as what money can free me from – being forced to do work I hate. I'm very lucky and I know it."

We walked through the living room to the great room at the back, complete with a gas fireplace and huge modern chef's kitchen. I was used to the elegance, but I knew Alexa wasn't.

In truth, at that moment, I could be happy being anywhere with Alexa – eating a hotdog in Central Park, getting a pizza slice from a storefront, eating fresh crab cakes at the beach. She was fun, she was smart, and she was real.

She'd be someone I could imagine getting involved with on a more long-term basis – if I was into that kind of thing. Which I wasn't.

Not any longer, anyway.

But if I was, Alexa would be it.

"What do I smell?"

"Dinner, my lady. Prepared especially for you."

She entered the kitchen and glanced at the pots on the stove.

"Fresh asparagus, steamed and almost ready. In the fridge is a fresh spinach salad and my grill on the rooftop patio will cook the two New York Strip steaks I got from my neighborhood butcher. In the oven is a fresh baguette heating up."

"I didn't realize you're a chef," she said with a smile.

"I enjoy cooking. My mother took a course from one of Julia Child's students when she was young and she and I used to cook together."

She glanced at me, an expression of sympathy on her pretty face. "You were young when she died."

"I was," I said, "but I had enough time with her to pick up her love of cooking and her appreciation for space. She was a maverick for her time, studying astronomy in school instead of how to find a husband."

"I doubt a rich woman with a fortune would have a hard time finding a husband..."

I laughed. "She didn't," I replied, thinking of my mother and father. "My mother was an heiress to a fortune and had all the money in their marriage. My father was a banker, but he wasn't wealthy in his own right."

"Your family is pretty convoluted," she said. "You and Dana are orphans."

"We are," I said with a sigh. "Neither one of us likes our adoptive parents. They're tolerable, but only. We have each other."

"It must have been hard to find out that Eric was cheating on Dana."

"I wanted to kill him," I replied and leaned against the counter. "Honestly, it was the closest I've ever come to violence. John had to hold me back from driving right over to their house and punching him in the face."

Alexa nodded and smiled softly. "John is a good friend if he kept you from doing it. That would have done no one any good. You'd be charged with assault. Your sister would be angry with you, and would probably side with Eric."

"I know, I know," I said, the thought still making my heart race, my blood pressure rise. "Luckily, cooler heads prevailed and I went to talk to a marriage counselor instead. She told me to let Eric know I knew about his infidelity and that if he didn't stop, I'd tell my sister."

"You thought hiring Lexxi911 would accomplish the same thing?"

I nodded. "Yep. I didn't trust myself alone with him. Honestly, I get angry just seeing his smug face."

"Violence is never the answer. Seriously. I know."

I examined her face. An expression of dismay crossed it. She'd only spoken briefly about her bad relationship. Her last boyfriend had been a control freak and that she felt she had to leave Portland because he was stalking her.

"Tell me more about Blaine."

She forced a smile. "I'd rather not. You know all you need to know about him. Let's say I escaped with my life and leave it at that, okay?"

"Sounds serious. Did he hurt you?"

She lifted her shoulder. "Not really badly but he would have." She sighed audibly so I knew it would be better to drop it.

"Sorry to pry. Let's move on to more happy matters. Like how do you like your steak cooked? And please, don't tell me well done with ketchup."

I grinned at her and she smiled back. Her smile was so infectious that I couldn't resist kissing her, and so I pulled her against me, my arms around her waist. She seemed a bit startled but leaned into my embrace, her arms slipping around my neck.

We kissed, our mouths meeting, the kiss tender at first, both of us smiling.

Soon, the kiss turned more intense and my smile faded. I was surprised at the intensity of my emotions when I kissed her. Arousal, yes. Desire, yes. But there was more.

It felt *right*.

Kissing Alexa, having her there in my apartment, fixing her dinner, felt right.

Once upon a time, I had been ready to be a married man, and had been planning for the day when Jenna and I would move in together and start our life as a married couple. I wanted someone in my bed every night and I wanted to wake up with that person every morning. I wanted to become comfortable with someone, passing time together, doing everything with her.

Doing nothing with her.

Then Jenna betrayed me and all those plans were gone in a heartbeat.

Every woman I'd been with afterwards was merely a means to an end – an orgasm.

I wanted that from Alexa, but part of me – a part I thought was gone for good – wanted more. I wanted everything else for a change and that surprised me to the center of my very being.

But I couldn't have her that way...

As much as I knew that I shouldn't allow myself to get any closer to her, I couldn't resist. For the first time since Jenna, I felt at home with a woman.

Instead of shutting things down – shutting myself down – I went full steam ahead, pulling her with me down the hallway to my bedroom, smiling the entire time, enjoying her playful resistance. When I picked her up and threw her over my shoulder, she squealed in delight, giggling as I laid her down across my bed.

I laid on top of her, my arms on either side of her face, and just stared down at her for a moment, both of us smiling like idiots.

"Why is this so easy?"

Her smile faded. "It's too easy. I know I'm going to have a broken heart out of the deal."

"Should we stop? End it now and say goodbye?"

I watched her, wondering how she'd respond. A range of expression crossed her face, from surprise that I said it, to concern, and finally, what I thought was a fuck-it face.

"To hell with it," she said and placed her hand behind my head, pulling me down for a kiss.

When she rolled me over and got on top, riding me like I was a bucking bronco, I didn't fight.

CHAPTER 19

ALEXA

I woke early when the sun was still just a warm glow on the horizon. Beside me, Luke lay on his stomach, a pillow over his head. His long arms were thrown up beside his head, and his body was naked, his glorious butt and legs on display for me to appreciate.

Appreciate them I did.

He clearly worked out to keep in such great shape. Plus, it looked like he'd spent time at the beach house in Westhampton because he had a decent tan everywhere except his ass and down to his mid-thigh where his swimming trunks would end.

I slipped out of bed and went to the bathroom for a quick pee, seeing everything again in the early morning light.

He was so wealthy. I felt somewhat in awe of the luxury in which he lived and part of me resented it. He was born wealthy, and had lived like this his entire life. It wasn't his fault, and I didn't

245

blame him for it. He'd had his share of sadness and pain. Money really didn't solve all problems, but I couldn't help but think money made the pain of life more bearable.

I finished up in the bathroom and slipped on my bra and panties, then tiptoed to the main living area to get a drink of water. I wanted to turn on the television and watch some local news, but couldn't find the remote. I searched through the drawers in the wall unit, looking for it, but it was nowhere to be found.

I did find a few DVDs and was curious about what he watched. Some of them were recordings, and I glanced at the hallway in case he was watching, but seeing that he wasn't, I checked out the label.

Various playlists for driving – sixties music, nineties music, and some metal. Then I found one DVD that had a hand-written cover with the simple name JENNA.

He'd made a DVD of his ex. I imagined it was a video recording of one of their happier days before they split. Once more, I wondered what happened and how it all went down. How did he find out that she cheated on him? Did someone tell him? Did he walk in on them after coming home early from work one day?

I held the disc in my hand and chewed my bottom lip thoughtfully, imagining it in my mind's eye. I searched through the drawer and found a photo album. At that point, I knew I should just stop and not snoop, but I was just too damned curious.

I opened the cover carefully, glancing quickly down the hallway, but there was no sign of Luke. He must have still been asleep. Unable to resist, I flipped through the first few pages of pictures from Luke's youth – snapshots of him on a surfboard, him skateboarding with a few friends, his hair longer, his body with that leanness of youth. Some of him working on a car engine, his hands greasy.

There were a few of him when he was much younger —
maybe seven or eight — standing with a dark-haired woman. His
mother, no doubt. It certainly wasn't his adoptive mother. This
woman had a pleasant face, pretty, actually, with a gentle smile.
She had one arm around his shoulder, and the two were smiling at
the camera. I felt a pang of sadness for Luke that he'd lost both
parents too early. No wonder he was so close with Dana...

Then, at the back of the photo album, some loose pictures
slipped out and fell onto the floor. I bent down to pick them up,
examining each one to see what was the subject.

Jenna.

Long dark hair and the face of an angel. Smiling at the camera,
a scarf tied around her head. She was in a convertible, her hands
on the wheel.

On the back was one word. Jenna.

The woman who broke Luke's heart...

There were nearly a dozen similar pictures of Jenna, in various
locations, but in all of them she was smiling at the camera like she
was perfectly happy. One showed Luke and Jenna together. He
pulled her closer, his arms around her and she kissed his cheek.

They seemed so happy. Why would she cheat on him?

I felt incredibly guilty snooping through his personal
possessions so I hastily slipped the pictures back into the photo
album and replaced it on the bottom of the drawer.

He still kept them – memories of his relationship – the woman
he almost married. I knew he was still not over her. He couldn't get
close to a woman, even now – almost a year later. He kept them all
at arm's length and focused on his business and his plans to sail the
world and then leave it for good.

A part of me wanted to cry after seeing those pictures of Luke.
He seemed so easy going and carefree, but I knew that deep down,
he had a lot of scars from the various pains in his childhood and

youth – his father and mother dying, leaving him an orphan cared for by adoptive parents, then his fiancée cheating on him with her ex...

I went to the bedroom, giving up on the idea of watching the news, and quickly dressed. I gathered up my bag and went to the kitchen. I scrawled a hasty note on a sheet of paper from my bag.

Thanks for the great night. This has been fun, but we both know it's going nowhere and that's not good enough for me. Have a great life and thanks for the memories.

Then I left the apartment while the sun began to rise and walked to the nearest subway station to take a train back home.

When I got back home, Candace was gone, so I changed into some jeans and a hoodie and went for a walk through the streets around the apartment, picking up a coffee on my way. I still felt sad and wanted to think through everything that happened between Luke and me. I decided to walk to the Hudson to watch the seagulls fly. The sky gradually brightened and I breathed in deep the cool morning air before it warmed up.

My cell dinged and I pulled it out of my hoodie pocket to see who was texting me, wondering if it would be Luke.

To my surprise, it was Dana, his sister.

DANA: Hey, Alexa, I hope you don't mind that I'm texting you. I got your number from Luke's phone. Ha ha. I pretended I wanted to google something. Hey, I'm his twin. I consider myself partially responsible for his happiness. Speaking of which, Luke told me you left suddenly this morning and pretty much broke off your relationship. Are you okay? I know Luke really likes you and I wanted you to know there is nothing between him and Jenna anymore in case you were worried about it. Sorry to butt into your life but I know my brother. He was really upset that you left and weren't going to see him again. I hope you two can work it out. He seems to really like you.

I read her text over, surprised that she felt a need to contact me. I mused whether I should text her back, but I decided I should, just to be polite.

ALEXA: I'm fine. Luke and I aren't serious. In fact, we're pretty casual. A relationship of convenience really, and so it's not a big deal if we stop seeing each other. Seriously – I'm fine. Luke is a free man, and he has plans for the future that don't involve me. I understand that, and we had some fun together, but he's not in my future and I'm not in his. Thanks for being concerned about me but really, I'm fine.

I read over my text and then sent it, figuring that would end the whole business and I wouldn't hear from her or Luke again.

I continued to walk along the river, feeling sad that nothing could happen between us, trying to harden my resolve. I felt so bad that I wanted to go back home and see my family, but I couldn't go back, because of Blaine. He'd find me if I showed up. In the small town where I had lived before moving to Manhattan, everyone knew everyone else's business. As soon as I drove into town, gossip would spread that I was home, and Blaine would know it. A court ordered restraining order couldn't keep him away – that much I knew for sure.

My parents often rented a vacation home on South Padre Island on the gulf coast of Texas. That was the only place I could go to meet with them and connect, given the problems that I faced when Blaine and I broke up before I came to Manhattan.

It was a time in my life I did not want to think about or revisit.

I sent my mom and dad a text, hoping I could visit them sometime in the fall during my break.

ALEXA: Hey, are you and Dad planning on going to Texas this fall for Thanksgiving? I need a break away from my studies and would love to see you.

She didn't respond right away, so I continued to walk along the river and drink my coffee.

When my cell dinged again, I expected it was her answering, but instead, it was Dana once more.

DANA: That's strange. I know Luke really regrets that you left early. I didn't get the sense from him that the relationship was one of convenience. He contacted me to talk, so I think he really likes you. So if it was a relationship of convenience, it was on your part, not his. I know my brother. I guess it's a good thing that you left after all, if that's the way you felt about him.

She got the wrong idea entirely, of course. She was too close to Luke, and was concerned for him, but of course, it was totally a relationship of convenience. I couldn't explain to her why and how we really met, so I was at a loss how I could explain it. I couldn't tell her the truth.

Your brother hired me thinking I was an escort that your cheating husband fucked while you were pregnant. He wanted to send a clear message to Eric that he better stop his cheating ways...

No, that most definitely wouldn't work.

I decided to text her back so she wouldn't push it any farther.

ALEXA: What I mean by convenience is that we both are really busy with our lives – Luke with with his business and me with my MA. We both understood that we would enjoy each other when we had the chance, but that there was no longer-term relationship possible because of both our plans. I'm going to move to Europe after I've finished my PhD and hope to join the diplomatic corps. He wants to go away for a year on his catamaran and then maybe take part in the Mars mission and eventually even leave on a one-way mission. So, we knew there was no chance that the two of us would stay together long-term. I care about him and he cares about me, but that's the extent of it. Sorry if I wasn't clear.

I put my phone in my pocket and started back to the apartment, wanting to get breakfast and try to put everything behind me. Before I reached the apartment building where Candace and I lived, my cell dinged once more.

DANA: Meet me for breakfast? I live just down the street from your apartment building.

I didn't know what to say. She seemed to be really invested in the idea of Luke and me being together.

ALEXA: Okay. Where do you want to meet?

DANA: At The Old Mill. It has a great English breakfast. See you in ten.

I was completely surprised that she wanted to meet me, but was willing to go and talk to her. She was really sweet and I knew she had Luke's best interest at heart. I had to convince her that it really was no problem that Luke and I weren't going to see each other.

So I went to meet her.

The Old Mill was one of those hole in the wall restaurants that had a busy breakfast and lunch crowd and then became a local watering hole for people after work. I entered and searched around, finally seeing Dana sitting at a booth in the back. I went to her and smiled when I saw her. She seemed really pleased to see me and so honest and open about everything. I felt sick that I knew about her cheating husband and couldn't tell her.

"Hi," she said and patted the booth beside her. "Come and sit down. They have a great British fry-up on the menu for breakfast. Eggs, beans, tomatoes, bacon, and toast. Plus, real hot tea. Usually,

Eric and I come here, but I told him it was a girl's breakfast for me this week."

I slipped in beside her and picked up a menu, deciding on the same thing she ordered when the waitress came to our table.

I felt Dana's gaze on me as I stirred my tea.

"So, I heard from Luke that you left his apartment early this morning without saying goodbye. I know you must think it's strange that I contacted you, but I liked you right away as soon as we met. I feel like we could be friends. Real friends."

I smiled back at her, feeling the same way about Dana.

"I do, too."

"So, tell me why you broke it off with my brother? You're the first woman he's brought to any family function since he and Jenna split last year. That has to mean something."

I shrugged, unable to tell her the truth. "Like I said, we're both really busy and agreed to only see each other when it was convenient for us both. There were never any long-range plans for us."

"He was really upset when she showed up at the beach house. Nothing happened between them."

I shrugged. "When I saw him with Jenna, I realized that he wasn't over her yet. This morning, I found a photo album in his bottom drawer in the living room wall unit and I had this sense he's still hurt and not ready to commit again. I figured I should break it off now before we get too far in. Even if he doesn't feel something for her, he's not ready for another serious relationship and that's all I'm good at."

She shook her head. "Look, I love my brother, but between you and me, all this sail around the world and Mars mission stuff is a way to distract himself from being lonely."

"That may be, but he's not ready to become involved in a serious way again, and frankly, I'm not interested in anything less."

"I know. I don't blame you. Look," she said and leaned closer to me. "Luke was hurt by what happened, devastated for a while, but the fact that Jenna had been cheating on him for months destroyed anything he felt for her before. Seriously. He feels nothing for her any longer. He told me you must have seen her touching him, but believe me, he did not touch her. He hates her at this point."

"Honestly, it's not that. Really. It's that I realized there was no future for us and I didn't want to get hurt when he leaves for his trip."

She frowned. "You could still see each other. He told me he'd fly you to meet him any time you had a break from your classes. He's going to be even more ridiculously wealthy once the deal goes through."

I felt frustrated, unable to tell her that it was all a sham. That we were pretending and that it was because of her bastard of a husband that we met at all.

Instead, I had to make up excuses.

She told me all about Luke and Jenna, going over everything I already knew.

I shrugged, never having heard of the Marshall family before or Jenna's family. "I didn't read the gossip pages in the paper. I had no idea who Luke was when I first met him."

"He liked that about you. He's proud of our family business, and of his own business, but he was never about the celebrity. He always wanted to do something bigger than himself." She sighed. "It was Jenna's betrayal that convinced him that he could never trust a woman to be faithful. Especially considering the one woman he thought loved him had been secretly fucking her ex for months..." She raised her eyebrows. "He was devastated, and then he was really reclusive for a couple of months, keeping his head down, working hard on the startup."

"I can't imagine finding out she cheated on him a week before the wedding."

"Jenna wanted to get married. Her ex didn't want to get married. So, she decided to start seeing Luke again. But she never stopped loving her ex, I guess. How someone could betray the person they were going to marry, I'll never know."

When she said that, I felt incredibly guilty that I knew about Eric cheating on her with the real Lexi911. It made my throat constrict, and I wished I could tell her the truth. But what good would it do? She was not far from giving birth for the first time – something she didn't think she could ever do. Finding out Eric cheated on her with an escort would only ruin what should be one of the happiest and momentous times of her life.

Then she turned to me. "What about you? Luke said you had some drama in your past around a former boyfriend?"

I smiled, but felt incredibly reluctant to talk about Blaine. "Luke told you, did he?"

"We tell each other everything."

I pushed my food around on my plate, knowing that in fact they didn't tell each other everything. "Blaine and I started dating in high school. He was a few years older than me and became really controlling once he graduated. Because he was no longer in the halls at school, I guess he couldn't be sure I was being faithful to him. Things went downhill from there and I was too in love with him to see it. What I thought was affection and attachment was really a desire to control me, it was sick instead of a sign of love. You know, the same old story..."

I didn't tell her the part about Blaine stalking me, eventually abducting me, and holding me prisoner, or of me escaping and going to the police. I didn't mention that they arrested him and that he went to jail. Nor did I mention that he got out of jail and started stalking me again. I had to leave home and move away without telling anyone where I was going except my parents.

That part I'd rather not tell anyone. I hated even acknowledging it myself because it made me feel like such a bad judge of character. How I thought I still loved him when he started trying to control my every move. How I had been so wrong and realized it only too late.

She gave me a soft smile and then reached out to squeeze my arm. "I know that love can blind you to the flaws in your partner. Believe me, I know Eric's no saint. He's a man with flaws like every other man." She turned back to her plate of food and cut some bacon. "One thing my mother told me before she died was that if I wanted to have a happy marriage, I had to decide what to fight over and what to let slide."

I watched her for a moment, wondering if she had some inkling that Eric had cheated on her during her pregnancy. But I couldn't imagine that a woman would look the other way if she knew her husband was cheating on her.

"How do you decide what to fight over and what to let slide?"

She took a sip of water. "I want a family. Eric's given me that. As long as he's good to me and to our child, I'll accept his faults and flaws."

"What flaws does he have, if you don't mind me asking?"

She laughed softly. "Oh, he's a bit pompous. Well, a lot pompous, to tell the truth."

I didn't know what to say in response. He'd struck me as a bit of a snob, but he was rich, and that explained a lot.

"And, he's obsessed with appearances," she added. "He cares about labels, and good press. He's vain, always looking in the mirror and worried that he doesn't look good from behind." She gave me this wicked grin. "I know it's true. I love him anyway.

Besides, I have my flaws too. If Eric expected perfection in me, he'd be really disappointed."

I smiled at her, wishing that Eric would realize what a gem he had in Dana. "What flaws could you have?"

"Oh, believe me," she said and chewed on a piece of bacon. "I have my own faults. Both of us look the other way. That's how we stay together. I think a lot of couples expect perfection in each other. They're bound to be disappointed."

"But you wouldn't blame Luke for being upset that Jenna cheated on him with her ex?"

"Could you forgive someone for cheating?" She turned to me and looked me directly in the eye.

"No," I said. "Cheating, especially when you're married, is the worst. I couldn't forgive it."

"Research shows that thirty percent of people cheat at some point in their relationships."

She didn't say anything else and the two of us continued to eat our breakfasts. Did she know Eric had cheated on her?

It sounded like she was willing to forgive.

"Would you forgive Eric if you found out he cheated on you?"

She continued eating, not meeting my eyes. "It would depend on the circumstances, I guess. Men can have sex without caring about the person much more easily than women. At least, none of the women I know." She shrugged. "Usually, if a woman's cheating on her husband or boyfriend, it's because she's emotionally unhappy at home with her partner. When a man does, it means he's not getting enough sex and probably couldn't care less about the woman he's cheating with."

At that moment, it almost seemed as if she knew Eric had cheated on her after all. Maybe all this charade Luke and I had been involved in was for nothing.

"I couldn't imagine it," I said, not wanting to give anything away. "Finding out that my boyfriend or husband cheated on me."

"You have to decide what makes you happier. Being alone or being with someone."

"Being alone," I said. "I was with someone who tried to control my every move and every thought. When I escaped, I realized that I would rather be alone than be with someone who was that obsessive."

"Did he hit you?"

I shook my head. "No he choked me," I replied quietly. "He threatened me when we broke up. I got a restraining order." I didn't tell her the rest.

"I'm so sorry. I agree that in your case, it would be better to be alone than with someone like that."

We ate in silence for a few moments, and I thought it was one of the strangest conversations I'd ever had with someone I barely even knew. Dana was so open and so easy to talk to, it seemed almost natural for us to talk about anything, even things you would only normally talk about with your best friend.

We finished our meals and the talk turned to more mundane things like her pregnancy and plans for the baby and how she'd manage juggling work and being a new mother.

I enjoyed our talk and sharing a meal with her, regretting that we wouldn't become more than just accidental acquaintances. She told me so much about Luke, filling in bits and details about his life before and after their parents died. It made me regret even more that he and I could never be a real couple.

"Well, I better go. I'm meeting Eric for a pre-natal class at the hospital." We stood up and grabbed our bags, then walked out into the warm morning sunshine.

She squeezed me briefly. "Don't give up on my brother. He's

one of the good ones, and I'm not just saying that because I'm biased."

"Thanks for breakfast," I said and waved as she walked away.

I made my way back to my apartment, my hands stuffed into my hoodie, regret filling me that Luke would soon be going and would be out of my life completely.

It seemed so unfair for us to meet the way we did – so accidentally, and then for us to enjoy each other so much to our mutual surprise.

And to have to now say goodbye.

Life wasn't fair.

CHAPTER 20

Luke

The note sat on the coffee table.

I'd read it over several times, debating with myself whether to text Alexa and protest. Argue with her that we should keep seeing each other to see where this relationship went.

Instead, I texted Dana.

She always had good advice.

Her advice?

DANA: *Do you want to see her again? Do you want to sleep with her again? Do you want to cook her supper again and spend time on the beach with her again? Do you want her in your bed again? Do you want to wake up with her again? If you answered yes to all those questions, then for fuck's sake, don't let her go.*

Of course, I answered yes to each and every one of those questions.

LUKE: I do but she's right. Our lives are going on separate paths. There's no future for us, so why get more involved?

DANA: You can always change plans.

I didn't respond. I wasn't going to change my plans. My cat was almost finished, and it made me incredibly sad to imagine not going on my trip around the world. To me, it was the one thing I couldn't change. I could delay it if there were problems with the deal going through, but I couldn't not go.

At the same time, I felt this deep-seated knot of something in my chest at the prospect of not seeing Alexa again.

Why couldn't I have it all?

I didn't text Alexa. Instead, I went for a run. I needed to work up a sweat and clear my mind. After I had a shower and cooled off, I spent the afternoon at the office, going over last-minute changes in the presentation we were going to make to the buyers. I outlined our projections for the next year and detailed how much the company had grown over the previous years.

It was pretty much a done deal, but we had to cross all the T's and dot all the I's before we could sign final papers. The other investors had to go to their own investors and justify the price they were going to offer. We had to make sure the deal was worth the dollar amount that was floated as a way to tempt us into taking their offer.

The fact that Felicia's brother Harrison had been one of the investors had worried me at first, but after he expressed concerns, the others convinced him to stay and things were back on track.

Thankfully...

After spending the afternoon going over the presentation, I went for a drink at a local pub with John, during which time we discussed the deal and the trip.

"So," he said, his eyes narrowed. "What's up with you and Alexa?"

I took a drink of my beer and considered John. His expression was far too interested.

"We broke it off. Or should I say, she did."

"What?" he said with a frown. "What happened? I thought for sure the two of you were going to get together..."

I shrugged. "How could we? I'm leaving and she's starting her PhD in a couple of weeks."

"So what? You can still see each other. She can fly to meet us when she can. You like her," he said and thumped his palm on the tabletop. "I know it. More than any other woman you've been with since Jenna."

"You and Dana seemed determined to match me up with her."

"Dana and I are smart cookies. You like her. More than usual."

I didn't respond.

He was right. But it was unlikely that we could make it work. Why cause each other needless pain? The closer we got, the more it would hurt when the time came to say goodbye.

"Enough with the matchmaking. Things are over between us. We've got other things to worry about, like the sale of Chatter and the Phoenix build."

"Yeah, yeah, yeah," John said and took a drink of his beer. "Whatever. You'll regret it if you let things slide with her. And that's all I'm saying."

He stood up. "Another beer?"

I nodded. "Hit me."

Then, he and I proceeded to get drunk.

It wasn't like I was drowning my sorrows.

Really...

The next day was just another day in my ordinary life leading up to the deal of the century and the trip of a lifetime.

By all accounts, I should have been the happiest I had ever been in my life – other than when I was engaged but blissfully ignorant of my fiancée's cheating on me...

Thing was, I wasn't happy. I was preoccupied at best, my mind filled with numbers and details. Even though I was trying to concentrate on the presentation, I felt this sense of gloom hanging over me, like everything I was doing was merely a distraction from what was really bothering me.

I shoved that out of my mind and tried to focus on the business at hand. John sat on a chair across from my desk, flipping through some papers, rearranging the hand-outs for the presentation to make sure they were in the right order.

"Are you ready for this?" He gave me a look from under a frown.

"Of course," I replied. "Do you doubt it?"

"You seem distracted."

"I'm totally present. I have the presentation memorized. I'm your man. The investors will be putty in my hands."

"I hope so. Blow them away, my friend. I want to see those big numbers roll into my bank account and the sooner they appear there, the sooner you and I can blow this popsicle stand."

My admin Stella buzzed my intercom, letting us know the investors had arrived and so we gathered our materials and joined them in the boardroom. After a round of handshakes and light banter about the weather and the latest ball game we got down to business.

For the next hour, I walked them through the business, the organizational structure, the business plan we'd drafted when we started, our balance sheet, the number of subscribers, our ad revenues and our share of the lucrative social media market.

Harrison sat at the far end of the table, watching as I went through the charts and tables on our financials, and the projections based on the past quarter's performance. I had to admit the presentation went smoothly. Questions were smart, and I answered them with ease. I knew my stuff and had a great product to sell, with a serious earning potential and room to grow the market.

They'd be foolish not to jump at the chance to buy Chatter and they knew it.

"If you have no more questions, I'd like to thank you for your interest in Chatter. Please, feel free to contact us with any further questions. We'll be glad to answer them."

Another round of handshakes followed and we walked them to the elevators and said goodbyes.

Harrison hung back, and waited for the next elevator.

"I was really impressed with your presentation," he said and clapped me on the back. "I had some second thoughts, but you've done a great job with Chatter and I'm feeling pretty confident that the deal will go through with no further problems."

"That's good to know," I said and we shook hands once more.

He took the elevator and as soon as the doors closed, I heaved a sigh of relief. When I turned around, John had this huge grin on his face.

"You did it," he said and high-fived me. "They seemed really impressed with the presentation and Q&A. I think we have a deal."

"I think we do as well," I said and felt adrenaline surge through me. "We should hear back in twenty-four hours. That was our deadline."

He nodded. "Let's go get a beer. It's time to celebrate."

I smiled. "Let me grab my cell. I'll meet you downstairs in the lobby."

He left and I went back to my office to grab my phone off the desk where I'd left it.

I sat on my sofa and read a text from Dana.

DANA: *What's up, o brother of mine? How did the presentation go?*

LUKE: *Looks like we have a deal.*

DANA: **Squee* We should all go out and celebrate once you sign. Bring Alexa. Our treat.*

LUKE: *Alexa and I aren't seeing each other any longer.*

There was a pause.

DANA: *Luke, she's a gem. She really likes you but is afraid of having her heart broken when you leave on your trip. She's a keeper. You're nuts if you let her slip through your fingers.*

I held my cell, re-reading her messages, then reading all my texts from Alexa again, for the third time that morning.

LUKE: *I'm going away for a year. I would only be able to see her now and then when she has vacation and I'm in port. Things don't look very good for anything more serious.*

That was it, really. I had plans. Alexa had plans. Our plans didn't mesh.

DANA: *Ask her to come with you.*

I frowned. Ask Alexa to come on the trip with me?

I had to admit my mind went there a few times. She and I could share the main bedroom. There was still enough bed space for the other guys, but they might not appreciate having a woman along on the journey.

Could I ask Alexa to come with me? Would she? She'd have to take a leave of absence and I doubted she'd want to do that, considering she was accepted into the PhD for the fall.

Sailing around the world was a once-in-a-lifetime thing. It was something you changed plans to do.

LUKE: *You're crazy.*

DANA: *You've already thought about it. Confess, brother. I know you...*

I laughed at that. She was right, of course.

LUKE: *You do know me.*

DANA: *See? I knew you really like her. I knew you were already thinking of asking her to come. *does the happy dance**

LUKE: *Don't be dancing too soon. Just because I passed the thought briefly over in my mind doesn't mean it's a plan. She might say no. She has big plans for her life you know.*

DANA: *Is the sex good?*

LUKE: *DANA!!! You pervert. I'm your brother.*

DANA: *Don't ask her if the sex isn't good.*

LUKE: *The sex isn't good. It's fucking great.*

DANA: *Ask her. She'll say yes. DO IT!*

I couldn't wipe a grin off my face. Yeah, the sex was great. It was fantastic. She was very responsive. She clearly enjoyed me. I couldn't get enough of her. But it was more than sex. I felt totally comfortable with her, like I knew her for years instead of less than a month.

The truth was, I had thought about asking her to come with me on my trip around the world. I wanted to see her response to all the places we'd go – The Panama Canal. The Galapagos. Tahiti. And all the other places I planned to visit.

I could talk to her about everything. She was as smart – if not smarter – than most of my male friends. And she was fun. She was playful.

Fact was, if I admitted it to myself, she was everything I could want in a woman.

Beautiful. Sexy. Voluptuous. Great in bed. Smart. Funny. Fun. Ambitious.

Goddamn...

What I really wanted was to text Alexa and get her to meet me at the pub for a drink with John so we could celebrate. I wanted to go out and dance with her and then I wanted to take her home and fuck her brains out all night long. I wanted to wake her up with my mouth on her pussy, and watch her writhe in delight the way I had that first night we were together.

I wanted to imagine her putting her plans on hold and planning the trip with me and the places we would visit. I could see her standing on the cat, holding onto a mast and enjoying the wind through her hair, wearing only a tiny bikini...

Crap.

LUKE: Just finished the presentation to the investor group that wants to buy Chatter. I think it went well. John and I are going out for a drink at Mulligan's. We'll be there at five thirty. I know we said we'd end things, but I would really love to see you, have you celebrate with us.

Then I slid my cell into my jacket pocket and left the office.

CHAPTER 21

ALEXA

I spent the day lazing around the apartment, feeling listless. I had thought I might spend time at the beach house with Luke and looked forward to pretending to be his girlfriend for a while, getting in as much sun and surf as I could before classes started later in the month.

Truthfully, I was also looking forward to spending time in Luke's bed. I was starting to get too attached to Luke. He felt too much like someone I could be with for the longer term, but he was leaving and I was staying behind.

I finally grew so restless that I had to leave the apartment, distract myself from my funk. Candy was at the library doing some research. I didn't want to be alone, so I decided to get out of the house and take a long bike ride along the Hudson.

Riding along the bike path skirting the Hudson, from our apartment close to Columbia down to Hell's Kitchen and back, would do the trick. I stopped and sat on a bench for a while, watching the joggers and pedestrians while the seagulls wheeled overhead. It was a beautiful day in Manhattan – late summer, the air was cooler than it had been in July and the sky was crystal clear.

I should have been happy. I'd passed my comps, I had two weeks off before my fall classes started and I was on track for getting my PhD in a few years.

Despite it all, I wished I'd never opened that email.

When I arrived back about an hour later, I walked up the stairs to our apartment after returning my bike to the locker in the building's basement. When I got to the top floor, the door was open and I frowned because it wasn't like Candy to leave it open. Maybe she was taking the garbage out and didn't want to take her keys. As I got closer, I saw that the lock had been broken, the wood torn, the frame partly broken off. I tiptoed inside and put down my backpack, only to find a hole punched into the plaster wall in the entrance.

It was then I got a surge of adrenaline and stopped in my tracks.

"Candy?"

I took a step closer and glanced around the apartment. Everything seemed in place, and the apartment was empty from what I could see.

"Candy? Are you here?"

I went down the hallway and saw that the main bathroom door was closed.

"Candy? Are you in there?" I put my hand on the knob and tried to open it, but it was locked.

Her voice came from inside. "Is that you?"

It was Candy, her voice sounding terrified.

"Yes," I replied. "What happened? Why is there a hole in the wall?"

The door opened and she came out, peering around the door like she was afraid.

"He was here," she said and went to the front entrance, glancing out. "The police should be here any moment."

"What? What happened?"

She took hold of me. "Blaine."

The blood drained out of my face and I felt dizzy. I sat down on the sofa, grabbing the arm rest, feeling like the world was spinning around me.

"Blaine?" I said, feeling numb. "How did he find me?"

She sat beside me, her arm around my shoulder. "I have no idea but he knows you live here. He threatened me. He said he'd find you, no matter where you went."

"Oh, *God*," I said, my throat choking up with emotion, tears finally overflowing. I covered my eyes. "How? How could he find me?"

"He said he made friends with the registrar at the University and knew where you got your transcripts sent. He searched my name and found me."

"What?"

Just then, we heard noise coming from the stairway outside the apartment. Two police officers appeared and knocked on the open door.

"Thank God you're here," Candace said and went to the door.

For the next hour, the two police officers took Candace's statement and all the information about Blaine from me. On my part, I tried to remain coherent, but I'd always felt so safe in Manhattan and to have that safety threatened crushed me.

"He did this?" the one officer, Constable Daley asked. He examined the hole in the plaster and turned to Candace.

"Yes," she said. "I told him that Alexa had moved away, but he found some of her things and punched the wall."

We discussed our options. While I had a restraining order against Blaine in Oregon, it wasn't in effect in New York state, so I'd have to get another one if I hoped to keep him away from me now that he knew where I lived.

"Everything was going so well," I said with a sob after the police had left and Candace and I were alone once more. "Why did this have to happen now? I can't stand the thought Blaine will be hanging around, stalking me again. It's been two years of peace since we came here."

She put her arms around me and hugged me, letting me cry on her shoulder.

"I called home after he left. My mom said he just got fired from his job," Candy said. "I guess that set him off. He obviously hasn't gotten over it."

"What are we going to do? I can't stay here," I said, glancing around. "He'll come back."

"You could stay at a hotel."

"I can't afford a hotel..."

"There's a student hostel you could stay at in a pinch."

I took out my phone, intending to call the hostel and see if there was a room available and saw that there was a message from Luke.

I read it over, surprised that he'd texted me.

LUKE: *Just finished the presentation to the investor group that wants to buy Chatter. I think it went well. John and I are going out for a drink at Mulligan's. We'll be there at five thirty. I know we said we'd end things, but I would really love to see you, have you celebrate with us.*

I handed my cell to Candy. "I got a text from Luke."

She read it over. "I knew it. He really likes you, sweets. You should go and stay with him."

"I couldn't."

"You sure as hell could. Tell him what happened. I'm sure he'd let you stay."

I looked in her eyes. "What about you? I can't leave you alone."

She shrugged. "I'll go stay with Jan for a few days until the cops find Blaine."

"Should I text Luke?"

"Yes. Do it. I'll call the landlord and get him to come and fix the lock. Then, I'll call Jan and make arrangements to stay there. You stay with Luke."

I hesitated, but then I decided to send him a text.

ALEXA: I know this is completely out of the blue but something happened and I need a place to stay. Can I stay with you tonight until I can get a room at the hostel? I'll explain later.

I sent the text off while Candy called Jan and talked to her about staying at her place for a few days. While she talked, I went to my bedroom and pulled a few things into my backpack – underwear, my nightgown, my makeup and toothbrush, and a few other personal effects. If Luke didn't want me to stay with him, I could stay at the hostel if they had a bed or in a hotel room, at worst.

My cell dinged.

When I saw it was from Luke, my stomach jumped.

LUKE: Of course. Can I come and get you? I'll be right there.

I responded right away.

ALEXA: Thanks. I'm really sorry about this.

LUKE: No problem. We can go out for a drink with John like I planned.

ALEXA: That sounds really good right now. I feel like I need a whole keg myself.

LUKE: That bad? What happened?

ALEXA: I'll tell you when you get here.

LUKE: I'll see you in fifteen.

Candy came back into the living room from the kitchen, where she grabbed a bottle of water from the refrigerator.

"You're looking better," she said and plopped down on the sofa beside me. "Did you hear from Luke? Tell me everything."

I nodded, wiping away the last of my tears. "Luke's coming to pick me up."

"I knew it," she said and held up her hand. "High five!"

"Candy! How can you be like that at a time like this?"

She grinned. "I love a good love story with a happy ending."

"There's no happy ending."

"Yet," she said and smiled.

Despite everything, despite the hole in the wall and the fact my violent ex ex-con of a boyfriend had found me, I couldn't help but smile back.

I grabbed my bag when my cell dinged and I saw that Luke was outside the building.

"I don't want to leave you here," I said, standing at the door.

"I'll go as soon as Mr. Johnston comes to fix the door. You go with Luke. I'll get a taxi as soon as the lock's fixed."

"If you're okay about it," I said, feeling bad that I was leaving her.

"You go. Relax. Have fun," she said and walked me down the stairs to the lobby.

"How did Blaine get inside the building?" Candy asked when we went to the door at the entrance. "Someone had to let him in."

"Probably Mrs. Frankenstein. I bet she left the door wedged open again."

"Yeah, I bet."

Mrs. Frankenstein, as we dubbed her, was really Mrs. Feinstein, but she looked like Lurch in The Addam's Family. She had a bad habit of putting a piece of cardboard in the back door so she could leave and have a smoke without bringing her keys along. I cursed her because she often forgot to take the piece of cardboard out, putting us all in danger. We'd complained to the building manager but nothing had changed.

Blaine would have found me either way. It was probably better that he came in when he did – when I wasn't there. I feared he would have hurt me if I had been in the apartment. That hole in the wall was probably a substitute for my face. Luckily, Candy had hidden in the bathroom when she realized who was at the door and scared him off by telling him she'd called the police or he might have hurt her as well.

She gave me a hug.

"Text me as soon as you get to Jan's, okay?"

"I will."

She waved at Luke, who hopped out of his car and opened the door for me, taking my backpack.

"Your steed, m'lady," Luke said as I got in the passenger side.

When he got in the other side and fastened his seat belt, I looked over and I realized just how glad I was to see him. He was casually dressed, wearing a pair of carpenter pants, a white cotton button down shirt, and a pair of dark aviator sunglasses, and I was struck once more by how gorgeous he looked.

He pulled his glasses down and looked me in the eyes. "What happened?"

"I'll tell you later," I said and leaned back, closing my eyes.

"Now, or I'm not driving."

I glanced at him and sighed in resignation. "My ex."

"What? Blaine?"

I nodded, and at that moment, all the anxiety and fear seemed to come back, completely out of my control and my eyes teared up.

"What happened? Did he hurt you?"

I shook my head and glanced way, slipping on my sunglasses, not wanting him to see my tears.

"He broke down the door to our apartment and punched a hole in the wall when he found out I wasn't there," I said, my voice wobbly. "Luckily, Candace locked herself in the bathroom and he left without doing anything worse. I was out riding my bike so he missed me by about five minutes."

He reached out and stroked my cheek.

"I'm so sorry," he said and leaned in. "Of course you can stay with me. As long as you need. We could go to the beach house, if you like."

"Thank you. I'd really like that."

Then he kissed me. It felt so sweet and tender that my emotions overflowed and I kissed him back more passionately, so thankful that he understood and was willing to help.

When he pulled back, he wiped a tear from my cheek.

"Whatever you need," he said. "You only have to ask."

We drove off, and he took my hand and squeezed. Even that show of tenderness touched me.

I sighed and watched the streets of Manhattan slide by.

CHAPTER 22

LUKE

We drove to my apartment because I wanted to pick up a few clothes and personal effects before we met John and then drove to the beach house. Alexa needed to escape the city and the beach house was perfect. Her ex had no idea we were together, and so he would have no idea where she was. The beach house also had great security so if, for some reason, he discovered that Alexa had been seeing me, and somehow found out about the beach house, we'd be forewarned and could call the local security company that monitored the property.

"Come inside while I get a few things for the beach house," I said and parked in the parking garage down the street. "I'll only be a few minutes and then we can go meet John if you feel up to it. If not, we can stay here. John will understand."

"No, please, we should go," Alexa said and took my hand. "You two deserve to celebrate and I need a distraction from what happened."

He smiled softly. "If you're sure. Maybe it would be good to have a drink, relax."

We walked down the street to the brownstone and I let us in, opening the door, admitting us into the cool interior. She wandered around the apartment while I went to my bedroom and pulled a few items of clothes into a duffle bag, then I went to the bathroom and grabbed my shaving kit, stuffing my things inside.

When I returned to the living room, duffle bag in hand, she was standing in the middle of the room, looking at her cell.

"What's up?"

She glanced at me and I saw there were tears in her eyes. "I called my mom, but there's no answer. Now I'm worried that Blaine did something to them. I know it's crazy, but she usually texts me right away or calls me back."

"I'm sorry," I said and pulled her into my arms. "I had no idea he was so dangerous. I'm sure they're okay and she's just busy. She'll call or text right away."

"I didn't think he'd find me," she said, a catch in her voice. "I thought he had to notify the sheriff when he left the county. I don't know why they didn't call my parents and let them know."

"That sucks," I said and stroked her cheek, wiping away her tears. "You'll be safe with me at the beach house. It has great security and a team can be there in five minutes if we need them. I'm sure he has no idea you even know me, so we can relax."

She finally smiled up through her tears. "I won't be able to relax until I hear from her."

"Shh," I said, embracing her in my arms, trying to comfort her. I was sure her family was fine and that it was just a temporary lapse on her mother's part. I hugged her more tightly, stroking her hair, her body warm against mine. One thing led to another, and our mouths found each other in a tender kiss.

Of course, my body responded immediately, my cock hardening from the feel of her breasts crushed against my chest, her tongue finding mine. She slipped her arms around my neck and pressed against my growing erection and although it pleasantly surprised me that she was getting aroused when she was still so upset, I wasn't going to fight.

Sometimes pleasure was the only thing that could wash away pain.

I continued to kiss her, my hands finding her breast over top of her sweater, cupping it, squeezing it before slipping lower to caress her hip. I pulled her against me, wanting her to know how hard I was and how much I needed her.

I broke the kiss and pulled her to the stairs and my bedroom.

"But John..."

I shook my head. "John's a big boy. He can wait. I can't."

She smiled at that, and that smile told me that she didn't want to wait either.

I led her up the stairs, my heart rate increasing at the prospect of a quick hard fuck – something I needed and that she needed as well. As soon as I got her in the bedroom, I pushed her down onto the bed and began to strip her clothes off, enjoying every moment of it, revealing more and more skin with each motion.

Her breasts were spectacular and I couldn't get enough of them, lavishing my attention on each one, my teeth soft on her nipples, nipping them into hard points. She groaned and squirmed beneath me, her arousal making my dick jump in response.

"I just went for a long bike ride and I'm all sweaty," she said, pushing me away. "I need a shower."

I kissed her belly, which was glorious, and ran my tongue around her navel. "You taste fine to me."

"Please," she said and struggled under me. "Just a quick shower. I won't be able to relax unless I do."

"I don't want you to relax. I want you all aroused and needy."

She smiled, her eyes closed. "I am all aroused and needy. But I also need a shower."

Then, she rolled under me and managed to get away, slipping off the bed and running to the bathroom, giggling as she did.

I followed her, stripping off my clothes, and by the time I was completely naked, she was in the shower and the water was running. I got in behind her, glad I spent the extra cash to get a two-person stall with a rain shower head. Within moments, we were both drenched, and she had a bar of soap out. We lathered our hands and began to wash each other, our hands slipping and sliding over the other's body, into every crack and crevice.

She giggled when I ran my soapy hands down her back and pulled her against me, but she became all dreamy eyed when I slipped my soapy fingers between her thighs. She paid extra attention to my erect cock, and I groaned in delight as she ran her soapy fingers around the crown.

We rinsed off and I couldn't wait, kneeling and kissing my way down her belly to her mound. I lifted one thigh over my shoulder and ate her, my tongue finding her clit and licking firmly, fingers slipping inside of her body to stroke her. She ran her fingers through my hair, rewarding me with a groan when I sucked the nub. I worked her up for a few moments, but I wanted her to come on my cock.

"Wait here. I have to get a condom," I said and left the shower, dripping all over the floor to my bedroom. I found a condom in my nightstand and slipped it on, then went back to the shower.

Once back in the shower, I lifted her up, positioning her just right so I could bury myself inside her hot wet tightness.

"Do you want it?" I said, rubbing my cock against her clit.

"Yes," she replied. "Fuck me now."

I did, sliding in deep, groaning at how tight she was and how intense it felt to be completely inside her once again. She gripped my shoulders as I began to thrust harder and soon, she gasped and I knew she was there. My movements were slow and steady through her orgasm, enjoying how she lost control, her eyes almost rolling up in her head, her jaw slack, her nipples hardening.

Watching her come on my cock sent me over and I thrust harder, faster, my orgasm starting, my own body tensing as I found my release. Pulse after pulse of white pleasure almost blinding me as I came.

I slowed my movements when it became too intense and simply leaned against her, her back against the wall, both of us breathing heavily.

"Fuck that was good."

I glanced at her face and she was smiling. "It was too good."

"Never. It could never be too good."

I kissed her and we remained like that for a few moments, the water still running, cascading over my back.

Finally, I pulled out of her and removed my condom, tying it off and throwing it into the trash can beside the toilet. When we finished rinsing, I turned off the water and we both dried each other off.

"I better text John and tell him we'll be right there or he might leave." I took my own cell and sent off a quick text to John.

LUKE: *Sorry bud, but I'm running late. Had to pick up Alexa and we had some business to take care of first.*

He texted right back.

JOHN: *Yeah, I can only imagine what business you had to take care of. BASTARD! Get down here. I'm already half-drunk.*

I grinned and showed Alexa the texts.

She smiled. "I feel guilty that we made him wait."

"We didn't make him wait too long. Damn, girl. You were fast."

"So were you."

I laughed. "I needed you."

"I needed you, too."

I kissed her again once more.

Alexa went to her pile of clothes on the floor and went through her bag for her cell. She checked her messages and smiled. "Look," she said and held her cell up for me to read. "It's my mom. Everything's fine. She was just out in the garden and didn't get my text until now."

"That's great. I told you she'd text you." I read it over, a twinge of envy that she had such a close relationship with her mother and father. I pulled her against me. "I'm so sorry this happened to you. You'll be safe with me at the beach house. The cops will find Blaine and you'll get a new restraining order. You'll see."

She sighed and leaned her head against my shoulder. "I hate that he knows where I am. I feel like I have to leave, go somewhere else to do my PhD."

"You can't do that," I said, frowning at the thought the bastard was going to derail her plans. Of course, it was then that my brain went there.

There.

I remembered my conversation with Dana.

She could come with me.

To French Polynesia. Tahiti. Australia. South Africa. Back home again. She could sail around the world with me, the way I didn't let myself imagine before.

Now, I could imagine it. I could see her lying on the hammock at the front of my catamaran, dressed in a tiny bikini, her skin tanned, her hair bleached in the sun...

"Come with me. Sail around the world with me."

She glanced up, her brow furrowed. "Are you serious?"

"Never been more serious," I said, my conviction that this was the right decision growing stronger with every passing moment. "Come with me. Sail as far as you want. Stop when you want. You can take a leave of absence from your PhD. I'm sure if you really want, you could go anywhere and do your PhD at any school."

"I don't know what to say," she said, her voice soft.

"Say yes," I replied. "I know it's sudden, but I've been thinking of it for a while now. I know our start was," I said and smiled, "unconventional, but now I don't want to lose you. I want to see the world with you. John is great, but you're special."

"It's a huge decision."

"I know, but if you have to change graduate schools, if you have to move away, why not take some time, see the world, and make a decision that isn't rushed? You're young. One year won't make a difference in the bigger picture."

She looked in my eyes. "You're serious about this? You really want me to come with you? I've never sailed before. We've only known each other for such a short time ..."

"Some things are meant to be. I feel like I know you better than most people I've known for years."

She smiled. "It never felt like an act for me."

I shook my head. "Me neither. At least, I wished it wasn't."

I kissed her again, deeply, pulling her tightly against me. "Come sail with me and be my love."

She smiled, recognizing my riff on a poem by the sixteenth-century poet Christopher Marlowe.

"You know Marlowe. Color me impressed."

"I'm impressed you recognized it. Don't be too impressed with me. It's the only poem I know so you better appreciate it." I grinned and kissed her again. "I had to memorize it when I took an English Lit class in High School. We thought it was a joke back then, but I understand it completely now." I stroked her cheek. "Come with me."

"I'll think about it," she said and played with my collar. "I have to make arrangements..."

"We have time. You'll stay with me at the beach house until the cat is done and we have all the details ironed out. Then, we'll sail off into the sunset."

"It sounds like a dream." She met my eyes. "Are you sure?"

"I'm completely sure. You know what? My sister suggested it to me when I was feeling down because it didn't seem like we were going to be together. She knew even then we were right for each other."

"She really wanted us to be together. You know she and I had breakfast together that morning after I left."

"You did? She didn't say anything. Sneaky..." I smiled, thinking about Dana contacting Alexa, trying to encourage her to continue to see me. "So, you'll come with me? Leave all your cares behind and sail the world with me?"

"As what? What will I be to you? You said yourself that you're not the type to be exclusive to anyone."

"I know what I said. I want you to be my real girlfriend." I stroked her hair, her cheek. "The performance is over. Now, it's real."

She sighed and kissed me. When she pulled back, our eyes met.

"I will."

We kissed once more and embraced and I knew then what I had known all along, somewhere in the back of my consciousness.

She was the one – the one who could bring me back to the world I once believed in and which I feared would never be mine again.

CHAPTER 23

ALEXA

I spent two weeks with Luke at the beach house while the Chatter sale was finalized and police tracked down Blaine. When they found him, they charged him with first degree aggravated harassment due to the threats he made to Candy and the damage to the apartment. Because he was on full parole, he didn't have to go back to Oregon and could stay in New York while his case was being prosecuted. The District Attorney's office drew up an order of protection on him.

It was great to know he couldn't come within one hundred yards of me or the apartment, so Candace could move back in. I'd keep paying my share of the rent while Luke and I were gone, in case I wanted to return early. I had no idea if sailing was my thing, being more of a landlubber, as Luke called me, so I wanted to have a place to land.

I didn't think I'd need it, but it was a second home for me if and when I needed or wanted it. At that point in our relationship, I didn't want to imagine us separating, but I had to be realistic – we had only known each other for a very short time. Although we both felt the same – that we wanted to be together – there was no way to know for sure we would for the long term.

When we got to the beach house, Luke sent the cook home and we had the entire place to ourselves. The only staff were the groundskeeper who mowed the lawn and tended the pool, and the housekeeper, who came every other day to do various cleaning jobs. It was amazing to spend time in the huge house, having it all to ourselves.

We christened every room in the place, making love wherever and whenever the mood struck, which it did – often. When we weren't having sex, we spent most of our time in the living room at night, or on the porch or beach during the day.

Candy came out to the beach house for the weekend before we set sail for our first big stop – Miami and then south to Key West and on to Havana. After a short stay in Cuba, we'd sail farther south to Panama and go through the Canal before heading out to the Galapagos and the South Pacific.

I still couldn't believe it, and often stopped to mentally pinch myself, especially when I woke up in the morning with Luke naked beside me in bed, his arm thrown over his eyes, his glorious body on display for me and me alone.

My mom and dad were planning to fly to Miami and spend a few days there with us so we could visit and they could meet this 'new man,' as my father called him, before we left the US. My father was happy that I had someone new, and the fact that Luke was one of the wealthiest men under thirty in the country didn't hurt. Fathers always worry about their daughters being taken care of, or so he said, so the fact that Luke could most definitely take care of me – if I needed it – was a relief to him. I told him that was terribly sexist, and that he wouldn't be worried about his son's girlfriend being able to look after him.

"Yeah, I'm a dinosaur, I admit it," my father said on the phone when we made plans. "You're my little girl and there's nothing that can change that. I don't want to think the guy you're with can't support you if you needed it."

"He can more than support her, dear," my mother said in the background. "And she can more than look after herself without him, and has for the past two years."

My mother understood how important it was for me to be independent. I could still be independent, because I could always come back at any time. My scholarship would still be there. I could delay my PhD for a couple of years if I needed, so I had a cushion of time in which to finish. That gave me the freedom to decide to go with Luke on the trip, but even if I didn't have that leeway, I knew if I got a scholarship to Columbia, I could go to most any university in the country and work on a PhD.

The day before the Phoenix was finished, we drove to the Alpha Yachts and took a tour of the cat and I got to see exactly where I'd spend my next six months to a year. The cat was large enough for four passengers comfortably with the ability to sleep six in a pinch on a fold down bed.

I'd thrown a monkey wrench in the plans for the trip but Luke would not stand any grumbling from the guys about my presence. I think they must have understood that Luke was serious about it and so if they resented my presence on the trip, they were quiet about it.

In fact, we all spent the weekend before the trip getting to know one another, spending time around a bonfire on the beach, or sitting at the large al fresco table on the beach house's porch, running through the trip itinerary, and what we would be responsible for. I offered to do all the cooking and cleaning, with the exception of any specialized meals the other guys were expert at preparing. Each of the four guys would do a six-hour watch so that the entire day was covered. Luke and I would do a watch together, only because I didn't trust myself to do a watch on my own.

I wasn't a seasoned sailor like the others.

The day of the big launch came, and we were all really excited. The guys spent the night at the beach house and even Candy came out for the launch. We woke early that morning, the sunlight streaming in, waking us up at five o'clock.

I glanced over at Luke and marveled at how intense our relationship had become so quickly. Since we decided to be a couple, I couldn't get enough of him and it seemed he of me. On the trip, we wouldn't have the freedom we had at the beach house, but we'd find a way. I thought it would make our encounters, such as they were, even more special since we would have to wait until we were alone and things were quiet or the guys were off on some excursion on land. We did have a bedroom on the cat that had a door so we could fool around if we wanted, but we'd have to be discreet, and quiet.

"If they hear us, neither of us will hear the end of it. They'll be merciless, so keep that in mind when I drive you wild with passion," Luke said with a grin.

I'd become so used to being able to say and do whatever we both felt like, it would be restrictive, but at this point, I couldn't imagine saying goodbye to Luke while he went away for a year at this point.

That last morning, Luke rolled over on top of me, and took my hands in his, his 'morning wood,' as he liked to call it, a pleasant hardness against my groin.

"Are you ready for this?" he asked, a gleam in his eye.

I pretended to act innocent. "For the trip?"

"You know what I mean," he said and began kissing my neck and throat, his scruff making me giggle.

"I'm always ready for you," I said, closing my eyes as his mouth moved lower.

It was the truth.

After a quick breakfast of eggs, bacon and toast, fresh squeezed juice and coffee, the six of us, including Candy, drove to Patchogue and Alpha Yachts to pick up the cat.

My stomach was all butterflies as we parked in the lot and removed our gear. There was a lot to do to get ready, including stocking the galley with food, getting all our gear stowed and taking the cat on its maiden run.

"I have the bottle of Champagne," Luke said and held up a bottle of Dom Pérignon we'd bought especially for the trip. "We can christen her before we cast off."

After speaking with the owners of Alpha Yachts and getting the keys, the six of us went to the launch where the cat was moored and Luke and I did the honors while Candy and the other guys, John, Andy and Ted, watched.

"I christen thee The Phoenix," Luke said. He popped the cork and poured us each a plastic cup of champagne. We raised a glass to each other and then Luke and I poured the rest of the bottle of Dom over the hull.

The time came for us to cast off and I had to say goodbye to Candy. I felt a bit teary eyed at leaving her behind, but with

Blaine safely in lockup, I felt comfortable that at least she'd be safe at the apartment alone. I offered to let her sublet my room to another student if she felt nervous, and she thought she might if she became too lonely.

"Have a great time," she said, hugging me tightly, both of us with wet eyes. "I'm so happy for you that finally, you found someone good. You can put the past behind you. Luke's great. He's a keeper."

"He is," I said and wiped my eyes. "Now it's up to you to find someone. What about that bagel shop guy? Is he a candidate?"

She grinned. "We'll see. His name is Zach and I'm seeing him this Saturday night. We're going to see the Rocky Horror Picture Show and if he dresses up, I'll know he's my type."

"I hope so."

We hugged once more and then I followed Luke to the cat and stepped on board. The cat was big enough that I felt secure on it and I watched while the guys cast off and Luke gunned the motors to pull out of the slip.

"Goodbye!" Candy called out as we drew further and further away.

I waved and watched as she grew smaller and smaller.

Finally, I turned and watched as we pulled out of the narrow channel leading away from Patchogue and started our journey.

"Come here," Luke said and waved me over. I went to his side and he pulled me against his body. "I'm so glad you're with me. When we met, you were just a way to teach my brother-in-law a lesson but you've become the love of my life. I had no idea how important you'd become to me."

"Me, either," I replied, a surge of emotion making me choke up. I leaned my face up for a kiss. When we pulled apart, I reached up and brushed his bangs out of his dreamy blue eyes. "You were a great story I was going to tell my girlfriends at Sunday brunch. I had no idea you'd become the love of *my* life."

He smiled and then turned back, one arm around my waist, the other hand on the wheel, steering the cat for open waters.

EPILOGUE

LUKE

Pape'ete, Tahiti

Six months.

That was all it took.

By the time we got to Pape'ete, Tahiti, I knew without a doubt that I wanted to spend the rest of my life with her.

Six months of knowing each other, a little over four of being together in close quarters day in and day out, tells you a lot and I knew all I needed to know about her – as a person, as a partner, as a lover.

Well, the lover part I knew would be even better once we were back on dry land and had the full freedom to explore each other without three other guys watching over us with jealous expressions in their eyes. As a result, we took every opportunity to stay in a hotel for a couple of nights at various ports just to be completely alone.

Now, while we were in Pape'ete for a few days, we sent the two remaining crew members, Andy and Ted, into the town to stay at a local motel on the beach so we could spend the night alone on the cat. John flew back to Manhattan earlier in the day to be with his mother after she discovered she had cancer and would be undergoing radiation treatment. He didn't want to miss any time with her because it was a late stage and she might only have six months to live.

So, as sad as I felt that he would be ending his time on the voyage, I understood completely.

That night, after we said goodbye to John, I had special plans and wanted to be alone with Alexa on the cat, in our anchorage for the night. With the guys in town, we were by ourselves, finally, and so we went about our routine of anchoring the cat, then we prepared a meal, grilling some fresh fish we'd bought at the market in town, along with beautiful baguette and salad. We sat at the table and ate, enjoying the quiet, talking about the future, the only sound that of the water lapping against the cat's twin hulls, and the occasional cry of a seabird flying overhead.

After we finished our meal, I opened a bottle of wine and we lay together on the forward trampoline, pillows behind our heads, and watched the sun set over the open ocean. Once the stars began to appear and after we found all the stars we knew of in the Southern Cross, I took her glass of wine out of her hand and rolled over on top of her. She smiled, knowing what was coming next – or at least, she thought she knew.

"You enjoying yourself?" I asked, kissing her chin, her cheek, her neck. She giggled, because my beard had grown a bit scraggly and I hadn't yet trimmed it back to its normal three day's growth.

"You know I am. I've never been so happy."

"Me, neither." I kissed her, deeply, and right away, my body warmed to her touch and from the way she moved her hips beneath me, I knew hers did as well. When her hand moved lower, grabbing my butt suggestively, I smiled.

"Not so fast," I said and pulled away. "I have other plans for tonight."

She frowned at first, but couldn't hide a smile on her lips. "What? What are you planning? I thought as soon as we were alone, you'd be all over me."

"Usually I would but tonight is special."

She nodded. She knew what I meant. It had been exactly six months to the day since I sent her that errant email that started everything between us.

"Six months," she said. "Who could have thought we'd be here, now, doing this when you sent that email and I opened it? I thought you were a total jerk."

"What?" I said in mock affront. "Me? A total jerk?"

"Oh, yeah," she said with a laugh. "Mr. Big Shot 69? I mean what kind of jerk has an email handle like that? And what kind of total ass sends a pic of his watch and Amex unlimited credit card limit to a woman?"

I laughed out loud, remembering how I'd sent those in an attempt to encourage Lexxi of 9-1-1 Escorts to accept the appointment with me so I could teach my cheating brother-in-law a lesson.

"I thought you'd be seduced by my unlimited credit and expensive watch."

"The washboard abs weren't too bad either," Alexa said. "Candace and I were rolling on the floor, wondering what kind of guy you were. A first-class jerk. That was certain. Who would have thought..."

She kissed me, tenderly, and I almost let myself get caught up in the kiss instead of what I had initially planned.

When our kiss broke, I was hard as rock, my erection pressing against her groin.

"I have something for you," I said playfully, wanting to trick her. In response, she grinned and her hand slipped down my back once more to my butt, squeezing one cheek, pressing her body up against mine.

"Not so fast, you insatiable vixen," I said, pulling away. "Later. Right now, I have something *else* for you."

Then, I reached beside me in a small compartment in the side of the hull and pulled out a tiny box wrapped in white tissue paper with a gold ribbon tied around it. I handed it to her and she took it and looked in my eyes.

"What's this?"

"Open it," I said. "It's special and is to remind us of our journey together."

She began to open it, her eyes wide. Inside the white satin box was a single black Tahitian pearl ring, the pearl surrounded by a crusting of diamonds set in white gold.

"It's beautiful." She slipped it on and admired her hand. "Thank you."

Then she pulled me back down for a kiss, her mouth meeting mine, her tongue finding mine.

We kissed for a long moment, the kiss tender and full of emotion.

"Alexandria Marie Dixon," I said, my voice choking with emotion, "will you marry me?"

Her eyes were even wider at that. "What?"

"I said, will you marry me? I've never felt like this for anyone before. I don't want to ever be separated from you."

She stared into my eyes, searching them. "But what about Mars?"

I laughed and kissed the end of her nose affectionately. "Mars doesn't hold a candle to you and to Tahiti."

"It doesn't?" she replied, a slow smile spreading on her lips. "How so?"

"Well, for one, there's no air."

I grinned and bent down, kissing her mouth. When I pulled back, I saw tears in her eyes.

"And for another, and more importantly, there's no you."

At that, she wrapped her arms around my neck, pulling me down for another kiss.

Above us hung the Southern Cross, below us, the South Pacific, and between us, there was nothing and there was everything.

THE END

Dear Reader!

Thanks so much for reading my book. If you enjoyed Mr. Big Shot and have five minutes, please consider leaving a review. They help spread the word about books you enjoy!

S. E. Lund

MATCHED: EXCERPT

Release Date: September 25, 2017

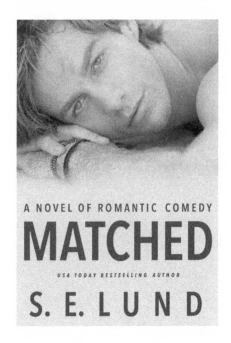

CHAPTER ONE

JON

We fist bump before she walks on the stage and she gives me that smile – the smile that says, *"I got this, Jon. Watch me blow their minds."*

I'm Jon.

Jon Anders Thorson. CEO of Pacifica Technologies Inc. We're a spunky little startup that's challenging Lockheed Martin's dominance of the aerospace industry.

That's my girl – India Louise Ward. Girl wonder at twenty-five years old. BS (Engineering) Stanford. MBA Stanford. My CTO – Chief Technology Officer. She's also my communications lead for the company. She's our public face because, why not put your best face forward and India is definitely Pacifica's best face.

She's fucking beautiful.

We're at the TechCrunch Disrupt conference and India is the speaker, talking about our experiences as a startup and how we went from my parent's garage in Pacifica, CA to a hundred-million tech business in Palo Alto. I'd be up there instead of India but I love seeing the audience when they realize that besides being smoking hot, she's smart.

Really smart.

Super smart. You can see it in her eyes. There's just so much going on behind them besides being pretty. They're hazel with flecks of green and violet behind thick lashes.

Not that I'm obsessed with her eyes, mind you. But I'm a man. I notice those things.

Back to India – you have to be whip-smart to be successful in this business and she's a fucking rocket scientist. She's one of the few women in the aerospace industry in positions of power.

Pride fills me as I watch her step up to the podium. There's polite applause, and the faces in the crowd I see are all interested. They've heard about the girl wonder at Pacifica Technology Inc. with the flaky name. Now they can see her in person and she's an eyeful.

India...

I mean, who the fuck names their daughter India?

Hippies, that's who. Her parents are old hippies, professors at Stanford, which explains India's brains. Her mom waited until she was forty to have children. Her father plays bongo drums for fuck's sake. Her mother has all these crystals lying around their house and is into yoga and eastern religions and took India to Machu Pichu when she was eight. You'd think that being exposed to all that airy-fairy stuff would warp a young mind...

Not India's. She's a straight arrow. Workaholic. Capitalist straight down the line.

Her parents must be so torn. They're typical flaky humanities professors. As a result, India didn't go to regular schools. No. She went to Montessori. She went into Stanford's Education Program for Gifted Youth program and was at Stanford doing a fucking engineering degree when she was six-fucking-teen. She's beautiful and she's probably one of the smartest people in the room.

Today, India's wearing a navy skirt to her knee and a white silk blouse. Over top is a navy blazer that hides curves like you wouldn't believe under her sober business suit. Her dark auburn hair is pulled back into a bun and she's wearing little makeup and black-rimmed reading glasses.

It's her disguise, as she calls it. She puts forward a totally professional demeanor but underneath, she's as crazy and geeky as the rest of us.

Here's the other secret she's trying to hide. She's five-foot five inches of babelicious woman. You should see her in a bikini.

Scalding hot. I mean, burn your retinas hot. Curves that would make a man kill to grab onto them and pump hard...

I know that each and every one of the men in the audience – at least those who are straight – want to bang her despite the disguise. Their puny brains get all mixed up when they see a beautiful woman like India. They can't keep two thoughts in their swelled heads because all the blood's drained down to their dicks.

They all want to fuck her. Every straight guy I meet wants to fuck her.

Unlike them, *I* don't want to fuck her. Sure, I mean, I *could* fuck her if the opportunity arose because she's sexy on legs and beautiful, but it never does. On purpose.

I need her to do her job.

We need each other to be totally professional.

We're practically best friends and have known each other

since our freshman year at Stanford. People joke and tell us we should just give up the pretense and fuck each other's brains out but no. We're business partners and more importantly, we're friends.

I was a hot young stud of an Army Ranger just returned from Afghanistan and was on the GI Bill, attending college to study business. Six foot three of hard-muscled killer. She was this pretty little brainy girl with a big laugh doing her engineering degree who stole my heart – in a brotherly-sisterly way – and who puts me in my place when I get too wild.

We took the same intro English class and the friendship began over coffee and then beer in the student pub. We did our MBAs the same year. Now, we're business partners.

I rely on her to run the technology department of Pacifica so I can focus on the financial side of things.

We don't go there.

I know what people think – they think I'm in love with India. I'm not.

We're best friends. People say you can't be best friends with a woman and especially not a beautiful woman like India, but we are the exception that proves the rule.

She's not into relationships either. I'm sure she looks up to me like the big brother she lost in the war. What we have is unique and I'm determined to not let something as crass as sex get in the way of our beautiful relationship or Pacifica's success.

I listen with half an ear as she wows them with our latest roll out, knowing her presentation about our latest satellite like the back of my hand. This one's destined for the military and will help soldiers on the modern battlefield. The contracts we're busy negotiating are huge. *Huge.*

I look out over the audience and I can see it as she finally wins them over and they're actually listening, their tongues rolled back up into their mouths. Behind her on the huge screen is her presentation, showcasing our technology. The music flares at the end and there's a huge round of applause for her. She smiles and bows to the audience, then leaves the stage, her face lit up, her cheeks flushed.

She's fucking *amazing*.

We fist bump again. "You rocked it, girl," I say, a huge smile on my face as she comes behind the curtain, grabbing the bottle of water I have ready for her.

"I think I did," she says and opens the lid, drinking down half the bottle. "They seemed to like it."

"Listen to them," I respond. I take her by the shoulders and turn her around so that she can see the audience, and bend down so that my face beside hers. "They loved you."

The audience is still clapping because the presentation was a combination of technology and patriotism. It was stirring, talking about mission and performance and making the world a better place and *rah rah USA*.

When the applause dies down, I let go of her arms. "You deserve a cold beer."

"I deserve a fucking *keg* of beer," she replies, grinning up at me, a twinkle in her eyes.

That's my girl. Huge brain. Potty mouth.

I love her.

Not in that way, of course. In the brotherly collegial and proud CEO way.

"Let's go," she says and grabs hold of my arm, her fingers gripping my bicep. I flex it because she's always kidding me about my workouts. I'm ripped. I work out daily. A habit I developed while in combat and I keep it up. No slacking off for me even though I'm no longer in a combat zone.

"I'm starving," she says, gazing up at me with those eyes. "I want to stuff myself with a huge piece of steak to go along with that keg of beer."

"Your wish is my command, CTO of mine," I reply but my mind substitutes *I want you to stuff me with that huge piece of meat you have, Jon...*

I can't control that part of my mind.

Give me a break.

We walk out the side of the auditorium, my arm draped around her shoulder in a brotherly way. I'm no longer interested in the last speaker and so we leave the conference for a bar where we're meeting the rest of our team to talk about the conference and our latest contract then we'll go for dinner and I'll make sure she gets her big juicy steak.

Life is good.

Two hours later...

Life sucks.

What the *fuck?*

Marina Clark, India's best friend from Montessori, and from forever, is sitting with us and as usual, she's frowning at me. She doesn't really like me. I don't know why, but she's always scowling at me like I've done something wrong. I check myself over. There's no food spilled on my crisp white shirt or silky blue tie. I run my fingers through my hair, which has a habit of falling into my eyes.

"What's your problem?"

She frowns. "You're working the poor girl to death."

"She's a big girl. She works herself hard. She's a winner."

Why Marina showed up at the bar, I'll never know. She's not in the tech biz. She's a psychologist. Doing her Ph.D. Sure, she's like India and is precocious and smart, but still. This celebration was meant for the team – not outsiders – even if she is India's best friend.

When India gets up to go to the bathroom, Marina leans closer to me.

"She's got a date tonight. Don't mess it up."

What?

"India has a date?"

I'm not the only one shocked by that announcement. The rest of my team members glance at me quickly like they expect me to be mad. I frown when they lean forward, eager to hear the details. Marina fills us in on this guy she's matched India with.

Like India needs help finding men... Every man she meets would fuck her, but she's not that kind of girl.

Besides, she doesn't want a man right now. She's focused on her career. I know because she told me that when we met at Stanford, back when I thought there might be something between us. She wants to make a hundred million dollars before she ever gets serious about a man and while we're definitely on our way to that hundred million, we're not there yet.

She's pure ambition – like me. Like the rest of us at Pacifica.

"She's lonely," Marina says plainly.

That hits me like a truck and I'm at a loss for words for a moment.

"How can she be lonely?" I say when I recover. I tip my beer up and take a long pull on it. "She's too busy to be lonely. She said so herself. She's focused on career. India says that men are superfluous. Those were her words, not mine, Marina. *Superfluous*."

"You think she's going to admit to you that she's lonely?" Marina gives me this derisive snort and takes a sip of her own beer. "She comes home to an empty apartment and is so lonely that she sleeps on the couch with the television on because she hates being alone in her king-sized bed. True confession." Then she points at me, her eyes narrow. "Don't tell her I told you that or she'll kill me."

I frown and imagine India sleeping on her couch instead of her bed. I remember when she bought that bed because I helped her pick it out. I even imagined the two of us fucking our brains out on it, but that's just an idle male thought. I'm as red-blooded as the next guy. But that was it. I imagined it one time, maybe twice. Less than a dozen times.

It's not like I think of sleeping with India often. I'm way too busy running one of the most successful tech start-ups in the past five years.

Speaking of her bed, it's hugely ostentatious with thick four posters and dark wood. Silk gray coverlet and throw pillows. In her huge master suite with the marble and expensive fixtures and the sliding doors that lead to her own personal deck overlooking the ocean.

She doesn't like sleeping in that bed?

I *love* that bed.

"She sleeps on the fucking couch?" I say, still dumbfounded at the prospect that India's lonely and wants a date.

Marina nods. "Sad, right? So, I've found this guy for her. I mean, he's right up her alley brains-wise. He teaches at Stanford, like her parents. He has a PhD from Harvard in Humanities. Philosophy."

"Philosophy?" I snort and make a face of disgust. "What the fuck is that?"

"You know – what is the good life? That kind of shit." She shrugs. "She filled out my questionnaire and his name came up among my subscribers as a match. I figured he was smart enough for her. Plus, her family is big in the whole humanities thing. He's coming tonight." She glances at her watch. "Any time now, in fact. I'm sure India's nervous. She's probably in the bathroom throwing up." She wags her eyebrows in this most annoying way.

"Throwing up? What the fuck are you talking about? Why would India throw up because she's meeting a pencil neck professor of philosophy?"

"He's not a pencil neck. He's really handsome in a professorial sort of way. She's shy, Jon," Marina says and that's the second time tonight I'm struck dumb by something she says. "You should know that. God, what have you been doing all this time? Ignoring India? See, that's what I mean by you work her too hard. You don't even know her."

"I know her better than almost anyone else."

I lean back, my blood pressure rising, my anger at Marina's meddling choking me for a moment. I sit steaming, unable to respond.

My India – shy? Nervous enough to meet some man that she'd throw up? I don't really even know her?

"This wasn't supposed to be a public event, Marina. This was meant to be a celebration for the team."

"India needs a man," she replies, shrugging like it's nothing. "I found her one."

"She doesn't *need* a man. She needs to focus on our business. On Pacifica. We have a big meeting coming up at the fucking Pentagon. I don't want her to be distracted by some flake from the Philosophy Department."

"No, *no*," she says and punches my arm. "She needs some, Jon. She's been out of circulation for way too long. You're always going on about how important sex is for well-being. Isn't that right?"

I sit and glower at Marina for throwing my words back at me, but she doesn't seem to notice the hate I'm sending her way.

"Oh, here he comes," Marina says and sits up straighter. "Be nice."

Be nice... Like I'm not nice.

Into the bar walks this tall fucker with dark hair and eyes, and a fucking goatee. He's wearing a tweed blazer with actual fucking leather patches on his elbows. And jeans. He must be forty if he's a day.

Old, in other words. There's actual gray in his hair at the sides.

"Him?" I say under my breath, giving Marina a glare. "He's an old man. Couldn't you find someone a bit closer to her age?"

"I did a really careful review of him, his values, his goals, his beliefs. They're a great match."

"You used the questionnaire?" I harrumph and lean back in my chair, taking a big drink from my bottle of beer. "I can tell just by looking at him he's not right for her."

"The questionnaire is an interest inventory that many of the dating businesses use. I've adapted it based on my understanding of psychology."

Yeah, I know all about Marina's damn dating app she's developing. I even agreed to help by filling one out so she can test the system. I had no idea Marina was this far along in the app's development.

"The app's ready?"

"Soft launch for the next month. We hard launch later, but I wanted to use India as a test subject. I've signed up about a thousand people to use as test matches. Most from Stanford and UCSF."

I watch the dickhead professor of philosophy walk in the bar. I don't know who this fucker is, but he's not the kind of man for India. That much I do know just by looking at him. How could he be? I can tell by the way he looks and dresses and walks that he's a stuffy old man. How could India be with someone like him?

"He's too old for her."

"Shush," Marina says and turns to the guy as he walks up to the table, all smiles. "Thomas! You made it. India's in the bathroom but should be right back."

"I did make it," Thomas says, his voice deep. "My flight from Boston was late but I managed to get an Uber driver who actually knows the fastest routes. I was giving a guest lecture at my old Alma Mater and we were late getting finished because I was hounded after the lecture by students wanting to talk. I missed my flight but was able to get on the next plane out. Barely made it."

He gives us all a smile, his teeth white over his goatee.

I hate him.

Marina introduces him as *Doctor* Thomas McAllister. Professor of Analytic Philosophy at Stanford.

He's not a fucking doctor. He's a professor. Doctors actually do important work in society, unlike professors of philosophy. I should know – my father was a doctor. I hate the way people call professors *Doctor* like they're something special...

"Pleased to meet you," I manage and shake the guy's hand, squeezing extra firmly. "So, tell me, what does a professor of analytic philosophy do? I mean, when you're not giving lectures."

"We think about how to think. It's meta," he says, smiling like he's made a joke.

I don't know what the hell he means, thinking about how to think. What kind of lame-ass job is that?

"Cool," I say, shrugging. "I already know how to think. Now, I just make shit. Shit that helps the good old USA win wars."

I lean back in my chair, folding my arms, and smile back at him.

Score one for the Viking...

If you enjoyed this excerpt, please click the link below and pick up your preorder copy now!

MATCHED AT ALL RETAILERS

S. E. LUND'S NEWSLETTER

Sign up for S. E. Lund's newsletter — she hates spam and will never share your info:

http://eepurl.com/1Wcz5

ABOUT THE AUTHOR

S. E. Lund writes erotic, contemporary, new adult and paranormal romance. She lives in a century-old house on a quiet tree lined street in a small city in Western Canada with her family of humans and animals. She dreams of living in a warm climate by the ocean where snow is just a word in a dictionary.

Other Books by S. E. Lund:

~

CONTEMPORARY EROTIC ROMANCE:
THE UNRESTRAINED SERIES
The Agreement: Book 1
The Commitment: Book 2
Unrestrained: Book 3
Unbreakable: Book 4
Forever After: Book 5
Everlasting: Book 6 (Coming FALL 2017!)

~

THE DRAKE SERIES (The Unrestrained Series from Drake's Point of View)

Drake Restrained
Drake Unwound
Drake Unbound

$\sim$

Military Romance / Romantic Suspense
THE BAD BOY SERIES
Bad Boy Saint: Book 1
Bad Boy Sinner: Book 2
Bad Boy Soldier: Book 3
Bad Boy Savior: Book 4 (Coming in July 2017)

$\sim$

PARANORMAL ROMANCE:
THE DOMINION SERIES
Dominion: Book 1 in the Dominion Series
Ascension: Book 2 in the Dominion Series
Retribution: Book 3 in the Dominion Series
Resurrection: Book 4 in the Dominion Series
Redemption: Book 5 in the Dominion Series

$\sim$

Prince of the City: The Vampire's Pet Part One (Coming in July 2017)

For more info:

www.selund.com
selund2012@gmail.com

CPSIA information can be obtained
at www.ICGtesting.com
Printed in the USA
LVHW100849180522
719091LV00013BA/49